THE
DUNG
BEETLES
OF LIBERIA

A NOVEL BASED ON TRUE EVENTS

DANIEL V. MEIER, JR.

BQB

Virginia

Published in the United States by BQB Publishing
(an imprint of Boutique of Quality Books Publishing, Inc.)
www.bqbpublishing.com

Printed in the United States of America

978-1-945448-37-9 (p)
978-1-945448-38-6 (e)

Library of Congress Control Number: 2019938864

Book design by Robin Krauss, www.bookformatters.com
Cover design by Rebecca Lown, www.rebeccalowndesign.com

First editor: Olivia Swenson
Second editor: Caleb Guard

PRAISE FOR THE DUNG BEETLES OF LIBERIA AND DANIEL V. MEIER, JR.

"Rugged, riveting, packed with exotic adventure and attitude, Meier's *Dung Beetles* is non-stop entertainment."

— Douglas Rogers, author of *The Last Resort*

". . . A fascinating evocation of 1960s Liberia, the novel explores the commonly accepted system of bribery and the arbitrary division between the masses. It will definitely appeal to fans of literary fiction as well as lovers of non-fiction. An engrossing read that is both informative and entertaining."

— *The Prairies Book Review*

". . . With a gift for portraying dialect, character quirks, and the intricacies of combining salient details of his youthful adventures with fictional flights of fancy, Meier flies readers on this soaring, literary saga that will leave them clamoring for a sequel."

— Kate Robinson, *The US Review of Books*

This book is dedicated to Charlene.

ACKNOWLEDGMENTS

Olivia Swenson, my editor, for her professionalism and assistance. Jane Knuth for reading the typescript, and for her encouragement and invaluable advice. Les Vipond whose knowledge and experience made this book possible. Teeja Meier for her faith, patience, endurance, suggestions, hard work, and love.

Dung beetles are beetles that feed partly or exclusively on feces. A dung beetle can bury dung 250 times heavier than itself in one night.

Many dung beetles, known as *rollers*, roll dung into round balls, which are used as a food source or breeding chambers. Others, known as *tunnellers*, bury the dung wherever they find it. A third group, the *dwellers*, neither roll nor burrow: they simply live in manure.

Dung beetles are currently the only known non-human animal to navigate and orient themselves using the Milky Way.

Source: Wikipedia

TABLE OF CONTENTS

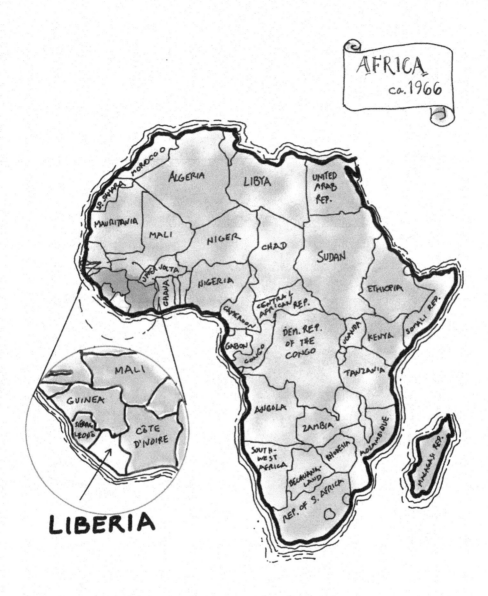

Map Illustrator: Rosana Keleher

CHAPTER 1

ISHMAEL

"Mr. Pilot! Oh, Mr. Pilot! Where are you, Mr. Pilot?" the nuns called as I squatted in the tall grass that grew around the airstrip. I had been on a trip up country to an area known as the Bomi Hills, which is about ninety miles north of Monrovia. On my way back from the diamond mines with an empty airplane, I felt it—the unmistakable cramping of an attack of diarrhea. Most whites develop intestinal problems if they stay in West Africa long enough. It is accepted the way getting a sunburn is accepted.

"Not here, not now," I muttered to myself. I knew from experience that when it hit you like that, you had maybe ten minutes.

I frantically looked around for a place to land. A large mission run by Catholic nuns should have been close by, and they had an airfield. Like some miraculous apparition, I saw the airstrip through a parting of the clouds—and I dove for it. I flew the airplane straight onto the runway with a couple of hard bounces, pulled it to a dusty stop, and set the parking brake. Leaving the engine idling with the prop turning over slowly, I bailed out of the cabin. I ran to the bush, which was mostly grass and weeds about chest high, and, with only moments to spare, relieved myself.

While this relief was occurring, I heard the distinctive *wuush, wuush, wuush* of dung beetles crawling through the grass. I had been told that they could hear a mouse break wind from five miles away and could follow the scent. With my pants around my ankles and the sun beating down on my head, I started a little hippy hop, hippy hop movement to keep away from them. And here came the good sisters in their Land Rover.

"Oh, Mr. Pilot! Mr. Pilot, Mr. Pilot! Where are you?"

I crouched lower, but now the dung beetles were visible, beelining toward me. I had hoped to spare the good sisters the sight of my naked bottom while trying to clean myself with my handkerchief, but then the dung beetles were upon me, crawling around my feet, and I didn't want them to start up my legs.

"Mr. Pilot! Oh Mr. Pi—!"

The nuns must have figured out what was happening because there was a pause, then they all waved like a car load of school girls and drove off. I got my pants up, shook a cluster of dung beetles off my boots, and got out of there as quickly as I could. Once airborne, I gave the nuns a wing wag as I climbed away.

On the flight back to Monrovia I thought about how I had gotten here. Not long ago, I had been a clean-shaven, ambitious college student at Cornell. Now I sported a three-day stubble, was badly in need of a shower, and had just finished scuttling around the bush with my pants around my ankles trying to avoid bugs and nuns.

I can't say for certain that it wasn't a damp, drizzly November of the soul or that I wished to be called Ishmael, but events had reached a turning point. I had made it to Cornell, and while I had been a good student in high school, this was a different environment altogether. For the first time since I had read it in tenth grade, *Moby Dick* started to make sense. I understood, or thought I did, why Ishmael ran away to sea and why Richard Dana left Harvard to join a whaling ship and later write *Two Years before the Mast*. I suppose it was because for nineteen years I had been encased in a world of security, protection, and expectation. Maybe I simply wanted to take some real risks of my own. I wanted to know what life was like outside of the silk cocoon.

I don't know when this process started. I think it was not long after Arthur's death. It was the summer of 1961; I had finished the first semester of my sophomore year at Cornell and had begun to realize that my future as a physicist was in considerable doubt. It wasn't that I could not have persevered and gotten my degree. It was that I knew if I continued, I would be a mediocre physicist at best. For reasons I've never been able to resolve, being mediocre seemed worse than failure. Then, too, winters are frigid in that part of New York State, and I was tired of being cold—bone chillingly cold. I didn't know what I wanted to do with the rest of my life, but I knew I no longer wanted to attend Cornell and that I wanted to go somewhere warm—warm all year round.

I tried my best to explain this to my father. He listened, unmoved, expressionless. He seemed to almost shrug, followed by a sip of coffee and a careful placement of the cup on the table. He always did everything carefully, as though every move was calculated. He then looked up at me accusingly, much as he had for the past year. A pall had hovered over our family since my brother's death.

"You mean to say that you are just going to give up, drop out of Cornell, and throw away two years of work?" His voice was measured and deliberate. I had heard this tone many times growing up, and it always made me tremble.

I took a deep breath. "Not give up. Postpone," I said. "I promise I'll go back and finish my degree—later. As for now, I love flying. I have a commercial pilot's certificate. I'm a rated flight instructor, and I know something about aircraft maintenance. I can use that. And I want to go someplace warm."

After that, he didn't say anything. He just stared at me. He knew.

Finally he said, "Well, maybe it's for the best." Then, "What did Jenny say?"

"She doesn't know," I said. "I'm going there now."

———————————

I had called earlier so it wasn't a surprise to anyone when I rang the doorbell. Jenny answered. Her long blond hair fell below her shoulders and seemed to shimmer in the backlight of the doorway. She was tall with sky-blue eyes. Her face looked as though it had been carved, very carefully, from flawless marble. At that moment she seemed more beautiful than ever. I thought of turning back, of not going through with it. She seemed, in that moment, the most important person that I would ever know.

"Want to come in?"

"Let's go to Bright's for a coffee and Danish," I said.

"Sure." Her voice elevated a little with uncertainty and concern.

We walked the block and a half to the coffee shop holding hands. Her hands were always warm and soft. She had long, elegant fingers that seemed more like beautiful decorations than simply fingers.

We each got a coffee and a cinnamon bun oozing with thick frosting. The coffee, as is said, hit the spot and had an immediate relaxing effect. I watched as Jenny bit gently into the cinnamon bun, getting just a little frosting on her upper lip. What was I thinking? Every time I looked at her, she was all I wanted. But I knew this wasn't the time for us. There was just too much history and a too uncertain future.

She smiled and looked up at me with those huge blue eyes. "Did you want to talk about something?" she asked, wiping the frosting from her lip.

"I've dropped out of Cornell."

She kept looking at me, waiting for me to explain.

"I'm still going to finish. I've promised my parents and myself that. It won't be in physics, however. I'm thinking more of math or engineering."

"But what will you do now?"

"I'm going to look for a flying job. I'm a pretty good flight instructor. I'll find something."

"Around here? There are a lot of small airports in this area," she said.

"That's just it. I don't want to stay here."

Jenny froze momentarily then looked at me with a wounded stare. "What do you mean?"

"I don't know. I just need to get away for a while."

"I'm in your way then," she snapped.

"Jenny, I'm not dumping you. I love you. I've never loved anyone like I love you! And besides, I'm not really leaving you. We can stay in contact."

"And for how long?" she interrupted. "A year? Two years? Five? These things never work out. And what am I supposed to do while you're out finding yourself?"

"Jenny, you're a free woman. You can do what you like."

I sensed immediately that I had said the wrong thing. Her eyes narrowed. I'd seen that look before.

"I do love you," I protested. "You mean everything to me."

"Then why are you leaving?" She hesitated then said, "I think it has more to do with Arthur. You've never forgiven yourself for his death."

"Yeah," I said, "and I know he loved you."

"And you feel guilty about that?"

"Don't you, just a little?"

"What happened between Arthur and me is long over. He is dead and will never come back. His death silenced everything and took away everything. But it was an accident. You have no reason to feel guilty."

"Maybe," I said. "It's just something I have to work through for myself."

"So you're running away? Christ! Why don't you become Catholic? They at least have a belief and a rite of absolution."

"Please believe me," I said. "It will only be for a short while. I'll be here for your graduation."

"Promise?" Her face relaxed and there was a flicker of a smile.

"Yes, I do promise."

It was one in a string of promises that I had no idea how I was going to keep.

A day in the public library looking through international employment publications and classifieds produced nothing. I knew that it would be a wasted effort, but I felt that I had to start somewhere. I went home. Sometime around 4:30 my dad came home, which was early for him. He was carrying a bunch of rolled up sheets of paper.

"Son," he said.

I looked at him.

He handed me the mass of documents. "West Africa."

I stared at him.

"You know I am concerned about this about-face of yours, so I called up some friends of mine in the aviation industry and told them about your wanderlust. We all agreed that West Africa is the place for a young man looking for a change. The economies are growing by leaps and bounds, most of the governments are stable, and it's warm. If I were young again, I'd be tempted to give it a try myself."

The rolled papers were maps and charts of West Africa. We spread them out on the floor. The charts covered all of the coast of West Africa down as far as the Congo. I found the northern part around the big bulge particularly interesting. It was obvious that these documents had been drawn a long time ago by people who were unable to penetrate the actual interior and survey it. Inland, there were many large, blank areas with no detail or relief data. This meant that no data was available, the modern equivalent of "*here be dragons*" found on some medieval maps that marked uncharted waters. Only the general locations of towns or villages were shown in white areas with no indication as to their size. The national borders were clearly marked but few rivers or roads. The best way in or out of the interior seemed to be by air, but no airfields were marked except on the coast.

I focused on Liberia. I knew that the US had a relationship with the country, and I was fascinated by some of the city names, like Sidi Ifney, Gbarnga, and others that I couldn't begin to pronounce. Looking at these maps, I felt I was looking at the edge of the world.

My dad thought it was exciting. I did too. I think he knew that a young man only gets one shot at freedom before living has to be taken seriously.

Fortunately, with his help, support, and connections, all the technical details went smoothly. I got a letter from a company that he had found through old friends, assuring me that they would leave "no screw unturned" to get me into the country. To me, it sounded a little ominous.

The next step was to get a passport and visa. I caught the bus that ran through our neighborhood of Silver Spring and joined the daily commuters. They had made this bus ride so many times that what went on outside the bus no longer interested them. They quietly occupied their time with crosswords or reading the latest romance novel. My only objective that day was to secure a visa at the Embassy of the Republic of Liberia. Soon I would be on my way to one of the few remaining blank places on the global map.

The bus rambled its way through the crowded streets of Washington, DC. It was a warm spring day and the bus windows were open, admitting a faint breeze as we accelerated between stops. The bus stopped near the supposed location of the embassy, but after walking up and down the block several times, I couldn't find it. At the address I had been given, there was a house of faded yellow brick with no markings of any kind indicating that it was anything but an unkempt, fully shuttered residence. After walking around it, I finally knocked on the door. Minutes passed, and then a child of about ten years old opened it.

"Do you know where the Embassy of Liberia is?" I asked.

"Yah, dis here," she said.

"I need to get a work visa for the country."

"Wait, yah." She let me in and disappeared. Inside I was thrilled by the strong, exotic cooking odors. I waited in the poorly lit foyer listening to the laughter and music that drifted into the room. Eventually, a very large woman dressed in a multicolored caftan and ragged flip-flops appeared in the hall and asked me my business. I explained my visa requirements and said I had all the required paperwork and pictures. Making no reply, she slowly shuffled back down the hall. I heard muted voices in a dialect that I did not understand, and soon a small man with a yellowish complexion appeared, smoking a cigarette.

"Visa cost money, ya know," he said.

I had, in my pocket, two envelopes. The first contained all of the appropriate application forms, signed and notarized. They had been procured for me by a Mr. Haddad, who I assumed was the deputy manager of the company that had hired me. He was the one who had promised to leave "no screw unturned" to ensure my prompt arrival into the Republic. The other envelope, which was sealed, was also for the embassy and bore official looking stamps and logos from the Republic's Ministry of Interior. I was to give this second letter to the embassy official only if visa problems arose.

The small, jaundiced man soon made it clear that the visa was indeed going to be a problem and might take much more time and money than the embassy had first stated. I handed him the second letter. He read it slowly then rapidly straightened up to his full height.

"Come back tomorrow. You will have your visa," he said. Of course, he indicated, it would require him to work overtime and would double the cost, but I could have my documents tomorrow.

On the return bus, a small red convertible passed and the two very pretty girls in it smiled and waved to me. I waved back. I was soon going to be on my way. It had been a good day after all.

The next day, the visa was ready, signed, and in order.

Jenny had just started a job as an administrative assistant at the Smithsonian and had agreed to meet me outside their offices on the Mall. I waited on one of the benches across the street. It had rained the night before and the grass on the Mall had turned to a richer, more translucent shade of green. I watched as office workers hurried past on their way to parking lots or bus stops. A few tourists in casual clothes, followed by weary children, ambled by looking at the buildings. I saw Jenny descending the stairs and walk toward me, her long blond hair flowing around her neck. I felt a sudden tightness in my chest and a near blinding realization of how lucky I was to have her.

"Would you like to sit?" I asked.

"No," she said, "let's walk—toward the monument."

We joined the others walking at a rambling pace, taking in the attractions tourists had come to see. The Washington Monument dominated the horizon.

"My new office," she said, "or shall I say desk, looks out on the monument. I was staring at it this morning and couldn't remember why it is made out of different kinds of stone."

"I think it was a combination of a number of things," I said. "They ran out of money, for one. Then there was the Civil War. The sad truth is that when work was finally resumed after the war, the builders couldn't find the same quality of stone. Like so much in this city, the monument has a long history of political and financial wrangling."

"And how do you feel?" she asked.

"Oh, I just think it was unfortunate—maybe a lesson to people in charge that when you start something, you should finish it."

We walked for a while in silence. She slipped her arm around my waist. "You didn't come here to talk about the Washington Monument, did you?"

We walked on a little farther.

"I'm going to Liberia," I said.

She stopped, her face blank. She bit her bottom lip, but her flood of words couldn't be contained. "Liberia! Do you know how far away that is? Do you know anything about it? Why Liberia?" she said, drawing out each vowel. She was just as angry as I expected she would be.

I took a breath and said, "It's about five thousand miles away. It's like a small version of America, I think. It was settled by former American slaves, now known as Americo-Liberians, in 1820 and was founded as a nation in 1847. They have a federal republic. The Americo-Liberians are in control of the government. Monrovia is the largest city and the capital." I paused to catch my breath, then continued. "William Tubman is president and has been since 1944. It's about the size of the state of Virginia and is covered in forest. It has mountains in the north and east, hardly any roads, and is rich in mineral wealth. How about that?" I exhaled grandly.

"That about says it all! So why did you decide on Liberia?"

"Because Africa is wide open now. The old European colonial powers are gone or going. And Liberia is rich—really rich. It's tied to the US by history and the currency is pegged to the US dollar. The country's being developed at an enormous rate, and, best of all, they speak English."

"Tell me about the job."

"Thanks to my father, I've been hired by an air transport operator called African Air Services. Other than that, I don't know anything about them."

We crossed 14th Street and walked up the curving paths to the base of the monument. Jenny and I looked up at the marble pyramidion that caps the obelisk and paused to watch small, puffy cumulus clouds drift slowly over it.

"When do you leave?" she asked.

"In two days."

"Two days," she said, almost in a whisper. "Only two days? Couldn't you have given us more time?"

We didn't speak for a while. Then she looked at me earnestly. "Kenneth, no matter where you go or what you do, I want you to remember where you come from and, most importantly, those who love you."

She kissed me and held me tightly for a long time. I still remember the delicious scent of her hair and her warm tears wetting my cheek. I felt like the worst kind of turncoat—like a man who walks out on his family when they need him the most.

I packed lightly—just a few changes of clothes, an extra pair of shoes, and some toiletries. I started to pack my sketch board with paper but decided that it would take up too much room and it was heavy. If it didn't fit into my carry-on duffle bag, then I planned to buy it when I needed it.

Packing is that first real step in travel. The ideas, the planning, the fantasies are over. Packing represents the transition from the dream to reality. I hesitated at first. There had been a flicker of doubt, but I closed my duffle and with one look back at my bedroom, the cradle of my innocence, shut the door and walked out to meet my parents waiting in the car. Jenny had arrived looking radiant as usual. We drove to the airport, Mother trying to talk to Jenny about her college plans, and my father commenting on the changes to the city. I felt like I was in a dream. Jenny held my hand in a tight grip until we were in the airport parking lot and stayed close by my side during the walk into the terminal building.

I checked in at the gate. The airport terminal was like a bus station. There were no body searches, no metal detectors, no X-rays. In the waiting area, Jenny sat next to me, still gripping my hand. My parents sat on the other side. No one spoke. Finally, the boarding call came over the public address system and I stood up to go. My dad shook my hand. He had a nervous smile and had difficulty looking at me. Mother wiped away her tears, and Jenny hugged me. I said as cheerful a goodbye to them as I could, hoping my voice would hold up, slung my carry-on bag over my shoulder, and joined the boarding line.

Just before going through the door that led to the airplane, I glanced back and felt a gut-wrenching panic. Jenny and my mother were wiping tears from their cheeks. My dad was absently wringing his hands and his face had gone tense. Had Ishmael felt like this? Yet I knew that my decision was necessary—that it was what I must do or not survive.

Approximate Boundaries of Liberia's
Officially Recognized Ethnic Groups

CHAPTER 2

AFRICA

My first sight of Africa was as we passed over a small island near the coast of Dakar. I gazed down out of the cabin window of Pan Am Flight 50, a state-of-the-art Boeing 707. Narrow dirt roads connected small, rough dwellings with an occasional thin column of smoke rising from them. We began our descent in a light rain. The landscape was a monochromatic grayish green. The first human I saw, as we were on final approach, was an old man, bent over as though he were in fear of being hit by the airplane.

We deplaned down a rusty metal stairway and hurried on foot through the drizzle to the terminal building. In spite of the rain and the high cloud cover, it was hot. Hot enough to make steam rise from the pavement in small, vanishing filaments. Eventually, we were shown to the transit lounge where we were to wait for our connecting flight. There was moderate chaos all around with people shouting and gesticulating. The odor of curry dominated the close atmosphere. Acrid cigarette smoke filled the lounge, turning the outside grayness, filtering through the window shutters, into grim bars of semi-light. Indefinable noises came from every direction. The overhead fans in the transit area did little but stir the heated, smoky air. I bought a draft beer at the bar and went back to my seat. Staring into the diminishing foam at the top of my warm beer, I wondered where this seemingly rash decision would take me.

When I looked up from my second beer, a woman with huge forearms and dressed in an official-looking uniform announced that Air Afrique Flight 156 to Monrovia was boarding. I emptied my glass just in time to join the crowd squeezing through the glass doors to the ramp where a dented, scarred, and faded DC-4 waited.

In the cockpit were two French pilots who looked as though they could do with a night's uninterrupted sleep and a square meal. The passenger cabin smelled faintly of urine, stale cigarette smoke, and aviation gas. The passenger seats were torn or worn through. In the rear of the cabin stood a disheveled flight attendant who spent most of her time glaring at us.

After a two-and-a-half-hour flight, we touched down at Roberts International Airport (known locally as Robertsfield) about thirty-five miles outside of Monrovia, in the late afternoon. Again, it was raining. The wet season had begun in tropical Africa and it would go on for several more months. I made it through throngs of people to the reception area of the terminal. The building was an open-sided concrete shed with bars on the windows, no glass anywhere, and plywood fastened over some of the openings. Customs and Immigrations were inside. People were yelling and shouting. Three or four men tried to yank my bag out of my hands, all loudly offering to carry it.

"I carry it for you, boss! I carry it for you."

But I hung onto it until I got into the customs line. I politely refused the offers. (I was told, before I left home, that I should always be polite. That would get me out of most scrapes). Then, about fifteen officials appeared and started marking passengers' bags with an X in chalk and began opening them. Mine was not marked and was not opened.

A large European who I had not noticed took me by the arm and said, "Are you Mr. Kenneth Verrier?"

I said yes. He had an African with him who picked up my bag. We went through the terminal past customs, walked around to the back of the building, and got into a Cessna 185 that was as ragged an airplane as I had ever seen. I was shocked and, for a moment, thought of not getting inside. It simply didn't look like it would fly.

Much to my disbelief the engine started and we took off and flew, surprisingly without incident, to Spriggs-Payne Airport, a smaller airstrip on the edge of Monrovia where a tall, dark-haired man with a soiled shirt and a cigar wedged in one corner of his mouth met me.

He extended his hand and said, "Mike McCoy. I manage the operation. I also own part of it. The pilots call me Mike or Boss. Everybody else here calls me Boss."

"Ken Verrier," I said. "You're American!"

"Yes, from Texas."

"Who is Mr. Haddad?" I asked.

"Oh, he runs a hiring agency in West Africa—got a lot of connections. Everyone hires their pilots though him."

Mike quickly showed me around what turned out to be a pretty small operation and introduced me to various people who worked for him. They hardly looked up from their tasks and did not seem interested in meeting me. The desks in the office were piled high with smudged and wrinkled papers. The maintenance area was dirty with machinery and tools carelessly scattered about. It did not look promising.

Mike then took me to my new accommodations. It was called a guest house and it was run by a woman named Lilly Gella who was part Dutch and part Indonesian. A number of African Air Service pilots lived there. Lilly would prove to be a good landlady, always attentive to detail. She reminded me of a good fraternity mom keeping a bunch of rowdy boys in check.

Toward evening we drove into Monrovia. The traffic was mainly a heavy concentration of people moving on foot along the sides of the road. The women carried something—a child, a soiled bundle on their heads—while the men trudged along ahead of them. Most of the vehicles were, as Mike told me, known as "money buses." Money buses looked like Volkswagen hippy vans, only twice as long with open sides and wooden bench seats. There were, of course, the more expensive taxis and independent buses, but most people crowded onto a money bus, paid their few cents, and took their chances.

We stopped at Heinz and Maria's, a restaurant and bar in Monrovia that catered to Europeans, but especially to Germans. It was an odd combination of West Africa and a German Rathskeller. On the bare concrete wall there was an empty picture frame with the words "Der Fuehrer" on a brass plate attached to the bottom. A large flag of the German republic hung over the bar. We ordered dinner—knockwurst and sauerkraut and several bottles of Krombacher.

"Finest beer in Germany. I don't think you can get this stuff in the States," Mike said, holding up the glass of golden liquid as though it were his most prized possession. After taking a long swallow and wiping his mouth with the back of his hand he explained what I would be doing for the next few days, which would be going through the tedium of getting all my paper work done—my work visa, my residency permit, my work permit, etc.— and obtaining an actual Liberian pilot's license.

"Essentially, African Air Services," he went on to say, "is an air transport company. We fly anybody and almost anything that will fit into the airplanes anywhere in West Africa. The company is very prosperous. You will be paid a flat salary, to start, of nine hundred dollars a month plus a percentage of the profits. There are five other air transport operators on the field and the competition is stiff. Actually, it could best be described as cutthroat and backstabbing, but," he chuckled, "that's to be expected where there is a lot of easy money. After all, TIA."

"What does that mean?" I asked.

"It means 'This is Africa.' The Europeans use it to explain or excuse things that seem illogical to them or are out of their control."

After dinner Mike offered me a cigar.

"I don't smoke," I said.

He congratulated me with a wry smile and lit a Cohiba, blew some smoke in the air and studied the smoldering cigar with satisfaction.

"The Germans prefer this place. Heinz and Maria are escaped Nazis. In fact, most of the people you see here are ex-Nazis. Only I'm not so sure the prefix 'ex' is appropriate. I personally like the food. The Americans and Brits like The Gurley Street Bar and Restaurant. The Israelis have their own places. The Spanish eat on the cheap from roadside vendors. I suppose it reminds them of tapas, diarrhea and all." He snickered.

He leaned toward me and looked directly into my eyes. "You're a very young man, so let me give you some friendly advice. Stay away from the local girls. The girls are sent out of their tribes down to the city to find a husband, so the second you invite one in to live with you, they bring the whole family. And you are expected to take care of them. Prostitutes, they're okay, but don't take a mistress or in any way get involved with the locals. If you do you'll be in a world of hurt you never even thought about. The Liberians have a word for it—*palaver*. It means a huge hassle, bullshit, expanding trouble—a real shit storm. Stay away from it." He took a long drag from his cigar.

"Also, just remember most whites are here because they want something. The Peace Corps is here. They want to 'do good' and have the Africans like them. If they stay to themselves and don't cause trouble with the locals, they should do all right. The missionaries want to convert the Africans to their brand of Christianity. Everybody else, including the international corporations—*especially* the international corporations," he emphasized, "is a hustler. They're going to do what you are probably going to do."

Before I could say "What's that?" he said, "Roll as much money out of this country as they can then bug out." He took another long draw on his Cohiba. "And another thing—you'll need a gun."

"A gun!"

Just then, Mike looked up and recognized the two men who had walked into the restaurant

"Deet, Joe, come over. I want you to meet our newest pilot." Two very handsome men somewhere in their late thirties waved and smiled, showing perfect teeth. They wore wrinkled and faded lightweight leather flight jackets with the imprints of former military insignia on them, and khaki shirts and trousers.

"This is Dieter Lothair Hoffman. We call him Deet. And this is Joachim Muller known as Joe. Gentlemen, this is Ken."

"Aha yes," Deet said, still holding his smile. "De American college boy, das is goot. Ve need to lift de standards around here." Both pilots laughed.

"Goot to have you aboard," Joe said, extending his right hand, which was badly scarred across the top.

"Ve need to talk to Heinz to see if he vill buy de drinks tonight," Deet said.

"Before you go," Mike said, "I want you to take Ken for a route check when his paper work is ready. I'll let you know."

"Ya, vor shore, I vill give him a goot check out," Deet said, his perfect teeth glistening in the light. Then he and Joe made their way to the bar where they were joined by two of the local bar girls.

"Ya know," Mike said with a slight smile, "I can't figure these guys out. They are Nazis to the core, yet they're the first ones to get tangled up with the local girls."

The next day Mike sent Paterson, a local who was somewhere between twenty and forty, to pick me up at the guest house. Paterson told me that for the next two days he was to take me where I needed to go, but after that I was expected to have my own transportation. I thanked him for the information and told him to take me to the Liberian Civil Aviation Authority. I got the clear impression that Paterson did not appreciate his new role. His father had been a taxi driver in Paterson, New Jersey, and he, Paterson, had been named after the city of his birth. The American connection gave him a slight edge over the native Liberians. I was also to learn that work status was very important among Liberians, and Paterson wore his faded white shirt and stained tie with pride.

To get to the office where a Liberian pilot's license could be issued, we had to walk down a side street, go through a very dark room, then climb a ladder to an upper room where an extremely gaunt man in his sixties took my twenty dollars plus the obligatory small bribe Paterson had warned me about. They called it "dash" or "Saturday." The way you did it was to say something like "Hey, let me help you out" or "Here's your Saturday."

The gaunt man typed out the license using an old Underwood typewriter. It was a small piece of paper with two misspellings. He wasn't the slightest bit interested in seeing my US pilot certificates. He handed the piece of paper to me, and I was a licensed pilot of the Republic of Liberia.

Paterson then took me around to complete the rest of the required tasks. He knew the system very well. He had, by this time, already spread the necessary dash. Absolutely nothing in government took place without dash. Sometimes the official would say, "You gotta help me. You gotta help me small." The bribes weren't big—a dollar here, five dollars there—but they were omnipresent.

The officials knew that our bribes would be bigger than the locals, so we were escorted by a large man in an official-looking uniform to the front of the lines. The lines were incredibly long, but no one protested our preferential treatment even though they would probably be there all day. When all this was done, I was at last able to go to work.

CHAPTER 3

LIBERIA

A lot of wealth was pouring into the country, mostly from international corporations. The national transportation system was still largely underdeveloped. Most of the roads had been built by international mining, timber, and rubber companies. These roads served the companies as well as the people of Liberia and were not paved. During the wet season they often became impassable. There was one national airline, Liberian National Airways, but it flew only to a few nearby destinations outside of Liberia.

There were basically only two ways to get around in the country: by boat, which took days and days, or by aircraft. The airstrips at the iron mines were carved out of the jungle, leaving a surface of laterite, which is an aluminum and iron based red gravely soil natural to Liberia. This type of soil was very hard on airplanes.

After a short time on these airstrips, the inboard wing sections above the wheels and tail surfaces became covered with dents and cracks. Wheel fairings were not used because they would not cover the oversize tires necessary for these rough field operations. The air service companies were always buying airplanes to replace those irreparably damaged by the soil. The average useful life of an airplane working in these conditions was three to four years.

I met Deet at the operations office at ten the next morning. The office was a rectangular structure built of concrete blocks that had been sectioned off to provide a waiting room and a sort of administrative office with a transceiver, a small briefing room with a telephone, and a workshop that also served as a hangar. The briefing room had an old National Geographic map of Liberia taped to the wall and a blackboard nailed next to it. Next to the briefing room was a toilet labeled "WC" with an actual flushing commode. A paper sign was tacked to the door that read in bold black letters:

PLEASE DO NOT THROW CIGARETTE BUTTS IN THE PISSER. IT MAKES THEM SOGGY AND HARD TO LITE.

Deet was lounging in one of the overstuffed chairs in the waiting room looking over a well-worn map.

"Come vid me to de briefing room," he said. Once there he pointed to a place on the map marked with a red map tack that was about sixty miles up the coast and ten miles inland.

"Dis is vere ve are going. It's a Protestant mission and, like most of dese places, a little village dat doesn't have a name yet has grown up around it. De old missionary lives by himself. De vife took off years ago. Dey said it vas vit one of de local boys, but I don't know. Ve supply dem vid vhiskey, cigarettes, scheisse paper, some girly magazines, and occasionally some food und medicine. Paterson und his boys vill load de stuff, und ve vill pick up de list from Mike in de office."

"Aren't we going to do a weight and balance?" I asked.

"A vhat?" Deet shouted with a short laugh. "I haven't done von of dose since I got here."

"Then how do you know that the airplane is not over grossed or within CG?" CG, or center of gravity, is important. If an airplane is loaded aft of the published CG limit it becomes unstable, pitches up after takeoff, stalls, and augers into the ground. No amount of correction will save it. If the airplane is loaded forward of the CG limit, it will be difficult or impossible to rotate off of the runway. If the plane does get off it will very likely pitch down, out of control, nose first into the ground.

"Dis is a Cessna von eighty. You can't over gross it and you can't get it out of CG. At least no one seems to have done it so far. Besides, if it veighs too much it von't fly. Simple, ya?"

"What about weather? Can we call flight service or does the company have its own weather service?"

Deet laughed again. "Look outside. Dat ist our vetter service."

Mike was in the office smoking a cigar. He looked up when we came in, then handed Deet a piece of soiled paper.

"Is that the manifest?" I asked.

"Yep, it's all in here," he said. "And, Deet, make sure you get paid before you let them unload the stuff, and for Christ sake don't bullshit the new guy. And get him back safe. And no side trips to see one of your whores."

On the way out of the office Deet stopped, turned to Mike, clicked his heels, and saluted. For a moment the old Luftwaffe professionalism came through—even though I knew he was doing it in mockery.

We walked out to the airplane. Paterson had just finished the loading. He was dressed in his usual pressed faded white shirt, soiled tie, and creased trousers, and his shoes were polished to a high gloss. Deet handed him the manifest. Paterson looked it over carefully, glanced into the cargo bay, signed the paper then handed it back to Deet.

He smiled at us. "Have a good flight, gentlemen."

Deet waved him off. "You'd sink dat black owns de company de vay he struts around. He doesn't own scheisse. I sink he even stole dat bicycle he rides to vork."

"He seems very efficient to me, and proud of his job. Who does own the company, by the way? Mike?"

"I don't know how much Mike owns, if any, but he ist de boss. De Honorable Williams owns at least fifty-von percent of dis company und several oder operations on de field also."

"Is the Honorable Williams a pilot?"

"No, but I tink he likes airplanes, und I tink he likes pilots. He likes to come out here und vatch takeoffs und landings, den go over to da airport bar und hang around vit de pilots. It's de law, you see. At least fifty-von percent of any companies licensed to vork in Liberia has to be owned by a Liberian. Dat vay de Big Men are sure to get deir cut. Mike says it's just von of de costs of doing business here. I don't tink Honorable Williams paid a pfennig. De oder owners simply signed over fifty-von percent to him und dey get vat's left over. It's still a lot of money."

I looked at him.

He continued, "Dese airplanes make over a tousand dollars a day. Fur most of us, dat ist a lot of Gelt."

The Big Men, I was to learn, held and controlled most of the wealth and sources of wealth in Liberia, which meant they also ran the government at its highest levels. It was easy to identify them as they were always immaculately dressed and were referred to as Honorable rather than Mister. Most of them could trace their ancestry back to Liberia's original settlement, descendants of former American slaves.

The Big Men tended to be well educated, many having gone to secondary schools and universities in the US or Europe. When they spoke to a European, their English was quite proper, but among themselves they spoke a version of English called Merico, an English-based Creole language. It sounds like English spoken with a Louisiana accent. They were Christian and most supported, as well as attended, the Episcopal Church. President Tubman himself was a devout Methodist.

The income gap between the Americo-Liberians and the native Liberians was enormous. I thought it strange that a population of former slaves would establish a system of government and social organization that mirrored the system that had enslaved them.

"Do you have much time in de one eighty?" Deet asked as we walked up to the airplane.

"I have a lot of time in my father's Aronica 7AC and some in a Cessna 140."

"Hmmm," Deet muttered. "Dose are small, tame airplanes compared to de von eighty. Vell, dey are all tail draggers so you should not have much difficulty."

He opened the doors and checked the cargo, which was piled to the overhead. He pulled at the cargo fasteners then tossed the manifest inside.

"Vell, it all seems to be here. Follow me around on de preflight, den ve'll get dis baby started and go." Deet looked up at the distant sound of an airplane engine. "Dat's Joe. I flew him over to Robertsfield to pick up a replacement airplane. I vunder vhy he is so late getting back?"

We watched as Joe entered the downwind leg; then opposite the approach end of the runway, he did a tight descending 180-degree turn. We could hear him pushing up the power.

"He's going to beat up de field. De Gott-damned fool," Deet shouted. We watched as Joe, in the new Cessna, roared down the runway just a few feet off the surface toward the other end of the runway. The airplane then abruptly pitched up and rolled to the left, and moments after it did so, most of left wing broke away. The airplane rolled inverted and dove, nose first, into the ground. It hit the ground near some palm trees and flipped nose over tail until it came to rest in a tangled mass of metal and undergrowth.

I didn't know it then, but that was the beginning of my stomach problems.

The airplane had snapped an unmarked communication cable at the end of the field. The severed cable whipped across part of the airfield like a scythe. It wrapped itself around the propeller of a parked plane, narrowly missing a man standing next to it.

"Gott damn!" Deet shouted. "Come vid me!" He started running and I ran with him, not knowing what he had in mind. We ran up to a Land Rover that had African Air Services painted on the doors.

"Get in!"

I jumped into the passenger seat at the same time Deet started the vehicle, put it in gear, and spun off down the runway toward the wrecked airplane. We bounced over the dirt ridge at the end of the runway, throwing clouds of red dust in the air as we slid to a stop near the wreckage.

Deet grabbed a fire extinguisher from its attachment on the floor of the Rover and leaped out. I followed, not knowing exactly what I was going to do. When we reached the airplane, Deet immediately began to spray the partially exposed engine with the fire retardant. The air was heavy with the smell of hot engine oil and aviation gasoline.

The plane was almost unrecognizable. The engine had broken away from its mounts and the fuselage looked like a crumpled mass of aluminum foil. The tail section had separated and lay some yards away. The right wing had also broken off and lay bent and twisted near the fuselage. The cockpit, including the cargo area, had retained much of its shape, which it is supposed to do by design, but it was clear that Joe was trapped.

His seat belt had failed, which, considering the force of the impact, would not have helped him anyway. He was pressed up against the instrument panel. The yoke had pushed his chest in. His seat was on his back. I could not see his lower arms or hands.

Things started to become very distant to me. "Let's get him out of dere," I heard Deet say as if from a long way off. After that, I could see Deet speaking, knew he was shouting, but I could not hear him. I saw him tearing at the door of the airplane, but I was unable to move. I could only watch Joe, trapped in that twisted mass of metal, his body trying to breathe through his bloody and mangled face, the exhalent forming bubbles in his blood. His breathing was labored, mechanical, like machinery still running after the switch is turned off.

Deet freed the door and pushed it open. I stepped back, and we carefully pulled Joe out and away from the wreckage. Joe was breathing in short, hard bursts now. Then, he stopped, there on the ground, where we placed him. His body was all broken up inside, and he couldn't be revived.

I became aware of Deet shaking me by the shoulders.

"Vat die fuck is vrong vid you?"

"I've never seen a man die before!"

"Scheisse! Scheisse!" Deet said looking past me toward the airfield. I turned and saw a crowd of local men and boys running toward us. Most of them either worked for someone on the airfield or simply hung around and hustled jobs where they could. As the crowd neared, Deet reached behind his back and pulled out a semi-automatic pistol. He aimed it at the oncoming crowd.

"Stay avay! Stay avay!" he shouted.

"We come to help, boss. We all come to help," a couple boys shouted back.

"You come to rob him. I know vat you come for."

"No, boss! No!"

They had stopped now. There were about twenty of them, but it seemed like more. They started to form a semicircle around us. Deet was moving the gun from side to side.

"I swear to Gott, I blow your fucking heads off if you come closer."

At this moment an old Chevrolet pickup truck skidded up next to the group, spraying dust and red gravel as it slid to a stop. Both doors flung open and Mike and a man in a police uniform got out. The policeman had his gun out. He fired it into the air once and the group of locals backed away.

"What the hell happened? What the hell happened here?" Mike shouted, looking at the wreckage. "Is he dead? Is he dead? Goddamn it!"

"Ya," Deet said, "he ist dead. Part of de left ving came off ven he pulled up."

"I warned him about playing cowboy," Mike said. "I warned him, Goddamn it, and now he's gone and destroyed a perfectly good airplane. Do you people think I can continue to operate like this?" He looked at Deet. Deet put his gun away behind his back and under his shirt. Without direction, we walked over to the remains of the left wing. Mike knelt down beside it, looking at it carefully.

"The wing's been cut, severed as cleanly as if someone had done it with a jigsaw."

"I tought he knew about de communication cable dat was put up yesterday," Deet said. "I'm sure I told him about it."

"Well, he obviously didn't know, or he forgot, and, of course, it wasn't marked. TIA, TIA, this Goddamned place. I swear!" Mike said. He stood up slowly then walked over to the group of locals. He called several out of the group by name and told them to get the body and place it in the bed of the pickup. He handed the policeman some dash and instructed him to keep the wreckage clear and asked him to wait until he returned. He then motioned for us to get into the Land Rover and follow him.

We all drove back to the hangar and, once there, put Joe's body onto several boards that had been placed over a couple of sawhorses. We covered it with an extra canvas tarp that had spots of paint and oil on it.

"I'll call Nathan," Mike said, "and see if he can fit us in. There just aren't enough undertakers in this country."

Paterson was in the hangar replacing the tools that his boys had left on the floor. Mike told him to put the tools in the truck along with an axe.

"We'll salvage what we can," Mike said to Deet. "I know it's not easy, but you do need to make the flight to the mission." They looked intently at one another for a few moments then Deet nodded.

"Okay, Mike, you're de boss." Deet motioned for me to follow.

"Wait," Mike shouted. "Do you know whether he had any relatives?"

"I tink so," Deet said. "A modder and a sister back in Germany, but I am not sure. It would be in his folder?"

"Yes, yes." Mike said. "I'll check that; see if they want his body. If not, we'll leave him here in Liberia."

We walked over to where we had left the airplane and finished our preflight inspection. There was a control tower at Spriggs-Payne. They would clear us to take off and land, but they had no real air traffic control responsibilities. Their only purpose was to keep a record of the air service companies operating into and out of the airfield, which included my company, then send them a bill for takeoff and landing fees.

We were cleared to takeoff, of course, and Deet slowly pushed the throttle to full power. The Cessna accelerated slowly at first, then faster, until I could feel the characteristic lightness of an airplane as it neared flying speed. Then there was that magical transition when an airplane rises up from the ground and is borne on the air.

We passed over the wreckage. Paterson's boys were busy chopping up the wreckage and loading parts into the truck. We did a climbing turn out toward the beach. I could clearly see Monrovia from the Cessna's right-side window. Deet turned to the right again and flew along the beach for a short distance.

"Dis country has some beautiful beaches. So far, dey're untouched and dere are houses you can buy or rent right on de beach. Monrovia, as you can see," he said, pointing, "is right off de nose. And dere is de Saint Paul River."

As we flew over Monrovia, Deet turned to follow the river.

"Das is vere all de Big Men live," he said. "Dey all have big houses dat look like dose Southern plantation houses in your country. Honorable Williams has one of dose."

"Do you know which one it is?" I asked.

"Nah! But it is von of dose."

As we followed the river I could see large, modern mansions with hints and traces of Greek revival architecture. They were surrounded by large manicured lawns with outbuildings, stables, and barns. There were a few people sitting in outdoor chairs who looked up as we flew over. Some waved. Then we climbed and flew along the river for about forty minutes.

"Remember dis," Deet said, pointing to a peculiar twist in the river. "Note your time und heading und maintain dis heading for fourteen minutes. You have de airplane."

Deet removed his hands and feet from the controls and glanced over at me to make sure that I was truly flying the airplane.

I checked my watch.

"I have the airplane," I said, as I had been trained to say to acknowledge the changeover. It was a supreme pleasure feeling the airplane in my hands. The Cessna 180 handled similarly to its lighter cousin, the Cessna 140. In fact, all Cessna aircraft have something of the same feel about them—even the turbo-powered Cessna Citation. I immediately felt comfortable and kind of at home with this much more powerful craft.

"You see dose clouds off to de north and vest?"

I nodded that I did.

"Dey vill be down on us in a few hours. De vet season began dis month. I'm surprised dat the veather has been so goot. You should see de airfield coming up in a few minutes. Vhen you do, circle de field. Dat vill take you over de willage und let de customers know dat ve are coming. Vhile you're doing dat, check out de vind sock at midfield. Den enter de downvind leg on de left side to avoid de higher ground on de right. Stay at fifteen hundred feet until you turn onto base leg. Den it's a normal landing. Do it at full flaps. I vill vork de flaps. Keep your approach speed at around eighty-five indicated. If you look like you're going to have trouble, I vill take over in de usual vay."

The Cessna gently descended toward the airfield, which looked like a orange ribbon lying on a green carpet. I flared the aircraft a few feet off the surface, and it floated down the runway for some distance then settled onto the ground with a muffled rumble, the spring steel landing gear absorbing the bumps from the uneven surface.

When the airplane had slowed sufficiently, I turned and taxied back to an open area next to the runway at midfield. A crowd of locals had already gathered. Some were smiling, others were laughing and jumping. Clearly they were happy to see us. I turned into the open area so that the airplane was facing the runway and away from the crowd. I went through the shutdown check list and switched the engine off.

"Stay vith me und don't say a Gottdamn ting," Deet said.

I stepped out of the plane and walked around the nose to where Deet stood with his hands on his hips. The crowd started to come toward us, and I wondered if Deet was going to go for his gun.

"Stay back until I speak vit de Head Man!" he shouted to the crowd.

An older man with white hair emerged from the crowd. He was very thin and wore a tee shirt, soiled trousers, and sandals. His presence seemed to calm the crowd as he approached with slow and measured strides. He came up to Deet and they shook hands in the Liberian way—a quick handshake with a snapping of your partner's fingertips as you release.

"What good tings you breeng today?" the old man asked.

"Here ist de list," Deet said, handing him the manifest.

"Ah, I see it's good. Many good tings." He had done this before and didn't wait for Deet to ask for money. He reached into his trouser pocket and pulled out a small roll of worn US bills and handed them to Deet. For a moment I thought Deet might pocket the entire roll, but he counted out the amount due and handed the remainder back to the Head Man. The man thanked him politely. Then he pointed to a small group of young men standing in front of the crowd and motioned for them to come to the airplane. He said something to them in the local dialect and they began to quickly off-load the cargo. He turned to us and asked if we would like some coffee while we waited. Deet said that would be excellent, and we followed the man to one of the nearby huts.

There were four short wooden stools placed around a loose stone hearth. A small fire was burning in the middle of the stones. The man removed a small bag from a wooden box and poured out the coffee beans onto an irregular shaped piece of sheet metal. He started grinding the beans into small granules with a large metal soup spoon. He then swept the ground beans into the pot and carefully placed the pot on the fire.

"Dat is de best coffee in de vorld," Deet said with a smile of satisfaction. My eyes were becoming more accustomed to the darkness. I could just see several sleeping mats along the cylindrical wall of the wattle hut. Other than that, it was void of furniture and personal items.

"How is de missionary?" Deet asked.

"Oh, he de same. He like his whiskey much. Since hees woman run off he like his whiskey much too much. He no give sermon now, always too drunk. A village woman come to clean and cook, but he no want her for anyting else." The old man shrugged.

"Dat ist too bad," Deet said. "Dere ist nothing more useless dan a drunk man of Gott."

The old man laughed, showing his yellow teeth. He then handed us each a metal cup; both were tarnished and had many marks and dents. He took the large soup spoon and ladled out the hot coffee grounds and dumped them on a piece of newspaper and poured the hot coffee into our cups.

We waited, out of courtesy and custom, for the old man to drink first. After he did, I sipped mine. The coffee was truly the best that I had ever had—rich, with a strong nutty flavor.

"Dis vill keep you avake on the trip home," Deet said, turning toward me.

"I say, ma fren, can ya take people back wit ya, oh?" the man asked.

"How many?"

"A woman an' her daughta. Her daughta vey sick and no one go to de mission anymore fo help."

"Sure," Deet said. "Is she going to pay?"

"De village got money for her. She mus' take her daughta to hospital in Monrovia."

"Fifteen dollars, US, for her und I'll let de kinder fly fur five."

The old man shook his head. "Oh, dat is very high price, but she mus' go jus now. I go now an' tell her to prepare."

"Tell her to bring someting to sit on. De cargo bay can get wery uncomfortable."

When I had finished my walk-around check of the airplane, the Head Man brought the "woman" over. She was barely fourteen and held a small child, less than a year old, in her arms. The child was asleep or unconscious. Its breathing was labored, and flies were constantly crawling around the mucus oozing from its eyes and nose. The Head Man put a sleeping mat in the cargo bay and took the child while the young woman crawled in and positioned herself on the straw rug. Then the Head Man carefully handed her the child.

Deet was already in the left pilot seat and was going through the prestart checks. He wasn't waiting. I quickly tied two of the cargo restraints around her and the child and told her to hold onto the restraints as best as she could. She started to tremble, and I could see that she was terrified.

"Don't worry," I said. "We will be in Monrovia soon."

Deet started the engine and we hurriedly taxied to the end of the runway. He ran the engine up to the recommended RPMs and checked each magneto and all engine instruments. The engine gauges were in the green arcs. After one check of the primary controls to determine if they moved freely, Deet lined the airplane up with the center of the runway, lowered takeoff flaps, and started the takeoff run.

We were airborne a little past midfield and turned to follow our route to the river, then headed home. When we reached the river it started to rain, a tropical rain with fat drops of water that hammered against the windshield. It was dark—not the dark of night but more like the dark when someone pulls down a shade. It was turbulent too. Deet was wrestling with the controls to hold our altitude and heading steady. I looked back to see how our passengers were doing. The young woman was holding tightly onto her child. Her eyes were squeezed shut and she was muttering something that was unintelligible to me. I supposed that she was praying.

At times we had difficulty seeing the river, so Deet kept checking his watch. Then he started to climb and we lost sight of the river altogether. In a few minutes I could see buildings below for possibly a mile out. Deet checked his watch again then turned left, and in a few more minutes we were out of the rain.

"Do you see dat building down dere?" He pointed straight ahead. I said that I did, although I wasn't really sure. "Dat ist de Ducor Palace Hotel. Use dat as your initial approach locator. Den fly due south until you cross de new road. At dat point turn to a heading of 270 degrees und descend to a tousand feet. You should see de airport in a few minutes. Once you see de runway, set it up for landing."

I took over the controls and did just as he said. And, although it seemed a primitive approach, under these conditions it worked. I landed the airplane and bounced it several times. The runway was wet with large puddles of water. As the wheels splashed through them, the heavy spray made a drumming sound on the fuselage. There was a second of silence when we stopped.

"I'll call a cab," Mike said as he met us. "I don't have time to take her to the hospital and I don't want you using the Land Rover to do it either. We have to call her a cab."

"How about an ambulance?" I suggested as we headed toward the office.

Both men looked at me with slight smiles.

"A cab will be much quicker," Mike said, reaching for his phone. "Hi Janice, could you send Jimmy? Village girl needs to take her kid to the hospital. Thanks." He placed the handset back on the phone. "Jimmy'll be here in a few minutes. Now I have work to do. Deet, stay here. I want to talk to you about the next trip to the iron mine."

I left Mike's office and closed the door. Paterson had helped the girl out of the plane and to the waiting room, where she sat clutching her child.

"They've called a cab for you," I said.

She looked up at me. Her eyes were wide with terror. I knew she had no money.

"Here," I said putting a few dollars into her hand. "Everything's going to be all right. How will you get back to the village?"

"I hav a uncle dat leeve in de citte. When ma baby ee well he wee pay ma bus." She stared at me intensely for a moment. "Tank you, sir. You verre kind."

"What is your name?"

"Sarah," she said, "like in de Bible."

"And your child, what is her name?"

She smiled. "I name her Mary, afta de modder of Jesus."

"That's a good name," I said.

When the taxi, an early Volkswagen Beetle with one fender missing and a smoking exhaust, came, I helped her into it and watched until they were out of sight. I hoped that her baby would survive.

CHAPTER 4

DEUTSCH PILOTEN

I met Deet, all smiles, coming out of the office. He slapped me on the shoulder.

"Vell my man, vhat you need is a vagon, a car, a means of transport, but most of all, a pussy vagon! Jump in and I'll take you to see a good friend of mine."

We drove to Heinz and Maria's restaurant. A middle-aged man was sitting at one end of the bar nursing a draft beer. His face was as red as a stop light and his swollen nose, a light shade of purple. Other than that he had all the indicators of a man who had been accustomed to power and respect but was now reduced to what he could carry in a small valise.

"Hans, I vant you to meet a fellow pilot, Ken. Ken, meet Hans."

Hans extended a weathered hand partially crippled by arthritis.

"Hans," Deet said, "dis young man needs a car und since you are leaving Liberia, I tought you might make him a goot deal."

Hans sipped his beer.

"Can we get a table?" I asked Deet.

"Of course," he said, signaling to Maria that we were moving to a table.

Hans moved uneasily in his chair; his eyes darted nervously around. I thought for a moment he was going to flick out his tongue to test the air.

"How much do you want for the car?" I asked.

"I vill take five hundred US dollars for it—in cash."

I shook my head. "Sorry, haven't got it."

"Vell," he said with an edge to his voice, "how much do you have on you, now?"

"Two hundred and fifty," I said.

"Gottdamn!" he shouted, slamming his crippled hand down on the table and letting out a small cry of pain. "Vhy did you bring him here, Dieter? Vhy did you? Vhy do you always vaste my time? Vhy?"

"You need de money, Hans. My friend here needs a car und you don't have much time. Besides, I don't see people standing in line to buy your scheisse."

This time his tongue did dart out and flick quickly from side to side. He rubbed his twisted hands vigorously together and looked at me for a long moment with predatory eyes.

"Vell I guess dat vill have to do. I have to leave soon. Come to my place tomorrow morning. Dieter vill show you." With that Hans rose from his chair, scanned the room quickly, and hurried out of the door.

"What is his problem?" I asked.

"He tinks de Jews are after him. I've tried to tell him dat he isn't dat important und never vas, but he doesn't believe me." Deet anticipated my next question. "He had some minor job in de Dird Reich. He vas a mid-level administrator in de Ministry of Agriculture. He didn't send anybody to de concentration camps. He didn't assassinate anybody—he doesn't even know how to use a gun. He's been a nervous bureaucrat all his life, und now he's convinced de Mossad is after him. Christ, I vish I could delude myself like dat vit Sophia Loren."

"Where is he going tomorrow?" I asked.

"He's catching de flight to Brazil. Varig Airlines operates a round-trip flight from Rio to Monrovia. It's usually filled vith Germans; some vith good reason to flee de Mossad, but most, like Hans, because of delusion and paranoia. By de vay, you got a good deal. I knew old Hans vould be anxious to get rid of it."

Maria came over to the table bringing a couple of beers on a tray. "Ve all heard about poor Joachim. It vas terrible, but he alvays vas a vild boy. Ve're having a celebration in his memory tomorrow night starting at eight. Vhy don't you and de handsome young man," she glanced at me, "come?"

Deet assured her that we would be there. We finished our beers and Deet left some money on the table.

"If ve have time, I'll take you to de Phoenician. It's von of the finest restaurants in town. It's run by a Lebanese family. Von ting you have to learn about are de Lebanese here. Dey own all of de stores and most of de restaurants—dat is, minus de fifty-von percent for de Big Men. De Lebanese are all through de interior. Dere's a Lebanese store at almost every mining camp in Liberia, und vat they don't own de Mandingos do."

Hans lived in a single room in a boarding house in a poor section of Monrovia. When he answered the door for us, his face was redder and his nose a deeper purple than it had been the day before. He motioned for us to come in. Inside, it smelled of alcohol and stale cigarettes. His bed was a US army cot, unmade and disheveled. There was one table and chair.

Hans was in a hurry. He had the necessary papers for the Volkswagen laid out on the table. He had signed in the proper places and indicated for me to do so also. After this I handed him the two hundred and fifty, which he quickly stuffed into his pocket and motioned with his hands that we should go, go, go. On the way out of the door his hat somehow fell onto the floor. I reached down to pick it up.

"*Vergessen sie es! Vergessen sie es! Schnell! Schnell,*" he shouted.

We took Hans to Robertsfield as fast as Deet could manage the roads and watched as Hans ran into the terminal, looking over his shoulders as he did so.

"A wery sad little man," Deet said.

Deet took me around to the various government offices to complete the paperwork and get my car and driver's licenses. I discreetly spread the necessary dash around. It was easier than I thought it would be, and the processes went relatively smoothly.

That evening I picked Deet up in my newly acquired vehicle, a 1951 VW Beetle, and drove to Heinz and Maria's. It felt good being mobile again, having my own wheels, feeling unfettered and independent.

Heinz and Maria's was decorated in honor of Joe. The flag of the Federal Republic of Germany had been placed on the wall next to the Liberian national flag. The Liberian flag has a single white star on a blue field in the upper left corner and eleven alternating red and white stripes; it is an unmistakable derivative of the US flag.

The bar was festooned with paper copies of the German coat of arms, the Bundesadler—a rather determined-looking crow showing his biceps. Underneath each coat of arms was a small square of red paper with a black swastika.

"Nobody cares about dat here," Maria said, "except de Jews and nobody in dis country gives a fuck about dem. They're here all right, lurking and spying, but dey keep deir heads down, I can tell you. And Tubman, he is no friend of de fucking Jews."

Maria was beginning to slur her words. Her English was good, but she still had trouble with her V's and W's. She had started drinking early. She would mix one drink for a customer then one for herself.

"Joachim vas a good boy," she continued. "He served his country, like his vatter. No matter what flag was flying over the Reichstag, Germany came first. Politics, he didn't give a fuck, like his vatter."

"How did his father serve?" I asked.

"Oh, his vatter vas an officer in de Keiser's army, den he vas a representative in the Bundestag during the Weimar Republic. But he died before Hitler came to power. Oddervise, I think he vould have done his duty and served der Fuehrer weddy vell."

Several of the tables had been pulled together. The waiters, all young Liberian men and all dressed in white shirts and blue trousers, had placed a long white cloth over the tables, giving the appearance of a single, long table. There were about twenty guests. Most were pilots who worked for one of the air service operators at Spriggs-Payne. Many were technical service people, and some were from the embassy. There was a sprinkling of wives and girlfriends—all Europeans.

Deet introduced me to several of the male guests. They were very polite in that practiced, old-world way, and it seemed a great struggle for the men to not click their heels when introduced. I met Fritz Werner. He too had been a fighter pilot in the Luftwaffe. Unlike all the others, Fritz had none of the old-world charm. His blue eyes locked onto you like an intense tracking device. His blond hair was thinning and turning gray. He combed it straight back down to his neck, and he handled himself as though every move was timed and calculated.

"You are too young to remember de var," he said. "Germany had its back to de vall und der Fuehrer vas de only von who gave us hope. You know," he said, hesitating with a slight smile stretching his lips, "I could never understand how de American pilots vere so goot. I mean, America is a mongrel country made up of all kinds of people, settled by religious fanatics und de scum of Europe. A nation of moral degenerates. How can such a people become so rich und powerful und produce such goot pilots?"

"Maybe Hitler was wrong?" I said almost as a reflex.

"If der Fuehrer's ideas had been allowed to develop, de vorld vould be a better place, I can tell you. Vat vould be so vrong, I ask you, with having a vorld made up of beautiful, highly intelligent people, free of genetic diseases and deformities? Vhat, I ask you?"

"I didn't know Hitler had any original ideas," I said. "I thought he made up his Nazi creed from the droppings of Nietzsche, Wagner, and the barnyard scatterings of Nordic mythology—all that nineteenth century romantic, sentimental, anachronistic stuff."

Fritz's eyes narrowed and his lips tightened. Just what I thought he might have looked like before pulling the trigger of the 20mm machine gun in the nose of his Messerschmitt BF109.

"Here, here, gentlemen, no politics please. Ve are here to honor a friend und fellow pilot," Deet said, showing me to a seat, and indicating to Fritz where he should sit.

After everyone was seated, the waiters began pouring beer from glass pitchers into large ceramic mugs. Then the meal was served—an assortment of German sausages, boiled cabbage, and a variety of mustards. There was a woman sitting across from me. She looked about my age, and I could not take my eyes off her. There are some women who are so beautiful that divine intervention in their creation seems to be the only explanation.

After a while she glanced in my direction, but I still could not look away.

"Yes," she said, with a symmetrically perfect smile. "And you are?"

"Quite dumbstruck," I said.

She laughed and, as I expected, her teeth were perfect.

"No, I meant what is your name?"

I told her, and to my surprise she seemed to want to chat. She was curious about life in the US and about my university experience. I learned that her name was Ana and that she had graduated the year before from Heidelberg University with a degree in economics and social studies. She had also studied English extensively. She was curious about why I came to Africa and whether I planned to finish college. I assured her that my time in Liberia was only a break from the regimen of higher learning. She said that she had come to believe that no one intends to remain in Africa, but that after a while, even though they say that they want to leave, they never do. It was her opinion that life was too easy for Europeans in Africa—everything and everybody was cheap and there was plenty of what one needed if you had money.

"And money is everything here," she concluded.

I noticed that the volume of voices had gotten much louder. Beer was flowing more freely and the pilots started singing old beer hall songs, then Luftwaffe fight songs. One of the pilots stood up, swayed several times, took a couple of gulps of beer, and started singing the German national anthem. Everyone joined in, including Ana. When that was finished a pilot, whose name was Willy, climbed onto the bar, rolled up his right shirt sleeve to reveal a tattoo of a red swastika on his upper arm with "*Deutschland Für Immer*" inscribed beneath it. He started goose-stepping up and down the bar giving the Nazi stiff-arm salute and shouting, "*Leben sie Langa, Liebe sie Langa, Fur Gott, Fuehrer und Vaterland, Machen Deutchland Wieder Groß!*"

The pilots cheered and toasted Willy with mugs of beer and then began a rhythmic pounding of their feet on the floor while shouting, "*Ein Reich! Ein volk! Ein Füehrer! Deutschland für immer! Ja, ja!*"

Ana seemed a little embarrassed. She glanced at me several times and smiled slightly then looked away.

"I have to leave," I said, getting up from the table.

"I am sorry," she said.

As I was leaving, I came up behind her and stooped to whisper in her ear. "Will you have dinner with me?"

"You don't waste any time," she said primly and smiled. Then, "Yes, you can reach me at the embassy." She wrote her phone number on a paper table napkin and handed it to me.

I drove back to the guest house feeling as though I had just witnessed a kind of satanic rite that, once seen, leaves one scarred forever. I started trembling and continued trembling until I crawled into bed, folded myself up into a comfortable fetal position, and waited longingly for sleep.

CHAPTER 5

MANDINGOS

I spent the next several days flying with Deet and other company pilots, learning the routes, procedures, and navigational landmarks to the mines, villages, and missionary stations that the company served. The iron mines were owned by large international companies, including some based in the US. The companies were all well capitalized and had the best airfields. The laborers were housed nearby in concrete block buildings with metal roofs, and there was often a small store owned and operated by a Lebanese merchant. The engineers and foremen had quite substantial and very comfortable quarters. The iron mines were in Liberia to stay.

In addition to the iron mines, there were four principal diamond areas in the country. They were fairly close together, maybe within a radius of a hundred miles, and all located in the northeastern part of the country near the Guinea and Sierra Leone borders. Foremost of these was at a place called Wiesau on the Lofa River.

There were no roads going to these mines as there were to the iron mines. Building roads to these places would have been extremely difficult and enormously expensive because of the mountainous terrain. Neither the government nor the mine owners were willing to bear the costs. As a result, these outposts were supplied by primitive airstrips only, which had been hastily dug out of dense forests.

The diamond mines were not actually referred to as mines—they were called potholes. Essentially, they were shallow holes dug in the earth. During the wet season, workers would wait for the potholes to fill up with rainwater, then they would pan for diamonds that might have been washed into the pit. It was like panning for gold. During the dry season, they would simply dig with what tools they had.

The area around Wiesua was rich in diamonds. The diamond mines in Liberia were strictly an African operation. The government would not allow the Lebanese or the Europeans in there at all. The Mandingos seemed to be the people in charge. The Mandingo people aren't necessarily Liberians but come from various parts of Central and West Africa. They were the ones with the money, and they ran the supply chains. Most of our payloads of rice, beans, and other staples went through the Mandingos. They also owned the stores at the diamond mines, but the big money came from the sale of rough diamonds.

Mandingos are a very tall and slender people. They wear long, colorful robes and are always clean and meticulous about their dress and appearance. They don't do manual labor, and they were, without exception, Muslim.

They were not part of the government but, owing to their wealth and business acumen, had much influence. The Liberian government was well aware of the contribution of the Mandingos. They always paid for their passage with cash and usually in small bills. There were several very wealthy Mandingos who had accounts with African Air Service, and we called them Big Men although in Liberia that term normally referred to Americo-Liberians of wealth in positions of power.

When the Mandingos transported diamonds with African Air Service, they would conceal the diamonds, wrapped in note paper, in their robes. We would fly them to Monrovia where they could get the best prices. The diamonds were raw and of different colors, grades, and sizes, and there were several diamond cutters in the city that could cut them.

The diamond mines were worked by local diggers. It was all voluntary labor. No one was forced. The laborers would dig and pan for the diamonds and the Mandingos would buy them at fairly low prices. Generally, the workers felt like they were getting a good deal, but I never learned how they were paid by the mining company. They did steal a diamond now and then, but the Mandingos let it go.

A digger could quit at any time, but to do that, he would have to walk through the bush for several days to get out. These laborers were mostly urban or village dwellers and did not do well in the bush. Nevertheless, if they survived the trek through the bush, they would typically wait until they were back in town, had sold their diamond, and had gotten sufficiently drunk, then announce they weren't going back to the mines. This trek through the bush did not happen often, and when it did the laborer would often return to the mines after sobering up.

At the end of my seven-day training period, Mike thought I was familiar enough with the country to let me go out on my own. I called Ana at the embassy. She answered with an official voice.

"Hi Ana, its Ken."

"Ken. Where have you been?"

"I've been learning the ropes, couldn't get away. I'm very sorry. Would you have dinner with me tonight?"

There was a long pause, maybe even a hesitation.

"I really shouldn't, but I do know how it is here." Then, "Sure, why not. What time?"

"I'll pick you up at the embassy at seven. I thought we could try the Phoenician. The guys say it's pretty good."

"Yes, I have heard of it. It has a good reputation. All right then, I'll be looking for you at seven."

There was a musical quality to her voice that told me that I was at least partially forgiven for not having called sooner.

I parked the little Volkswagen Beetle outside the embassy about ten minutes before seven, and at seven sharp Ana came through the gate. She saw me and waved. She was dressed in the normal business attire for the tropics—loose blue skirt, which went below the knee, and loose white blouse. She jumped into the passenger seat and smiled brightly at me.

"You can't believe how happy I am to get away from there. It's like a prison sometimes," she said.

On the way to the Phoenician she told me, in a brief and guarded way, what working at the embassy was like. I parked as close to the restaurant as I could and before I could close and lock the door a street boy, possibly near my own age, was standing beside the car.

"I watch fo you, boss. Keep bad men way." Somehow I sensed that I had better take him up on his offer or certainly confront a couple of flat tires when we returned. I put a quarter in his hand. "Many thanks," I said. The young man looked at the coin, smiled—the dash was acceptable—and put his hands in his pockets.

Feeling somewhat relieved but not certain that the car would be there or usable when we returned, I put my arm through Ana's arm and we walked over to the Phoenician. The owners had gone to considerable lengths to emphasize the Middle Eastern tone and atmosphere of the place. There were oriental rugs on the floor and walls, and each table supported an ornate brass tray. A polite waiter with a soft voice showed us to a corner table, and we settled into overstuffed upholstered seats. Ana ordered a bottle of wine for both of us.

"I'm told they import the wine from Lebanon," she said.

"I didn't know they produced wine in Lebanon."

"Oh, yes. It all started there, you know—in the Middle East. It was so important that Christ himself turned his host's drinking water into wine. You've certainly heard about that."

"Yes, I remember something about it," I said. "Are you religious?"

"No, I don't think so. I don't think anyone in Germany today is. Oh, a lot of them go to church, but I think they're there for the music. It helps them not think about their next meal or if they can afford the rent. Even though it's been sixteen years since the war ended, things are still bad in Germany. It's odd, you know. A lot of people got jobs cleaning up the damage from the war. Old Berlin is now a great mound of rubble, covered with dirt and grass. These mounds are all over Germany. That's where most of prewar Germany went—and in the cemeteries. Now the rubble that was once German cities has been cleared away and, slowly, new buildings are being put up. The common laborers who did the cleanup work are now out of a job."

"Do you think there will be another fascist movement in Germany?" I asked.

"No, not likely. Hopefully, after two bloody world wars, Germany—and Europe for that matter—has learned its lesson. If anything, and if history is any guide, Germany will swing the other way, which it seems to have done. In fact, I think all of Europe has moved to the left, partly as a reaction to the war and partly because fascism is so self-destructive"

She lowered her eyes and her brow wrinkled for an instant. "I want to apologize," she said.

"For what?"

"For that vulgar display at Heinz and Maria's."

"You mean the goose-stepping and heil Hitlers?"

"Yes, that and the whole attitude of those guys. It's as though they haven't learned a thing. That vicious war and the horrible people who brought it on us. Germany will be hated for a long time to come."

Her eyes were brimming with tears, and I could see that she was fighting for control.

"Please don't apologize," I said. "I understand how you feel. Look, I try not to make judgments about anyone, but I have to admit that I was a little out of place there when the singing started. Pilots are lousy singers, and for the most part, they tend to see things in straight lines, in black and white. I went to an air show once at Andrews Air Force Base when I was in high school. There was a section of the ramp roped off where spectators could get close to the airplanes and the pilots, all dressed in their flight suits and silver braided hats. One person standing near me asked about navigation and the pilot tried to explain the electronics used in navigation. When he saw that he wasn't getting very far, he paused, then he explained it as a point on a graph. 'You are only a moving point on a graph. That's all you are,' he said.

"When it comes to politics, great social movements, or interpreting history, pilots can be the most naive people in the world. Our American hero, Charles Lindbergh, is a good example—brilliant pilot but naive as a child about politics."

The wine came and the waiter told us that it was Chateau Kefraya from the vineyard at Mount Barouk. It was the smoothest, most delicious wine I had ever had.

"Do you have a girlfriend back home?" she asked.

I hesitated. I couldn't describe what I was feeling, but I knew it wasn't good.

"Yes," I said.

She raised her eyebrows slightly.

"Are you engaged to her?"

"No. Not yet."

"And what does that mean?"

"I think she wants to get married, have a family and a house in the suburbs."

"And you don't want that?"

"For now, let's say I'm not ready for it. That's part of the reason I'm in Africa," I said.

"What is the other part?"

"Let's just say it truly was a dark November in my soul with a ghost I need to exorcize."

"You sound like a poet rather than a pilot."

"Thanks, but I'm really a failed physicist."

"You're not interested in art or literature?"

"Yes, of course, but math, physics, and the sciences make the world sensible for me. To me, the sciences deal with unambiguous truth and beauty. I have a hard time dealing with illogical or subjective concepts."

"Emotions, feelings, make no sense?" she asked.

"Insofar as they can't answer the question of how, yes, they make no sense. But I have to admit, emotions and feeling are strong motivators. I think of them as colors that an artist uses to paint pictures and those pictures could well be our lives."

"And what about that dark November?" she asked with a slight smile.

"As I said, it's certainly part of the reason I'm here and as soon as it makes sense, I guess I'll leave."

"Sounds like you're a bit of an artist too. Do you paint or anything like that?"

"Very perceptive of you. I prefer to sketch, but I also paint in acrylics."

"Are you good at it?"

"I think I'm a fairly good sketch artist and a fair painter. It's a hobby really—a way to deal with the boogieman."

"And does it work? Does it keep the boogieman away?"

"It helps but, then again, I have many ways of keeping the boogieman away."

"You'll have to tell me about them sometime."

"Be happy to, but only when I know you better."

She laughed. We talked for a long while about Cornell, and I think I convinced her that my decision to come to Africa was based partly on logic and partly on the dark November. She planned to return to Germany and get into the film industry. Germany, she emphasized, was going to grow, and she wanted to be a part of it. She wanted to get into the production side of the film industry because she believed that was where the real value lay. She was convinced that Germany was going to lead Europe in film making. Performing, as a career, she believed, was too ephemeral, based as it is on youth, appearance, public whims, and an enormous quantity of luck.

"And besides," she said. "I'm afraid of being in front of the camera."

The dinner was excellent—malfouf (a stuffed cabbage roll) and baba ghanoush (roasted eggplant with garlic and tahini sauce). It was satisfying without being filling, and I was pleased to see that she didn't light up a cigarette afterward. We chatted for a while over coffee, then I drove her back to the Embassy and walked her to the Embassy gate.

"I'm going to be busy for a while, but can we do this again?" I asked.

She hesitated, looking me directly in the eyes. "Yes, I would like that."

I drove back through Monrovia to my guest house. Lilly was up finishing a large glass of rum. Since all of her guests were pilots, who by the nature of their work were coming and going at all hours of the day and night, the rules were slack about coming in late or leaving early. Lilly waved at me but didn't speak—probably because she couldn't get her lips to form the words. I went up to my room and crashed onto my bed thinking I really needed a place of my own.

CHAPTER 6

TOO FINE

When the Peace Corps act was passed by Congress on September 22, 1961, it was a particular boon to Africa Air Services. The company was able to add these Peace Corps volunteers to its long list of contract passengers along with technical service people and Liberian government officials. Although passenger service was lucrative, it was usually simple coastal routes that were considered less desirable by the AAS pilots. So it was not a great surprise to me that most of my trips in the beginning were coastal.

My first solo trip was about an hour's flight down the coast to a small town by a lake and close to a mountain. It was a beautiful place, and the sea was nearby. I decided to hotdog a little, so I flew along the beach and veered in and out between palm trees. It was a rush I hadn't felt in a long time! I had a couple of missionaries on board and a lot of general cargo. The missionaries were silent and unconcerned.

This airplane was designed to carry a thousand pounds as maximum payload; however, we usually took off with twelve hundred pounds. If we were operating from an especially rough or short field, we would stay within weight limits. The company would have pushed us to fly with more than twelve hundred pounds if they could have, but they had discovered that any more than twelve hundred pounds and the plane just didn't fly.

After offloading my cargo, I started back with two new passengers. But before I turned on course for Monrovia, I circled the lake. It was easy and beautiful, just as I thought it would be.

The custom in Liberia at the time was that whatever a Big Man wanted, he got. Mike asked me to fly over to Robertsfield and pick up Honorable Williams and members of his family. They were due in on Pan Am Flight 51. Pan American ran Robertsfield, and they provided the air traffic control. I took off from Spriggs-Payne and shortly afterwards called the tower at Roberts and told them that I was about fifteen minutes out. A snappy controller's voice called back and said, "We use Zulu time here," so I asked him for a Zulu time check. He gave me one and I proceeded in to Robertsfield. I was cleared to land and after landing I turned off at the first intersection and starting taxiing. The controller came back with his snappy voice:

"Cessna 180, you were not given permission to taxi. Report to the tower when you have completed your final check. And make it quick."

I climbed the ladder to the tower, which was on top of the terminal building and was let into the glass enclosure of the control tower where the controllers had a complete view of the airfield. By this time, Flight 51 had pulled up on to the ramp below. The "snappy" controller was an American—a short, red-faced man.

He deliberately made me wait while he finished some paperwork, then turned to me and said, "I'm in charge here and I'm thinking of filing a violation against you."

"For what?" I asked.

"Well, you don't seem to know what time it is in this country," he said.

I suppressed my anger as best I could. "I know damn well what time it is."

He continued, "Or obey instruction coming from the tower. I'm probably not going to give you permission to fly out of here."

"That's very interesting," I said. "You see, I have some important passengers to pick up."

"I don't really care," he barked. "You're not going anywhere right now."

I didn't see any point in continuing this. I left the tower and met Honorable Williams in the terminal. He was a handsome man. He stood over six feet tall and was impeccably dressed in a blue, lightweight suit. His dark eyes showed both intelligence and kindness. At the moment, however, after a long trip and accompanied by his family, they showed fatigue.

"We have a problem," I said after introducing myself. "The man in the control tower won't let us take off."

Honorable Williams said, "Oh, is that so!" He really did not want this irritation. He turned and spoke to a Liberian army lieutenant who was nearby. The lieutenant motioned to a couple of his soldiers.

"Go an' bring heem down," the lieutenant ordered. The soldiers immediately went up to the tower and brought the controller down to face Honorable Williams. "This is the man who said you can't takeoff?" he asked, looking at me.

"Yes," I said.

Honorable Williams rubbed his hands. "Do you need him to tell you how to take off?"

"No."

Honorable Williams turned to the soldiers. "Take him into the customs room and hold him until you hear from me."

By the expression on his face, the controller knew that he had made a big mistake. I smiled at him, but he was avoiding any eye contact with me. We did take off and I flew Honorable Williams and his family members back to our airfield. Later, I heard that they let the controller go free but, at about three o'clock the next morning, soldiers went to his house and "interrogated" him. Then they took him to the local constabulary and he was gone on the next flight out. He had learned too late that one did not cross or refuse a Big Man.

When the company had enough confidence in me, I was assigned to what I thought of as my first real trip. I was to transport supplies for a store owned by some Lebanese in the interior. It was at the end of the railroad to a new mining camp. This was a serious money-maker.

The mining camp was part of the Liberian-American-Swedish Mining

Company (LAMCO). LAMCO was the first large iron mining operation in Liberia. With mines in the Nimba mountain range in the eastern part of the country bordering Guinea and Ivory Coast, the mining company had built a 156-mile-long railroad to transport the ore to Port Buchanan.

There were no facilities in Liberia, at that time, for filing an instrument flight plan or expecting radar coverage or air traffic control (ATC) guidance. You simply loaded your airplane, did your preflight checks, and took off. If there was somebody else up there flying around at your altitude, you didn't know about them and they didn't know about you.

Ascending slowly from Spriggs-Payne, I crossed the crumbling remains of the outer ring road, originally designed to bypass Monrovia but never finished. The road, an orange band of bare laterite over a green carpet, passed slowly by the cockpit window until small rice farms started to appear. There was a small hut next to each green patch of rice. Occasionally, their roofs would flash in the sunlight. After some minutes, the Saint Paul River came into view. I was well inland by this time. My flight path would cross the river nearly at right angles. Its brown flow seemed to be more like a wide highway than a river.

Scattered along the near bank lay huge decaying mansions, ironically reminiscent of the last vestiges of the antebellum South. This was one of the early and misguided choices for a settlement location. Over a hundred years ago, the original black settlers who migrated from the United States tried duplicating the plantation homes that they had known in the Old South. Now, the crumbling buildings had been taken over by the jungle, leaving only roofless ruins—a decaying echo of a system that should never have existed.

After crossing the river, the rice farms began to disappear. Civilization fell back and beneath me. The world below was a more primitive place now. The matted mangroves of the coast steadily gave way to the forest of the rising plateau. The farms that remained were small and isolated. A thick double canopy of the high rainforest now covered the land. Only the bravest villages, diamond mines, and missions, supplied by bush plane, dared the forest. From here to the savanna 150 miles to the northeast, the escarpment of vegetation resisted human passage and all signs of civilization vanished in the jungle. I was bound for the rim of the Savannah and beyond. The great forest itself soon disappeared into the opaque clouds below as I sought cooler altitudes nearly a mile above the jungle.

To get to the mining camp I had to clear mountains with peaks somewhere near three thousand feet. The mountains had not actually been mapped, so three thousand feet was just a guess. Not very high as far as mountains go, but the cloud ceilings were usually down around fifteen hundred to two thousand feet during the wet season. I estimated my position by dead reckoning, held my course for the estimated time then started letting down, hoping that I would see the St. John River before I hit something. Once I had it in sight, the usual procedure was to spiral down over the river so as not to lose sight of it, then fly up the river to the estimated position of the mining camp and hope that the airstrip came into view. If you missed it, you had to fly down the river and back up again until you saw it.

To transport their heavy equipment, LAMCO had cut a rough road for about 150 miles through the jungle. The bright orange laterite indicated the area was rich in iron ore. LAMCO was the wealthiest business interest in Liberia, so lack of money was never an issue. They used a large number of bulldozers and other heavy equipment on these sites to build an airstrip and to clear away the jungle for open pit iron mines. These mines looked like terraced rock quarries, some about the size of a midwestern town in the US.

This particular mining camp was all open air and populated with local laborers and wild-looking Europeans. When I arrived, a European man was standing on the edge of the jungle slowly shooting his pistol into the bush for no observable reason. I decided to do my business and leave quickly.

My trip out of the area was tricky too. And I knew that if I were to go down, no one would ever find me.

About every couple of months an air service operator would lose an airplane. Sometimes the pilots would survive, but most of the time they would not. I decided to never let down below 2,500 feet unless I had the river in sight. If I couldn't spot the river, I would have to go back with my load. One pilot, Johann Muller, always went in, no matter what the conditions. One day he didn't come back. Neither he nor the airplane were ever found. The jungle swallowed them up. I came to the quick realization that my life was worth more to me than a load of mining supplies.

Over two weeks had gone by since our dinner, but I had spoken to Ana several times on the phone. There was a soccer match coming up the following week at the stadium, and I asked Ana if she would like to go. She said yes. In the meantime, I had a flight up the coast to a small village near the Sierra Leone border.

I was to meet a group of Peace Corps volunteers and fly them up the coast to Gola village. They arrived on a chartered bus from Robertsfield around noon. There were three women, all young, white, and recent college graduates. There was also one man who was older and seemed to be in charge.

It had been a long series of flights for them with no real opportunities for rest. I knew how they must be feeling. They had been dropped into an alien world of heat and humidity with no sleep, bad food, and strange sights and smells. They off-loaded their bags from the bus and, looking bewildered and disheveled, flopped down on them. The man walked over to me, probably because I was the only white man there. We did not wear uniforms or any form of designation such as silver wings pinned on our shirts or epaulets with gold stripes on them—no suit of lights for the pilots of African Air Services.

He extended his right hand and smiled. "Are you the owner?" he asked in a clear masculine voice.

"God no, I'm just one of the pilots. I'll be flying you to where you want to go."

"Good, good," he said, shaking my hand vigorously. "I'm Chuck Townsend. I'm the director and, as you can see, my guys are pretty beat. How far is it to the village?"

"About an hour, give or take ten minutes."

"Great, great! So if we could start getting everything and everybody loaded," he said, his voice rising as he turned to the huddled group.

Paterson had arrived with two of his loaders. He called these boys his "rollers" because they rolled the equipment carts around. They pushed the empty four-wheeled cart toward us. Paterson said something to them that was unintelligible to me and then very politely asked the women to stand away from the bags. The women wearily struggled to their feet and stood patiently while Paterson's boys loaded the bags onto the cart. With all the bags teetering on top of each other, one of the boys pulled while the other pushed the cart over to the airplane.

Paterson handed me the passenger list and loading sheet, which read 1200 lbs. I called all the names and they all answered like a Girl Scout troop, saying "Here!" when they heard their name.

The company had recently acquired a Cessna 185 with a cargo pod fastened under the belly of the airplane. It was a bigger, heftier airplane than the 180 and required more takeoff room. The speeds were a little higher than the 180, but other than that it was laid out like most Cessna aircraft—comfortable, easy to read, and made to fly.

After the boys had loaded the bags on the airplane, I waited for the passengers to seat themselves. Chuck took the front seat next to me. It was obvious that we were overweight. In the US this would be a violation of the aviation regulations and, therefore, the takeoff weight limitation is usually strictly observed. But this was West Africa, and all the rules hadn't been written yet. I was learning you did what had to be done.

I taxied to the very edge of the bush at the end of the runway to give myself every available foot. I double checked to make sure everyone had their seat belts on, then started the takeoff run.

The airplane accelerated more slowly than I expected, but it steadily gained speed. We reached rotation speed about two thirds down the runway and I slowly pulled the nose up. The airplane struggled into the air and the stall warning light came on immediately. The loading sheet had been fudged of course.

I eased off of the back pressure and the light went out. The airplane continued to accelerate but wasn't yet ready to climb. The end of the runway was coming up fast; the palm trees looked like they were reaching out to grab us. I did not want to end up in a pile of crushed aluminum in the same spot where Joe did.

I held it down, gaining speed, as long as I dared then eased back on the yoke and the airplane started to climb nicely. We cleared the cable and tops of the palm trees by what seemed like inches. Chuck looked at me with an expression of relieved terror.

"Just a day in the life of an African bush pilot," I said, hoping my weak attempt at humor would relieve the tension in his face.

The young women behind us seemed unconcerned. Most gazed out of the windows in wonder at this "brave new world." The weather was good, and I was able to gain enough altitude to safely fly over Monrovia. After passing over the city, I dropped to a lower altitude to fly along the coast. Chuck had indicated on the map where the village should be. The head men had been informed, by radio, of our arrival and had put a large cross made of bed sheets on the runway. I reached a point where I estimated that I should turn inland. Ten minutes later I saw the village.

I could clearly see the cross, and as I circled the runway, people started to remove the sheets. It was a dirt strip with puddles of rain water scattered over it. I suspected that the ground was soft, so I set the airplane up for a soft field landing, which means, in aviation jargon, hanging the airplane on the propeller and dragging it in at plus five knots above the stall speed with full flaps. Since I knew that the airplane was overweight, I added an extra five knots and made the approach as low as possible, skimming over the tops of palm trees. Chuck looked terrified again, as well he should have.

As the airplane neared the ground I added a little power to reduce the rate of descent, then, as the plane settled, a little more, and a little more until the wheels began to touch the ground very gently. I slowly reduced power and the wheels began to sink into the mud, splashing fanlike sprays of muddy water onto the wings and tail. Once on the ground, the speed dropped rapidly. I did not want the airplane to come to a stop and sink deeper into the mud so I kept it rolling, turned with some difficulty, and taxied on the runway to a grassy area beside the runway near a large mud hut. I shut the engine down. Chuck seemed relieved.

Villagers began crowding around and I opened my door and asked for the Head Man. I saw him making his way through the crowd. He was, as expected, older with graying hair and bad teeth. I stepped out of the airplane and the man greeted me with the unique Liberian hand shake with a snap at the end. We introduced ourselves.

"Helloo ya! Ah Mulbah," he said.

"Hello Mulbah, I'm Ken. Could you get some of the boys to help with the bags?"

He looked back and made several quick gestures with his walking stick. Several boys pushed their way to the airplane, and he said something to them in a tribal dialect. One of the boys ran to the cargo pod and opened it as though he had done it before. By now the women had started to deplane and gather near the tail. Chuck was with them.

Again Mulbah said something unintelligible to the boys, who were now lifting the bags onto their shoulders, and pointed to the mud and grass hut with his stick. They pushed through the crowd, each carrying a bag on his shoulders. I went behind them, followed by Mulbah, Chuck, and the women, almost in single file.

The hut was a fairly large rectangular structure of dried mud and wattle, a roof thatched with palm leaves and several small rooms, each with an open window. There was a single entrance. Each room had a cot, a wooden stand with a metal wash basin and a metal water pitcher. The few pots, pans, eating utensils, and linens in the hut were shared. There was no electricity, and each room had an oil lamp and a large grass rug on the dirt floor. Oil, Mulbah emphasized, was strictly rationed.

Mulbah showed the hut off as an object of pride, and the women, as well as Chuck, did a good job of hiding their shock and disappointment. When the tour was over Chuck thanked him for his generosity and kindness and directed the women to select rooms and do the best that they could. Chuck said he would walk back to the airplane with me to make a final check, but I suspected that he wanted to jump into the front passenger seat and get out of there.

"I have to admit," he said on the walk to the airplane, "I don't think the girls are quite ready for this, despite their training."

"What are they going to do here?" I asked.

"We have two teachers and a nurse and more arriving next month. All very young, very enthusiastic, and sure they can make a difference. These volunteers know they are ambassadors. They know their work and behavior is going to be scrutinized."

"Is that your job, Chuck?"

"No, no, I'm more of a facilitator. The volunteers are going to be watched by the host country and by the skeptics in the US government, and believe you me, we have a lot of them. Some of them are already referring to us as a cult of escapism. But we intend to make the idea of a crossroad for Africa work. We see ourselves as a bridge from our country to theirs."

"Do you have any male volunteers coming in the next group?"

"I don't know yet, but I can assure you that all of our volunteers are dedicated to the goals of the Peace Corps and are certainly not trying to escape anything," he said with just a tinge of stridence.

We reached the airplane. I looked around to make sure there were no obstructions.

"Look Chuck," I said. "I haven't been in Africa all that long, but I've learned enough to know that a woman, on her own without a male protector, is fair game here."

"These women are here to help and they have each other. Besides, we have the assurance of the Liberian government that they will be safe, and considering the historical ties with the US, I believe they will honor their commitment."

"I don't think the Liberian government knows or cares what goes on outside Monrovia. Your volunteers are in the bush and the rules are different—more basic, more elemental. Do you understand what I'm saying?"

He nodded slightly but I had the feeling that he was not ready to step out of his ideal world. I climbed back into the airplane.

"Can you come back for me in a couple of days?" he asked.

"Sure, you guys have a contract with us and we are at your service whenever you want."

"Good, I have to get the office in Monrovia started up. We're expecting volunteers all over this country by the end of the year."

I closed the door. Chuck stepped away from the airplane and I started the engine. As I taxied away I saw Chuck wave. He looked completely out of place with his expensive tropical attire, his clean shoes and his confident smile against the background of mud huts, soiled clothes, undernourished people, and limping domestic animals.

CHAPTER 7

PRESIDENT TUBMAN

I landed about an hour before dark and tied the airplane down. I turned in my trip report and drove back to the guest house dead tired. There was a letter from Jenny in my box. Jenny was a good correspondent and had written regularly. I had written occasionally, but I had to admit, not often. I was immediately overcome with a feeling of both guilt and joy. Guilt because I had to admit to myself that I hadn't thought a lot about Jenny since I arrived and joy, of course, from hearing from her. I opened it in my room and sat down at the small desk to read it.

Darling Kenneth,

It's been forever since I last saw you. But I can fully understand why you haven't had time to write—I've been busy too. I did some research on Liberia and realize that you must be knee-deep in this new and confusing world.

As far as I can tell, President Tubman is a strong leader and good for the country. I read that he is the first president of Liberia to include all sixteen indigenous tribes in the government. He also established the "Open Door Policy" that brings in tons of international investment. Your last letter said you were flying into iron mines, and according to what I've read, Liberia is very rich in mineral wealth and that the government collects billions in leases, fees, and contracts. Plus, it says, that Liberia has the fastest growing economy in Africa! It sounds like there is plenty of work to go around.

I can't wait for you to tell me all about it!

Kenneth darling, I'm still having trouble getting over how I felt the last time I saw you. I have this permanent picture in my head of you at the airport, with your duffle slung over your shoulder, walking to that airplane. And even though you were with a crowd of others, you looked so vulnerable, so alone. I had this awful feeling in the pit of my stomach that I would never see you again. Please don't let that happen. Please take care of yourself. And write to me, write to me.

All my love,

Jenny

I carefully folded the letter and put it into the desk drawer. She seemed so far away. I felt like she was writing to someone else, to a different Ken. I'd promised I wouldn't be gone long, but it was looking like that might be one more promise broken. I didn't want to end up like Deet or Mike McCoy or Joe—especially not Joe—but I was now being treated differently—not like a student or someone's son, but like a grown man whose skills were respected, who could be looked upon to get the job done.

I thought about Jenny for a long while. The possibility of keeping her, as well as my new life in Africa, seemed remote. My earlier joy waned, but the guilt was still there.

I decided that a change of mood was in order. Deet had said that the Gurley Street Bar was a favorite hangout for British and Americans. Maybe I needed the company of my countrymen and our British cousins for a while.

The bar was crowded, noisy, and filled with cigarette smoke. It was early enough that the drinking had not begun to take its toll. I made my way to the bar and ordered a beer. In what seemed like an instant, the bartender plopped a beer in front of me and popped the top off with the adeptness of a magician's hand.

"You stay hee fo while? You wanna tab?" the bartender asked.

"Yeah, sure. Could I get something to eat?"

He placed a rather worn and smudged menu next to my beer.

"I'd recommend the prawn sandwich."

The recommendation came from the flushed faced man on my left. I turned. He was an older man, possibly in his mid-forties with a dark indentation in his forehead that was partially hidden by thinning blondish hair.

"You must be a newcomer, mate."

"How can you tell?"

"Let's just say that you still have that washed-and-dried look. Kinda like one who hasn't looked into the pit and seen the real shit at the bottom."

"Thanks," I said. "What part of the UK are you from?"

"I'm not. I'm a Kenyan, but I went to school in England and flew in the RAF. So I suppose I consider myself British."

"RAF . . . as a pilot?"

"Of course, lad, there is no other way to enjoy the RAF."

"So, what are you doing here?" I realized instantly that was not the sort of question one asks here. I started to apologize, but he interrupted.

"It's all right, lad, I understand. But to set your mind at ease, I fly for Monrovia Airlines. And you?"

I told him who I worked for. His eyebrows narrowed a little, and he asked me how long I had been there.

"Just a few months," I said.

"Take my advice," he said, "and watch your six o'clock with that guy. He can be as slippery as an eel and as mean as a rhino. Hell, he doesn't even bother to wear a mask when he robs you."

The waiter brought my prawn sandwich.

"There's a table free over there," I said, pointing to a recently emptied table. "Would you like to join me?"

He looked hesitant for a second. "The next one's on me," I said.

"Certainly, lad, certainly. I never refuse that kind of invitation."

I tried the prawn sandwich. It was excellent. "My name's Ken. Ken Verrier."

He extended his hand, which had a missing forefinger. He noticed my attention and said, "It happened when I punched my way out of a mangled aircraft five years ago. So you're Canadian? The name's Colin by the way." He lit a cigarette.

"Actually, I'm an American but my ancestors were French Canadian. Did you work for Mike?"

"No, but I know some what did, and he royally fucked every one of them. I'm just advising you to watch him, that's all. Look, lad, you can't trust anybody in this country, especially the fuckers what's in charge. This place is a great fucking grab bag. People like your boss are here to grab what balls of shit they can and get out. They don't care what kind of mess they leave behind."

"He seems to have some good people working for him now," I said.

"That bunch of fucking Krauts? They are all unredeemed Nazis to the core and old McCoy knows what will happen to him if he tries to fuck with them. I heard you lost one?"

"Yeah, Joe. An accident. He clipped the new communication cable near the end of the runway. He didn't know about it."

"Well, don't expect any tears from me. We should have killed all those goose-stepping bastards when we had the chance. There is one bit of irony though, and forgive me for smiling a little—they are all scared to death of the Jews. You know, the Mossad. The Israelis around here are keeping an eye on each one of them. But the Jews, they have to be careful too, because of Tubman."

"Tubman? Why? It was my understanding that President Tubman has been good for this country," I said.

"Tubman would be a Nazi himself if it were not for the fact that he's black. Let me tell you something about Honorable Tubman. He loves the krauts and he's smart enough to learn from old Adolf's mistakes. He's got this problem with the country people. They all have tribal affiliations. They don't like him or any of his friends. So instead of rolling his storm troopers into their lands and shooting all of the tribal leaders, he goes to see 'em like he is one of their long-lost cousins and buys 'em off. It's the old custom of dash around here, magnified. As long as he does that, he'll have no serious trouble from them."

"Yes, but throwing money around doesn't earn respect, and I get the impression no one really challenges anything he does. Sounds like a pretty nice guy."

"Bollocks, mate! I'll tell you the kind of nice guy he is. Several years ago

'Honorable' Tubman had this Kraut girlfriend. This was about the time that a gang of thieves in Monrovia developed a tactic of ram, rob, and run. They would pick out somebody they thought was a rich American or European. They would wait until the right moment, then ram the unfortunate victim with their car, rob them, and drive away. Normally, Americans and Europeans are not molested here, but these guys decided they would branch out, defy convention, and go for the real money.

"So, the president's Kraut girlfriend flies in one day from the fatherland and Tubman sends one of his cars, a white Mercedes, to pick her up. Now the car isn't marked with a government symbol or anything like that. It looks like an ordinary rich white man's car. The thieves, who had been cruising the airport, you know Robertsfield, spot the car and follow it. Then, when they think it's all in their favor, they ram the car, steal her jewelry and what cash she had on her, then took off. Well, that was the worst mistake they could have made. Within an hour, the thieves were rounded up and thrown in jail."

He chuckled to himself. "You see, it was bad enough that they assaulted and robbed the president's girlfriend. Had she been just another European, it really would not have mattered that much. Tubman would have given another one of his anti-crime speeches, the boys might have been slapped on the wrist, and that would have been the end of it. But by attacking the president's honey, they attacked the president himself, and that is the very thing Tubman will not tolerate—a challenge to his authority or an attack upon anything that belongs to him. It's one and the same to him."

"So what happened to the thieves?" I asked.

"Tubman decided to make an example of them, so he announced there would be a Justice Day. And when that day came, justice was to be held in the football stadium. It was done at night for full effect. You know, like the Nazis used to do at Nuremburg with their torches and vertical lights. Herr Speer called it the ice palace.

"It was like a sports affair. Vendors were selling cotton candy, beer, shit like that. And just at the right moment, he got up into the speaker's stand and called for the criminals to be brought out. The same white Mercedes was driven out onto center field and two policemen got out. They opened the rear door and dragged out three guys who were handcuffed and chained together. Then Tubman made this long speech in the style of der Fuehrer about how he was going to put an end to crime and, after a timed pause, he extended both arms and said, 'Now let justice be done,' and the crowd went wild."

"The cops dragged the three guys around to the rear of the car, opened the trunk and threw them in, and slammed the trunk lid down. A pickup truck drove out to the scene and the cops started offloading five-gallon cans of petrol. They must have dumped fifty gallons of the stuff in and on the car. Tubman gave the signal by suddenly lowering his arms, and the cops lit the car off. At that point the crowd let out a scream that made what's left of my hair stand on end. I've never heard anything like it. It was like ten thousand people at the height of supreme ecstasy.

"Toward the end, when the car finished bouncing and the flames were dying down, the crowd in the bleachers started throwing their empty bottles down on the people standing on the ground. It's a sort of custom. That's why the groundlings always bring a piece of metal sheeting with them when they go to a football match. It's like an umbrella to deflect the rain of bottles."

"Why on earth do they throw bottles down on the people below?" I asked.

"Haven't the foggiest, mate. I suppose it's a way of showing the groundlings what their place in this society really is. Can you imagine being so obsessed with a sport that you're willing to stand under a rain of beer bottles? And make no mistake—other than public executions, football is the number one sport in this country."

I smiled slightly at Colin and turned toward the barman and motioned to him for another round. "So tell me about this company you work for."

"Monrovia Airlines? It's really the same type of operation that you work for, only bigger and with more aircraft. I think it's owned by an Israeli company and, of course, the Honorable Williams. The boss's name is Andre. He prisses around like a frog and he wants you to think he's a frog, but he's really a Eurasian. His father was French and his mother was Vietnamese. He was sent to France for his education, and after the French were defeated at Dien Bien Phu, he stayed. I understand his parents didn't make it out. Not sure how he ended up here." He paused. "The pay's good and, I have to say, Andre runs a tight operation."

Colin was interrupted by a man sitting down at our table. Colin didn't look surprised.

"Max," he said. "This young man is Ken. He's American and he's working for McCoy."

Max looked at me and smiled slightly but did not extend his hand. "It's time," Max said to Colin.

"Sure, Max," Colin answered.

Max rose to leave and looked at me. "Nice to meet you."

As Max walked away Colin leaned toward me and said, "I know what you're thinking. You've got to remember, in this country, you don't ask too many questions. Max isn't a pilot; he's a kind of freelance. He gets things done for people. That's all I know and all I want to know." Colin rose to leave. "Stop by the operation sometime. I'll introduce you to Andre."

I said that I would and watched him disappear into the crowd of the Gurley Street Bar.

CHAPTER 8

ANA

Soccer, or football as it's known in Liberia, can be said with considerable accuracy to be the national sport of Liberia. The Lone Star team, named to recall the lone star in the Liberian flag, is meant to represent Liberian pride. Winning football players are venerated with the same idolatry that baseball heroes are in the US. And it is those Liberians near the lower rungs of the economic ladder who are the most passionate followers of the game. They would spend their last penny or endure all varieties of hardship to watch their favorite matches.

President Tubman, possibly seeing no way out of it, built a football stadium with a capacity for ten thousand people in the city of Monrovia a few blocks southeast of Gurley Street on United Nations Boulevard. He wasn't a huge fan of soccer—no more so than the rest of the Americo-Liberian elite. However, he did understand the power of giving the people "bread and circuses" and made sure that enough government funds were diverted to subsidize the price of rice, the staple food in Liberia, and to keep the price of tickets to football matches cheap. To make sure Monrovians knew whom to thank for their low-cost food and entertainment, he named the stadium after his wife, Antoinette Tubman.

I met Ana at the stadium as planned and we climbed the steps to the covered seats. Ana had played soccer in secondary school in Germany. She wasn't exactly a "fan" in the American sense of the word. She didn't follow matches and she didn't know many of the names of the star players, but she enjoyed the game and cheered loudly when the Lone Star team scored a goal.

Every seat was taken in the covered section of the stadium, and almost everyone was drinking a beer or soft drink. The people, sitting and standing on the ground below, all had their assorted shapes of sheet metal by their sides. After the first Lone Star goal, the crowd went wild, followed shortly by a rain of bottles. We could see them arching out from the open seats in a wave of slow moving projectiles to shatter on the metal plates below. It was just as Colin had described. I looked at Ana.

"Are you all right?" she asked.

"Yes," I said. "I just realized that a story a friend recently told me was true." The cheering was so loud that it nearly drowned out what I was saying.

The Lone Star team won the match against Ghana. The sound of ten thousand human voices roaring with all of their power reminded me of the roaring intensity of the wind near the vortex of a hurricane. I wondered if it had not been similar at the Coliseum in Rome when a favorite gladiator defeated another and the crowd roared for his death. I thought of the American football games that I had attended in the US and heard people in the bleachers shouting "Kill 'em!" "Stomp 'em!" and "Murder 'em!" during tense moments.

The shouts somehow seemed more serious here than in the bleachers at Cornell. Ana and I were both experiencing a heightened sense of excitement. I looked at her and at that moment she looked breathtakingly beautiful.

"Would you like to try the restaurant at the Ducor Palace Hotel? It has a beautiful view," she said. "And I'm told the food is exceptional."

"Absolutely!" I said.

The hotel had been finished the year before and it was located on the top of Ducor Hill. It overlooked the Atlantic Ocean and the Saint Paul River. It also had a commanding view of most of Monrovia. It had been built by an Israeli contractor and was the last word in accommodations and luxury. One could easily say that it was the jewel of Africa. I had remembered to bring a tie and blazer, which I had folded in the back seat of my car. My suspicions were correct—they required a tie and jacket. Ana wore a light cotton, sleeveless pale blue dress good for any occasion.

"We're here for dinner," I told the parking attendant dressed in chauffer's livery, all in white with gold buttons and braid. He regarded the rather faded and battered VW with a tolerant smile. He opened the door for Ana. I handed him the keys wrapped in a dollar bill. He bowed slightly, and we walked into the hotel. Another hotel attendant, immaculately dressed in a tuxedo, very formally pointed the way to the restaurant. Although it was still a little early for dinner, Ana suggested that we find a good table and enjoy a bottle of wine and the splendid view.

Since it was early, there were empty tables and attentive waiters.

"I'm in the mood for steak and potatoes," she said.

"That sounds great—very American."

"Yes, but it's very German too."

A young Liberian waiter, looking rather formal in his white shirt, black bowtie, and black pressed trousers, asked what we would prefer to drink. Ana looked intently at the wine list for a few minutes and recommended the Mosel. I looked up at the waiter, who couldn't disguise the amusement in his eyes, and said the Mosel would be just fine. He jotted it down, then turned like a soldier doing an about-face and marched toward the kitchen.

"German wines are not so difficult to get here," she said, "and Mosel is my favorite. I like to think of it as a real, living touch with history. The vines were brought to Germany by the Romans who needed to supply their troops. It was too expensive and too difficult to transport barrels of wine from Italy, so they grew their own grapes and, in the process, created a huge modern industry. You know, people in those days substituted the stuff for water. It's a wonder the Roman army won a single battle much less conquered most of the Western world."

She chatted for a while longer about the Mosel region and that it was her hope to one day live there and enjoy "real" seasons once again. The waiter brought the wine, showed us the label, and opened it with some ceremony before pouring about an ounce in my glass. I tasted it, not really knowing a good Riesling from a not so good one, but able to determine that it wasn't yet vinegar. I nodded to him that it was okay and he proceeded, without further ceremony, to pour.

"I particularly like this northern vintage," she said, after sipping from her glass. "It's not too sweet or alcoholic—just right."

Our conversation touched on all sorts of things as time floated by. The wine, the view, and the soft evening tropical air enveloped me in a light sense of euphoria. She was mesmerizing, and I couldn't stop talking. She wanted to know about my work, and what I had seen of the interior. I told her about flying to the missions, the mines, the Peace Corps volunteers. By the second bottle of wine she wanted to know about New York.

"I always think of New York as the most exciting place in the world. I imagine it's like what major European cities used to be—alive, vibrant, and untouched by war."

I agreed, not knowing what European cities were like before the war. That New York was vibrant and probably the most culturally and intellectually productive place in the US, I was sure, but before I could elaborate on the qualities of New York, the waiter returned for our dinner orders.

It was getting dark as we finished our meal. We lingered over a cup of coffee, not wanting the evening to end. The soft lights of various parts of the city were beginning to switch on. Maybe it was the effect of the candlelight and the wine, but her blue eyes had taken on an intense shimmer, and she seemed to radiate near lethal levels of warmth and sexuality. I had to shake my head to get over it.

"What's the matter?" she said.

"Nothing, just a little overcome by the tropics," I said.

She smiled. "I would like to continue our conversation," she said.

"So would I."

"I don't have to be at work tomorrow." She hesitated. "You don't have to take me to the embassy if you don't want to."

I tried to appear cool and calm, but I was nearly trembling with excitement. "Would it be all right with you if I got a room for us here?" I tried to say without stammering.

"I think that would be very nice," she said.

CHAPTER 9

BELLE YALLA

The weather was beginning to improve and, as a result, the company's business picked up. I had flights scheduled almost every day. I tried to call Ana when I could but did not always have access to a phone. When I did find one it usually didn't work.

It was a Friday afternoon when two policemen brought a prisoner, in handcuffs, to the airfield and said we had to fly him to Belle Yalla, a prison in the northeastern part of Liberia maintained by the government. It was a very bad place to go. Mike told them that we couldn't fly him until Saturday—no airplanes were available. Then he asked what the man was charged with.

"Na yo binness," said the policeman with the sergeant's stripes on his shirt sleeve.

"Who is he? Where's he from?" Mike asked.

"Dat too, na yo binness," said the policeman.

More than likely the man had said something against the president or had crossed one of the Big Men, or possibly it was a tribal issue. So, they sent him to Belle Yalla, where there was an excellent chance he would never be heard from again.

Since we couldn't transport the prisoner until the next day, the two policemen agreed that as far as they were concerned the prisoner could wait until Doomsday. They proceeded to handcuff him to an old VW engine block that had been placed outside the hangar.

"Dat be too fine! See ya Sattaday," the sergeant joked as they drove away.

It had started to rain so Paterson had some of his boys give the man a piece of thin sheet metal to hold over his head with his free hand. I found a couple of bananas in the office and gave them to him. I got the assignment to fly him out so I was at the airfield around 10:00 a.m. the next morning. When I arrived, I noticed a long, deep groove cut in the dirt leading up to the road. Neither the prisoner nor the engine block was anywhere to be seen. The groove ended abruptly at the road. I suspected that he had dragged the engine block the half mile to the road, gotten on a money bus, and paid his ten cents. Nothing and no one rode for free on the money bus. I'm sure the bus driver charged him another twenty-five cents for the engine block, probably telling him that it was ten cents for him and twenty-five cents for the "jewelry."

When Paterson arrived he, of course, found the prisoner missing and followed the telltale groove to the road. Paterson's rollers and field boys expressed great admiration for the prisoner, commenting excitedly about his strength and determination.

"My-oh! Da boy ee buku buku strong, oh!"

I must admit to feeling some admiration for him myself. It took more than I had in me to drag a hunk of metal that distance then take a chance that a bus driver would accept me and an engine. It could have been the bus driver knew something of the legal system in Liberia and decided to give the man a chance.

The police were very upset when they saw what had happened. I thought they might be angry with us and try to blame Mike or one of the boys, but they ignored the missing prisoner almost entirely and just shouted at Mike about the handcuffs.

"Now we mus buy new cuffs, oh! Handcuffs are spensive, you know, mon, vey vey spensive!"

That evening I managed to reach Ana by phone. She had rented a cottage on the beach for the weekend. Since I had been working steadily for the last two weeks, Mike granted me leave for a couple of days. I grabbed a change of clothes and underwear, jumped into my trusty VW, which I had named Junebug, and struck out for the beach. The wet season had ended and I was looking forward to drying out in the intense sunshine.

I found the cottage after a few wrong turns. It was about as I had imagined—a minimal living area with an adjacent bedroom, a small bath, and a very small kitchen. But the refrigerator was working and there was a radio in the living area. It was airy and clean. The ocean breeze flowed through the large open windows and doors, keeping the place cool and saturated with the salty, organic smell of the ocean.

Ana greeted me at the front door. She was dressed in a thin cotton gown popular with the native women. She usually wore her hair pulled up in a twist, which was expertly done, but on this occasion, she had let it down and it flowed freely and delicately over her shoulders. Her smile was radiant, and seeing her there, she looked like an unnamed beauty from a medieval tale of chivalry. I dropped my small bag and took her in my arms.

After the lovemaking we lay for a long time enjoying the breeze and listening to the gentle sound of the surf washing up onto the beach. She held up my hand, looked at it, and then kissed it.

"What have you been doing? This is not the hand of a pilot," she said.

"I've been doing some maintenance work for the company. Mike lost his head mechanic and asked me to fill in until he can find another. There's a lot of digging into hard-to-get places and rolling stuff up into neat bundles. It can be rough on the hands."

"I like a man with a man's hands," she said, placing my hand on her breast. "Use those hands," she whispered in my ear.

Ana had hired one of the local women, Tina, as housekeeper and cook. Tina seemed to understand what was expected of her. We only saw her at meal time and for an hour in the morning when she cleaned the cottage. We took our meals under a large umbrella on the beach, then read or slept in the shade. Since we had been warned against swimming in the ocean due to the strong undertow, we played "catch ball" in the surf, or simply let the surf tumble over our bodies. Tina would clear away the plates and utensils after each meal then discreetly disappear. I never knew where she went, but she always left and returned silently.

During that weekend Ana and I made love in almost every place that we could—on the beach at night and in every room in the cottage except the kitchen. Ana had rented the cottage for two nights and it was then, the last night, while we were enjoying a glass of wine after dinner, that she told me she would be going back to Germany.

I hesitated. I hesitated a long time. Then asked, "When?"

"After Christmas; I won't be here for the new year. I've been offered a job with a film production company."

"Doing what?"

"In their accounts department." She paused. "I know it doesn't sound very exciting, but it's a start, and it's what I want."

I had known this would come. It had to come. Ana had a vision of her future that did not include me. And I couldn't ask her to share what I had, which was an uncertain future at best. She told me what she wanted from the outset and she had not wavered in that.

"Would you be my guest at the Christmas party?" she asked. "The Embassy always gives an excellent Christmas party." She paused. "We can say our goodbyes then."

I left early the next morning. Ana was still in bed, though awake, and Tina had not arrived. I kissed her and told her that I had an early flight. She smiled and said, "Call me when you can and let's talk about the party." I said that I would and left.

Truth is, I did not have an early flight. I had no idea what was on the schedule for that day. I did know, however, that I needed to leave before I said something foolish, before an unrealized feeling boiled to the surface. I couldn't deny that I was viscerally hurt, that a part of me screamed for her not to go. The rational side, however, the logical side, said that what I wanted with Ana couldn't be. It simply wasn't to be our reality. I would call, of course, but I resolved not to see her until Christmas.

CHAPTER 10

SEPTRO

When I got to Spriggs-Payne, Mike had a surprise for me. He had, without anyone's knowledge, agreed by contract to train selected Liberian candidates to fly. Since I was the only one of his pilots with a US government-issued flight instructor's certificate, the task was given to me. The program was funded by USAID, as were a great many programs in Liberia at the time. The Cold War was raging, and both the Mali and Guinea governments were known to have strong communist leanings. Through USAID, the US was able to pour a huge amount of money into Liberia in the belief that it would establish a US democratic stronghold in Africa.

It was an interesting concept to take someone who had probably grown up with little knowledge of machinery and teach him how to handle something as complex as an airplane. Nevertheless, I assumed the prospective students could drive. They were in the national army, so somebody selected these young men for training. I was given four students, and four weeks to get them soloed and ready for more advanced training.

I started out with five days of ground school. We met in the hangar and, using a blackboard and chalk, I drew and explained the theory of flight, aerodynamics, vectors, weather, and load factor. The next week, we got into the airplane. That was when I was able to see how much of my instruction had failed. Three of the students had no understanding as to how a compass worked or, more importantly, what its significance was. What does the polar magnetic field mean to someone who has grown up in the tropics, lived within a ten-mile radius of his remote village and, if lucky, taught the rudiments of reading and writing?

I worked with these young men for two weeks every day, all day, but out of the four candidates I was only able to solo one. I later discovered that these men had not been specially selected at all; they had been picked completely at random. None had ever expressed any interest in becoming a pilot. Their officers worked on the military principle that when a subordinate is ordered to do something, that person will do it.

My one success, Septro, turned out to be a reasonably decent pilot with a lot of natural talent. After his solo flight, the army then sent him to the US for additional training. He was supposed to come back at the conclusion of his flight training and be what they referred to as the presidential flight pilot.

The president had an airplane, but he never used it. It was a Cherokee 180, a single engine, low wing, light airplane manufactured by Piper. He was afraid of flying. A local witch doctor had told him that he would die in the airplane.

When Septro returned a year later from the States, he strutted around with a new sense of importance because he had a US commercial pilot's certificate. He was the first Liberian charter pilot. We were all very proud of him as he passed his new certificate around for everyone to see. It was marked "not valid within the continental United States of America."

He found that his duties were limited to flying the president's girlfriends around and the occasional official visitor. I was happy for him since I knew that these trips were well within his capability. Septro's aviation career was short, however. He was told to take a couple of government officials down the coast to the town of Harper on Cape Palmas. The passengers were Americo-Liberians and fairly high ranking in the government. To go down the coast you keep your left wing over the land and your right wing over the water—pretty simple. On the way back, apparently he forgot which way he was going and continued heading south. He ended up in the Ivory Coast. When they landed at the airport, he realized his mistake—all the signs were in French. So he took off and went back the other direction. He managed to get back from where he started, but by then it was starting to get dark. It began to rain. The visibility dropped, and his passengers were getting nervous. According to Septro, one of the passengers tried to take the controls away from him, but he yelled and fought back, eventually regaining control of the airplane. He tried to keep going up the coast but soon lost sight of the coast altogether. The airplane finally crashed, ending upside down in the jungle.

Miraculously, everyone lived and walked to the nearest village on the coast. During the post-accident investigation, the passengers swore that Septro had gone insane and foamed at the mouth. They said they had told him, "De watta ee ova dere!" and he'd said, "No, no, no, das no right!" Given the military's intolerance of mistakes or embarrassments, this abruptly ended Septro's aviation career. In addition, the army decided they didn't need to train anymore pilots.

Since all of my company time up until Christmas was involved in training these young men, I had weekends free. So I threw my resolution out of the window and spent every weekend with Ana. We took advantage of every minute we had together. I simply tried not to think of her leaving and focused only on the moment. I savored it like one would good food or a favorite drink after a long abstinence.

She wanted to see Monrovia from the air, so I rented a Cessna 180 from Mike, packed a picnic lunch, did a preflight inspection of the airplane, and waited. She arrived exactly on time. It turned out to be a beautiful day, no rain showers, and hardly a cloud.

I flew her over Monrovia. She was thrilled to see the embassy from the air. I circled it a couple of times, then flew out around West Point and back over the city, passing over the football stadium. I then turned to fly over the beach. Ana was transfixed with the sight of the surf rolling up onto the beach as we flew along it. After about ten minutes we were at a relatively empty stretch of the beach. I did a quick scan for obstructions, turned, slowed to flap speed, put the flaps down and landed the airplane on the hard sand. It was a little nerve-wracking at first since the beach had a little slope to it, but it was controllable. The thought flicked through my mind of just how quickly Mike was going to fire me if I damaged the airplane.

I got the airplane stopped in a reasonable distance. Ana was smiling with pure joy. And so was I. We had just enough time for a picnic lunch and a few moments to enjoy the beach before we had to throw the remains of the lunch back into the basket. We jumped in the airplane and started the takeoff run. Since the beach slopes a few degrees down to the surf line I had to manage the takeoff so that we would not run into the surf. I succeeded with some difficulty until I knew I had flying speed, then pulled the airplane gently into the air and in an instant swept out over the breaking surf.

When we got back I did one last turn over Monrovia for Ana then on to Spriggs-Payne. Once back at the operations ramp, I saw Ana to her car. I could tell she had enjoyed herself. She smiled brightly and her eyes shone with delight. I kissed her through the open driver's window and waved goodbye.

Mike was in a spin that I had kept the airplane longer than agreed and promised to take the overrun out of my salary. I shrugged and waved my hand in the Liberian way, which is a nonverbal way of saying "I don't give a fuck."

That evening Deet stopped by my room. He said he wanted to talk to me and could we go to Heinz and Maria's for dinner and drinks. I knew Deet well enough to know there would be very little dinner and lots of drinks. I didn't want to take a chance on not getting back to my room, so I said I would go on the condition that I drove. He agreed.

As we walked to my car, Deet wanted to know what I had named it. I told him that I had decided on Junebug after the first modern airplane designed and built by Glenn Curtiss.

"It looks more like a dung beetle," he said in his typically irreverent way.

We got a good table at Heinz and Maria's. Deet ordered a scotch and soda and told the waiter to keep them coming until he could not say stop. I decided not to drink since I had an early flight the next day. I had been drinking too much in the last few days and I could feel its cumulative effect, and I wanted to shake it off. I wanted to feel alert and normal again. Deet was into his second scotch and soda when he started telling me his suspicions about Mike.

"I'm sure he's planning to dump de business und go back to de States. Vhere ist dat fucking place he comes from? Taxes?"

"How do you know?" I asked.

"He's got de look of a man getting ready to run. Believe me, I have seen dat look before. He's on de phone a lot. Paterson, who sometimes stays late to tidy up, told me dat he saw Mike taking some boxes out to his car. If he's planning somezhing like dat, you'd tink he would have de decency to say somezing to us."

"He may," I suggested. "Let's wait and see."

"I tink I should get the fuck out of here. I tink Brazil would be nice. I know people there. I have connections. It's a developing country—lots of opportunity."

"No extradition?" I asked.

Deet did not take it humorously. For an instant I saw that look of the wolf in his eyes, that same momentary stare that I have seen in all successful fighter pilots' eyes.

"You're new in dis country. You'd do well to pay attention to vhat I'm telling you."

We were joined by several German pilots who worked for another company on the field. It didn't take long for the singing to start and the toasts to the fatherland and der Fuehrer to begin. It had the same discordant ring as the conversations that I had had with some of the Southern students at Cornell—the South was constitutionally correct and the federal government was the aggressor. They saw the South as a virtuous woman that had been violated by brutes.

Coca cola was no substitute for a good beer, but I was determined to stick to my resolve and stay sober. I was not in the mood for old Nazi antics, so I decided to leave. I asked Deet if he could get a ride home. He said not to worry about him, that he would be okay. I left, intending to stop by the

Gurley Street Bar just to see who was there—still vowing not to drink. It wasn't too far to walk.

The sun had set hours before, but the oppressive heat remained. The night air seemed thick and unusually dark. I hadn't walked very far when I noticed a young woman standing near a doorway. In the sparse street lighting she seemed more like a shadow than a person. Nevertheless, I was sure that I recognized her.

"Sarah, is that you?" I asked, coming closer.

She stared at me. She had changed. She was dressed like a prostitute, her face heavily made up.

"Sarah, don't you remember? I was the pilot who flew you and your daughter down from the mission. How is your daughter?" She glanced away for an instant. Her lower lip began to tremble slightly.

"Ma daughta Mary, she die. She die at hospital. My uncle, he not got good way. He say she be better off wit de voodoo man."

"Then what are you doing here? Why didn't you go back to the mission?

"Ma uncle, he say I mus' pay him back. He say I owe 'im. I owe 'im for hospital and for funeral. He say I mus' earn money. Dis is de only way I get nuff money to pay him. I should be grateful, he say."

"Sarah, do you want to go back to the mission?"

She hesitated for a long moment. Her lips tightened.

"Ma uncle, he say de mission not accept me now. He say dat I am disgraced. He say no one would look at me now."

"Sarah, I think your uncle only wants you to earn money for him. A good uncle should not make his niece do such things. A good uncle gives; he does not take from his niece. How much do you earn in a day?"

She shrugged. "Twenty, twenty fie dolla maybe."

"Here," I said, handing her a twenty-dollar bill. "Go back to your uncle. Give this to him and don't tell him that you saw me. If you want to go back to the mission, I will fly you there. Your uncle did not tell you everything.

The people at the mission are Christian people, are they not?" She nodded. "Then they will forgive you, whatever you've done. They will accept you back. Do you remember the story of the prodigal son?"

Her eyes searched mine.

"You will be the prodigal daughter and they will welcome you back as the prodigal son was welcomed back."

A flash of excitement, or maybe it was hope, came into her eyes.

"This is money for a taxi to the airport." I said, giving her another five dollars. "Do you need more?"

"No," she said. "I save ten dolla."

"Good. Come to the airport tomorrow morning. Do not bring anything with you and, this is most important, do not tell your uncle where you are going or what you are going to do. If he finds out he will keep you here, and you will never be able to leave him. This may be your only chance to free yourself. If you stay and continue to do this, I promise you that you will get sick, very sick."

A look of fear swept over her face. "Ah mus' go," she said. "Ah mus' go." I watched as she disappeared into the night. I thought that I would never see her again.

I didn't feel like going into the Gurley Street Bar after that. I didn't want to listen to a bunch of old, drunken, washed-out World War II pilots airing out their grudges and feeding their self-delusions with the cheapest booze they could find. I went back to my Junebug and drove home to Lilly's, took a much-needed shower, and climbed into bed.

The next day I was a little surprised, but happy, to see Sarah in the waiting room of African Air Services. She was very frightened. I had some light cargo to deliver to the mission and I paid for Sarah's fare, telling Mike that she had given me the money. Paterson's boys finished loading the airplane and I put Sarah in the front seat.

She seemed not to notice the takeoff or the flight up to the mission. She was silent throughout the journey, and for most of it she stared straight ahead, hardly seeming to notice anything. Her initial fear of flying had been wiped away by something much more terrible.

We landed at the mission where the usual crowd stood waiting. Sarah looked up at me.

"No one knows anything," I said to her directly. "You simply tell them that your baby died, and that's it—nothing else. Let the truth come out later." She nodded slightly.

The village Head Man was there to meet me. I jumped out of the airplane and greeted him in the usual way and said that Sarah had returned. Several of the women, seeing her sitting in the airplane, came to help her out onto the ground. The Head Man looked at her curiously.

"Her baby died," I said. A momentary expression of concern swept over his face. "Please treat her kindly. It was not her fault. She has suffered much."

"Be it so," the Head Man said. Then in a voice heavy with authority, he spoke evenly to two of the young men standing behind him. They immediately ran to the airplane and started unloading it.

He must have also said something of Sarah's condition because the women standing with her began to rub her shoulders and say things to her in soft voices. They then quickly led her away toward the center of the village.

Although now she was relatively safe from her uncle, I knew as I watched her walk away that she was walking into a life of backbreaking labor, another pregnancy, and probably an early death. Such was the normal cycle of life and death for young women like Sarah in Liberia. But I consoled myself thinking I may have made a positive difference in someone's life—maybe she would beat the odds.

I had been in Liberia for a couple of years now and had learned where all of the airfields were along the coast. I made a habit of visually locating them just in case the trusty Continental engine decided to cough and sputter. They were not marked on the chart—hardly anything was marked on the chart. We would often draw a circle where we thought they were, but that was only the general location. These airfields were usually a part of a village or mission, neither of which was indicated on the chart. In fact, our charts were really maps with no reference at all to latitude or longitude.

One time, as I was passing over one of these airfields, I noticed a large white flag waving. This was a request to land—someone needed air transportation, and it was the company's policy to comply with such a request. After all, I told myself, that's why I'm here—to provide air transport. I circled the field a couple of times to check it for wet spots and obstructions. It looked good, so I set the airplane up for landing, which went smoothly. I taxied to a stop in the cleared area off the runway and shut the engine down. As always, there was a group of people gathered there to meet me. I stepped out of the cockpit and was approached by an elderly man and woman.

"Suh, please, ma sista, she mus' go to Monrovia. Her son, he no be fine self; he be hurt bad an' is in much need."

The woman came up to me and gently, almost reverently, removed the cloth that contained her money and held it toward me. I could see that she didn't have enough.

"The fee is fifteen dollars," I said to the man.

"Suh," he said getting down on his knees and taking my right foot in his hands. "Yah mus' take her. I hold your foot, suh. I hold your foot!" This is an expression of extreme humility.

I looked at the woman. Her lips were trembling as she clutched the folded cloth over her few coins.

"Ohhh, my," she said softly. "Da way too many!"

"Okay, mama." I used the term of affection for older women in Liberia. "Okay, get in and I will take you to Monrovia. Keep your money. You will need it there. Where in Monrovia is your son?"

"He in hospital," she said.

As we taxied for takeoff, I looked back. Her brother was still on his knees, his hands held out, cupped, as though to hold my foot in case I changed my mind.

A few days later I had my first accident in a company airplane. It happened at one of the iron mines in the interior and, as with most engine failures, it happened during takeoff. I was flying a Lockheed AL60, a large single-engine airplane great for hauling large volume cargo. I had just lifted off from the runway. Everything was running on max. Without warning, the turbocharger blew up, causing the engine to seize. I put it down on the airfield but the airplane nosed over and went onto its back. When that happened, my shoulder strap failed, sending me face first into the instrument panel. I was still strapped in my seat at the waist, hanging upside down, when they got to me. My face had swollen so much I could hardly see, and I was covered with blood.

Nearby workers were quick to get to me and took me to the mine's medical clinic. The facility had been set up primarily to treat mine worker injuries, and it was the only clinic for miles. A Swedish first-aid worker cleaned my face and sutured the gash on my forehead with the deftness of one sewing up an old leather bag. He stripped me of all my clothes, handed me clean garments, and led me to a room with four beds set end to end around the room. I chose one and fell asleep instantly.

I awoke the next morning to the sound of children playing in the yard outside. The heat of the day had settled in, and my gown was soaked through with sweat. My head and face throbbed and I felt an immense pressure in my lower abdomen where the seat belt had held me upside down. I tried to sit up. Then decided to lay back down. I stared at the corrugated tin ceiling above and the concrete walls and tried to remember where I was.

"You have been asleep for eighteen hours."

I looked up to see a young Swedish woman smiling at me.

"You have a significant cut on your forehead and two cracked ribs, but other than that, you are fine."

Memories of the crash came flooding back. "Does African Air Services know what happened?"

"Yes," she said. "They wanted to know how badly the airplane was damaged."

I smiled and laid my head back on the pillow.

"I will bring you something to eat and some more medicine for your pain," she said on her way out the door.

I stayed in the clinic for a few days. Then the company sent a plane for me and a truck to haul away the Al60, which was repaired and back in service within a month. It took about the same amount of time for me to feel myself again, though after a couple of weeks the doctor declared me fit for flight, and I was back at it.

CHAPTER 11

FROEHLICHE WEIHNACHTEN

My wounds had almost healed by the time of the Christmas party at the German Embassy. Ana looked radiant. She positively shimmered in her evening gown. I had managed, at the last minute, to rent a tuxedo, which was badly pressed and had a faded stain on the cummerbund. The swelling in my face had gone down somewhat but the scars, while fading also, were still visible. It occurred to me that I was beginning to look more like my World War II Luftwaffe colleagues than a college boy from Cornell.

"Aah, you must be Ana's American friend," said the director of Ana's section. "How do you Americans say it?" He hesitated as though in thought. "What does the other fellow look like?" At this he burst into restrained laughter, sloshing his drink around as he did so.

"I wish it were something that interesting, but unfortunately, it's the result of a slight mishap in an aircraft," I said.

"Well, I'm so glad that you are not worse off. Although, I must say, German women," he glanced over at Ana, "do tend to like a man with a scar on his face." He laughed again. "You must excuse me," he said, nodding to Ana. "Do enjoy yourself Mr.—" He paused, trying to remember my name.

"Mr. Verrier," I said.

"Yes, yes of course, and help yourself, Mr. Verrier, to the American bourbon. We have it straight from your state of Kentucky."

It was an immense house, possibly one of the largest houses in Monrovia, with heavy stuffed chairs and sofas all around. A crystal chandelier hung in the center of the great room. A tall Christmas tree, flown in from Germany, almost touched the ceiling in one corner of the room. A quartet, playing

Christmas music from the German Baroque period, was stationed on a second-floor landing. We were the youngest couple there. Everyone else looked middle aged, very prosperous, and familiar with one another.

"Who is here?" I asked.

"Invitations were sent to most of the embassies and legations. A few did not respond—the Russians, the Cubans, the Chinese—pretty much anyone with an ideological ax to grind against the Western world. The Israelis came. You can see them over there." She pointed to a well-dressed man and woman. "I don't know what his job is at the Israeli Mission. He's probably here to check on all of the bugs his spies have planted. They're still searching for war criminals, you know. I think the woman is his wife, but then that might be a cover."

"Is that why I haven't seen any of my pilot friends here?"

"I think so. I think the Israelis secretly regard them all as war criminals. Maybe they are too small to fry, but I suspect that when they run out of big fish, they'll go after the little ones. We also have some representatives of industry here. Over there." Ana pointed to a group of elegant, well-groomed people standing near the punch bowl. "European steel, and rubber, mostly."

"Any chance of modernish dance music? I want to ask you to dance."

She smiled. "I might be able to do something about that, but only after enough schnapps has been served."

We chatted for a while with various couples then Ana excused herself to go to the "powder room." I watched her easily make her way through the crowd of guests.

"She is certainly a beautiful young woman," a male voice said near my right ear. I turned to face an impeccably attired man enveloped in an essence of expensive cologne.

"I am Major Ahud," he said. "And this is my wife Nouga." Nouga smiled. "I am attached to the Israeli Mission here and you must be the new, young American pilot working for African Air Services?" I was startled and must have shown it. The major continued, "Please, don't be concerned. It's my job to know who the newcomers are."

"Then you must be a busy man."

"Yes, yes I am. Monrovia is, as you Americans say, a happening place—lots of foreigners, lots of money, and lots of things valuable to the West." The major had a military bearing—square shoulders, direct eye contact, and a firm jaw. His wife looked European and watched me carefully as the major probed. "You know," he continued, "there is a lot of traffic going through Monrovia in the way of escaped criminals and others wanted by your government and mine. There is a pipeline, so to speak, from Europe to South America directly through Monrovia."

"Why here? Why Monrovia?" I asked.

"Just look at the map," he said. "This part of West Africa is the closest geographical point in this hemisphere to South America. It's a relatively short flight and, as you probably know, Liberia is, shall we say, very liberal in its treatment of—"

"I wouldn't know about that," I interrupted. "I do contract flights to the mines and missions, but I haven't seen any German war criminals on my airplane."

"Yes, but your colleagues—some of them have very interesting histories."

"I didn't know that it was a war crime to fight for one's country."

"Oh, but it is if you murder innocent civilians or unarmed prisoners of war."

"I'm sure you're right, Major, but the former Luftwaffe pilots that I work with here were just very young men fighting in the air for their lives. And, really, do you think it's appropriate to talk about such things here?"

"As you wish, my friend," the major said. "But I would like to meet with you later, at your convenience."

"I don't think I can help you, Major. If you'll excuse me." I looked at his wife. "Nice to have met you, ma'am," I said. She smiled without parting her lips.

I made my way to the bar, hoping to get as far away from the major as I could. The bartender was a local who spoke German and English very well.

I asked for a gin and tonic and in a few moments he had it sitting in front of me—an excellent job. From my position at the bar I scanned the room for Ana. I saw her chatting with an older couple. I made my way toward her through the growing crowd of guests.

She smiled at my approach and introduced me to Sir Reginald Hooper and his wife, Alice. Sir Reginald was an executive with British Petroleum.

"Well young man," he said, extending his hand, "Ana tells us that you're a pilot."

"Yes sir, I am," I answered giving his hand a couple of light pumps.

"Did you fly during the war?"

"No sir, I was only six months old when Pearl Harbor was bombed."

"Yes, yes," he said laughing with just a little bit of embarrassment. Alice laughed too—a very restrained, controlled laugh. "All you flyers look so young. Some of our RAF chaps from the war look like they haven't aged a day."

"That's from flying Spitfires, sir. They fly very fast you see and, as you know from Einstein's special relativity theory, the faster you go the slower you age."

"Really!" Sir Reginald said looking genuinely astonished. "Do you think so?"

"Oh, without a doubt," I said. "Take jet pilots for example. Their airplanes fly much faster than Spitfires, so they age much slower. Surly you've noticed how young those guys look."

"I never thought of it that way, young man, but you may have a point. Yes, indeed you may have. I'll have to see about taking flying lessons." Sir Reginald waited politely for the laughter to die down. "Well, it was lovely to meet you, young man, but we must be moving along—lots of people to see. Cheerio." Mrs. Hooper smiled at me and blew a slight kiss at Ana.

"Did I scare them off?" I asked.

"I don't think so. I doubt that Sir Reginald knows much about relativity, but he is a specialist in public relations and schmoozing politicians. I think this party is an opportunity for him."

"Ana, I'm sure there are a lot of interesting people here, but this will be our last night together."

"Let me say hello to a few more and then we can go." She touched her index finger to her lips then touched mine.

The next morning, after breakfast at the hotel, I took Ana to Robertsfield and watched her get on an old DC-4 bound for Cairo. She had said that I could meet her in Germany any time I wished. I didn't answer. There was, of course, Jenny, and my behavior with Ana had not been exemplary. I had convinced myself that I would never see Ana again—that is, until I saw her climb up the stairway and disappear into the aircraft cabin. I found myself clutching the paper on which she had written her address with great care.

CHAPTER 12

JUJU

I had a flight scheduled in the morning, so I drove back to Lilly's. It was a few days before Christmas. I picked up the latest copy of the *Washington Post* lying in her living room—it was several days old—and saw that it had snowed in Washington. There was a picture of the Capitol building taken from a snow-covered mall. In Monrovia it was 85 degrees and steam was rising from the streets after a recent shower.

I had tried to make it a point not to drink before 6:00 p.m. except on celebratory occasions, but I needed something to dull the pain of Ana's departure. I mixed myself a large gin and tonic, flopped in my stuffed chair, and stared out of the window trying to imagine snow falling outside. Eventually, I fell asleep in the chair and the empty glass slipped from my hand and fell to the floor.

Later that night I was awakened by screams and shouting. It was like emerging from a dream but as I sat there, fully awake, I realized that the commotion was coming from just outside. I quickly stepped out into the hallway. Boarders and staff alike were running toward the back of the house. I joined them. There was great confusion going on in the backyard, focused around a group of people crowded around a tree. I pushed my way through the group. One of the house boys that I recognized was propped up against the tree. The lower part of his body was covered with blood. His abdomen had been slit open.

"It be de Leopard Men," someone in the crowd said.

"Bad juju," another said.

Others mumbled, "Ya, bad juju."

Lilly came running out of the house. When she saw what had happened she started yelling and pulling at her hair. "Zhey killed Josef! Schijt! Schijt! Zhey killed Josef and I have already paid him a month's wages in advance."

One of the roomers standing near me whispered, "That's Lilly. Always concerned about money. It's not like she has a problem. There are always three or four more boys waiting to take his place."

As I stood there trying to process what was going on around me, the police came and looked over the scene. They questioned Lilly for a few minutes and left. After Josef's body had been taken away I learned from Miguel, one of the Spanish pilots staying at Lilly's, that around Christmas time a group called the Leopard Men, also known as the juju people or Heartmen, would capture young men or teenage boys, kill them, and cut their livers out. They would then eat the raw livers during a ritual meal for society members. They believed that eating the boys' organs would restore youth and sexual vigor. Miguel believed that most of the Leopard Men were witch doctors.

"Until now," Miguel said, "I thought the Leopard Men were just a myth. But it's true. And I now believe the other things that I was told."

"What other things?" I asked.

"That all the locals truly believe it. They tell their children, 'Watch out for the Leopard Men! They will get you when you walk alone!' Also that your best friend could be a Leopard Man and you wouldn't know it.

"It's a very secret organization. The local papers don't report on the Leopard Society, but everybody seems to know about it. You will never find anyone who admits to being a member or even to publicly admitting that such an organization exists."

Miguel assured me that the society wasn't interested in white boys and, as he was quick to point out, I was too old anyway.

Just when I was beginning to think I understood the Liberians, something like Josef's needless death would shake me to the core, leaving me confused and unbalanced. For me, everything was unexpected. One day there was a group of men and women dressed in green palm fronds dancing happily down the street. I never found out why, but I think it was a happy event—what they call good juju. Another day there was a group of pubescent girls tied together, naked from the waist up with the upper part of their bodies covered in white clay, being led by a black man in western dress. The girls were silent and solemn. Was it a rite of passage? Were they on their way to being sold? Again I never knew, but I think that was definitely bad juju.

There had been a series of thefts from a local post office, so a witch doctor was summoned by the post master. He was a small, shriveled man with snow-white hair and watery, yellow eyes. He was there to sort out who was stealing mail from the post office. The police knew well the power of juju. They lined up all the post office workers, generally referred to as boys. Any native man who did manual labor was call a boy. There were five of them in t-shirts, shorts and sandals, standing up straight. The police made sure that they stood straight.

The witch doctor slowly walked in front of all five men and locked eyes with each one.

"Okay boys," he said, "which one o' you be de rogue?"

No one moved.

"I smell a rogue here, an' I know one o' you is it."

Still no movement. The witch doctor had an iron pot filled with white hot charcoal. He stuck his panga (African machete) in the pot until in glowed with heat. Then he smeared a patch of white clay on each of the workers' legs. The witch doctor then pressed the flat blade of his hot panga hard on the leg of each man where the clay had been smeared. You could see the smoke and hear the flesh sizzling, but each man stayed absolutely still—until he got to the fourth man. As the witch doctor approached, the man screamed and tried to run away. The police caught him and brought him back. The man admitted to the thefts. This was juju. Everyone believed in juju.

CHAPTER 13

I PUT YOU DOWN

We were well into the dry season in Liberia and could expect good flying weather most days, except for when the Harmattan wind hit. When conditions are right, it blows down from the Sahara Desert and brings a blinding, choking dust that looks more like a yellow fog. It grounds everything that flies—even the birds. It gets in your throat, clogs your nostrils, and contaminates the food and water. It penetrates anywhere there is a chink big enough for a microscopic particle to get through.

This gritty veil of dust could wax and wane with any particular day or hour. It could roll in at any time during the dry season, and all of Monrovia would be forced to wait it out. This time it came up as I was headed to the airfield. I quickly turned and started back for Lilly's. By the time I got there, I was in need of a bath and change of clothes.

The next day, after the Harmattan wind had passed, it was an unusually perfect flying day—clear with unlimited visibility and temps in the midseventies. Paterson and his boys had cleaned most of the grit from the airplanes. The rollers had my airplane loaded by the time I got to the airfield. It was a parts delivery to a new gold mine in the area of Gbarpolu in the northern part of Liberia. It was one of the few mines in Liberia that wasn't an open pit. The gold miners of Gbarpolu burrowed tunnels to get at layered veins of glistening wealth buried deep within the mountains.

I checked the load manifest, did the weight and balance calculations, and was on my way to the airplane when Deet stopped me.

"I heard about de boy. A terrible ting vhat des people do to von anodder.

Look, some of us are getting togedder and renting a house on de beach. Vould you like to join us? You can get avay from Lilly's. No more boys vid der livers cut out und room enough to entertain a lady now and den. Vhat do you say?"

"Can I let you know tomorrow?" I said, holding up my weight and balance data sheets to show that I was busy and in a hurry.

"Ja, sure, no problem. I'll tell dem to hold it von more day."

"Thanks," I said and walked to the airplane. It was overloaded as usual and the takeoff had to be done carefully—nursing the struggling craft off the runway and accelerating in ground effect until I had sufficient speed to clear the trees at the end of the field.

The trip went according to plan without a single glitch. On the way back I couldn't resist playing with a few clouds. I circled the fluffy columns, looking down the sides of these white towers as though skirting the side of a mountain, occasionally climbing steeply up and over the tops then down the side and, puff, into the column itself. Then, enveloped in white mist for a few moments, I would pop out of the other side to see the green-and-brown checkered ground thousands of feet below.

All good things must come to an end, however, and soon I was back at Spriggs-Payne completing the paperwork. When I had finished and everything was signed and sealed, I jumped into Junebug with the intention of asking Deet to show me the house. But, since it was late afternoon and I hadn't eaten anything since breakfast, I drove to the Gurley Street Bar. I was enjoying some corned beef and rice with a nice cold Coke when Colin, my new best friend from my last visit here, and a couple of his friends dropped into the empty chairs.

"Hello mate," he said. He then introduced his friends, Ozzie and Simon. Ozzie was a white Kenyan with reddish hair, pale blue eyes, and leathery skin. He wore the usual khaki shorts and open shirt. The corners of his eyes were wrinkled from squinting, and he seemed to squint now from habit. His eyes locked on to you and did not let go. I was never clear as to what Ozzie did except, I was told, that he sometimes worked for Max, the guy who "gets things done for people." I assumed that this was a bit exaggerated but, nevertheless, close to the truth.

Simon was an Australian and had that happy, smiling, welcoming nature of many Australians. He was an "importer/exporter." His taste ran a little loud as he wore a bright Hawaiian shirt, long yellow, slightly stained trousers, and leather sandals. Colin introduced me as "that young American pilot who's taking a fucking from McCoy." The three of them were on their way to a party and wanted me to come along as their token Yank. The US army had a survey team based about twenty miles outside of Monrovia, and Colin had heard that they gave great parties with lots of food and drink.

I gulped down my corned beef and Coke, paid the bill, and followed them outside. The wind had picked up and dust and bits of trash were being blown around in swirls. I could see lightning in the distance but couldn't hear the thunder. Colin managed to hail a taxi and we all piled in—Colin in the front seat while I sat squeeze between Ozzie and Simon in the back. The driver was a big man, probably a Nigerian since they controlled most of the taxi business in the city. He acknowledged Colin's direction with a nod. He didn't speak.

We started on our journey to the survey station. Dust and bugs were sticking to the windshield and the wipers were smearing the accumulation into a thin opaque film. Colin withdrew a flask of whiskey from somewhere, took a pull on it, and passed it around. After a while, when we were all beginning to feel a little happy, Simon started singing bar songs. Soon, we had all joined in, except for the cab driver.

We had gone about fifteen miles and were well into the second verse of "Waltzing Matilda" when the cab driver pulled to the side of the road. We were far outside the city and it was pitch black but for the occasional lightning flash. I thought he was going to complain about the singing. Colin looked up and asked the cab driver what was wrong. No answer.

"What's wrong?" Colin repeated.

The cab driver said, without turning his head. "I want more money, mon, or I put you down. I will put you down, mon!"

"What? What did he say?" Ozzie demanded.

The taxi driver folded his arms and stuck out his chin. "You got one minute, mon, or I put you down."

I later learned that this meant that he would put us out of the cab. Ozzie must have thought it meant something else. I saw his hand move quickly. It was dark in the back of the cab, but I could see the reflection from the gun as he pulled it up and placed it next to the cab driver's ear. I forced my head down behind the seat, and then there was a flash that momentarily lit up the cab and an explosion that deafened me. There were the sounds of braking glass and crunching metal.

I waited for a few moments, dreading what I might see. Slowly I looked up from behind the front seat through the thinning, drifting gun smoke. The taxi driver was gone, and the windshield was missing. I thought I saw the taxi driver running down the road, but it was only for an instant. Then he disappeared in the darkness. My head was ringing from the discharge of the weapon.

Ozzie got out of the cab. "Would you look at this shit!"

Then the rest of us jumped out of the car. "Hey, mon!" we all started to shout. "Where are you, mon? Come back, mon!"

"I should have known better," Colin said. "Those Nigerians, they like to use intimidation to jack up their fares."

Ozzie shrugged and put his gun back from where he had retrieved it. We were all soaking wet from sweat, and the bugs were beginning to annoy us. We found the windshield. It had a bullet hole in it and it was cracked throughout like a jigsaw puzzle. The cab driver had apparently pushed it out and scrambled out over the hood to escape. Amazingly, it was still more or less in one piece, so we wiped it off and placed it back in the windshield frame and drove off.

I thought the lightning flashes I had seen when we left the city might have been dry lightning. They weren't. And after one particularly heavy discharge, which sounded more like a high intensity explosion, it started to rain in torrents. The windshield leaked around the edges where we had tried to press it against the ruptured sealant, and water poured in through the bullet hole, but it did keep the heavy rain from pelting us. Someone said something about it being the dry season and we all laughed and continued to sing "Waltzing Matilda" until we got to the survey station. Ozzie decided to leave the keys in the cab with the engine running and took bets on how long the cab would be there. The car was gone in about thirty minutes.

CHAPTER 14

PARACHUTERS

I decided to go in with Deet and one other pilot on the beach house. It was right on the beach and fairly near the Ambassador Hotel. I could walk to the Ambassador in about thirty minutes, and I found I liked walking along the beach to their beach bar. Lilly wasn't broken hearted. She shrugged and said that I would be back. "Zhey always come back to Lilly's," she repeated.

All of my worldly goods went back into my duffel bag, which I tossed into Junebug before driving the few miles to the rental house. One thing I thought I would miss was Lilly's cooking, although as it turned out one of the guys, Tony, was a very good cook. Being a good chef is a gift, like being a brilliant physicist or pianist—you either have it or you do not, and it isn't something that you can fake.

Tony was also a major alcoholic, which was nothing unusual among gifted cooks and pilots. He was from somewhere in New York—Syracuse I think—and somehow ended up in Africa. I was careful not to probe. Some said he was escaping an angry ex-wife. Others said he was escaping an outraged husband. I suspected that it was both plus the relentless hounding of creditors. Whatever the reasons, he was here and had gone into business for himself. He had a Cessna 180, and he'd fly around and do light charter work on his own. There was always plenty of work for him, but he only did enough work to pay for the plane, the gas, and his booze. He didn't really stress himself, and even though he seemed rather old to me, he probably wasn't more than forty or forty-five. He was burnt out. His face was bloated and red, and he had a giant 1959 rusted-out Chevrolet sedan. His favorite activity, after flying all day, was to go into town and drink until he was, as we would say in college, completely blotto. Somehow he would make it back to his room, sleep it off, then repeat the process the next day. He had been doing this for years before I met him.

The three of us got along much better than I had expected, and after six or seven months we had settled into something close to a routine. Tony was strangely quiet when he was drunk, which was most of the time, and Deet turned out to be upbeat and pleasant to be around. In the mornings on the weekends when we weren't flying, I would sometimes borrow Tony's car to go down to the local bakery to pick up some sweet rolls and coffee. One morning I got in his car and noticed that there was a smear of dark brown stuff all over the windshield. I got out of the car to wipe it off and, for no logical reason except a persistent gnawing suspicion, happened to walk around to the front of the car.

I saw that the grill was smashed in and there was a tennis shoe wedged in it. I pulled the shoe out and threw it in the back seat, then went to his room to wake him up. He, of course, was terribly hungover—he usually slept until noon. "Tony, Tony!" I shouted. "Something has happened to your car! I think you hit someone last night!"

Tony rolled over, looking dazed, then said, "Oh my God! I thought it was a dream."

"It looks like you got the windshield wipers going."

"Yeah," he said, looking more alert. "There was stuff all over it and I had to run the wipers so I could see to get home."

I thought a moment and said, "I think we should report this to the police."

Tony panicked. He pleaded with me not to, saying over and over, "This is not the US, man! This is not the US!" Then, "It'll only lead to more palaver that I can't afford. Even if the person I'm supposed to have hit complains or his family complains to the cops, nothing will be done about it—unless the cops figure it's some white guy with dash money. Then they'll burn me good and, I tell you honestly, I haven't got dash money. I'm shit out of luck."

Had we been in the US or Europe I would have reported it, but I had to admit that he was right. It was becoming hard for me to draw a line between right and wrong here. I was learning that life could be cheap in Liberia. The ethics and morality that I thought were universal had a price here.

I knew that the probability was that one day Tony would takeoff in his airplane and never be heard from again. The drinking or the jungle would eventually get him. Was it worth putting balm on my conscience to get the police involved and watch as they threw Tony into some dark pit and leave him there because he couldn't pay the dash?

"I swear," Tony pleaded. "I won't do it again. I won't drink and drive again, I promise."

I knew he thought he was sincere. I knew he believed he meant it, but I also knew that he wouldn't live up to it.

"I think you'd better clean your car up, Tony, just in case."

"Yeah, yeah, I'll do that right away," he said with relief.

Toward sunset I decided to go to the Gurley Street Bar downtown. I wanted to shake the feeling that I had somehow been corrupted by a foul and smelly deed. I felt knee-deep in it and wanted to get clean.

A very attractive woman in tight jeans and a t-shirt was sitting at the bar talking to the bartender. The ever-present heat and humidity were exaggerated by the crowd of sweaty bodies. Her damp clothes looked like they had been painted on. She spoke excellent English but with a slight French accent that I couldn't place exactly. I used that as my opener.

"Are you from Quebec?"

"Is it that obvious? I always thought I had sort of a mid-Atlantic accent," she said, clearly happy that I had spoken to her.

"There are so many different accents around here I guess I'm getting pretty good at it. Are you waiting for someone?"

"Yeah, my husband. He plays guitar at another bar down the street. We just arrived in town so I'm thrilled that he got a gig so fast. I usually wait for him here rather than go back to the hotel."

"You mean, you don't have a place to stay permanently?"

"Not at the moment, but it's no big deal. We always seem to get by. I'm

Belinda, by the way, and my husband is Barry. He's Australian—an Aussie guitar player who plays American country western in West Africa!"

"Hah! Glad to meet you, Belinda. I'm Ken. I'm a pilot here."

"A pilot! Who do you work for?"

I paused. "For a guy I don't trust, in planes I don't completely trust. But at least I have a place to live."

"Lucky you," she said.

"Actually, we do have a spare room. If you guys are good for the rent, I can check it out with my house mates. I have to warn you, they are pilots as well, so it can get pretty rowdy at times."

"Don't worry," she said. "We know rowdy!"

That night I brought it up with Deet and Tony.

"Sounds like a couple of parachuters to me," Deet said.

"Parachuters? What are they?" I asked.

"Parachuters. You know. Dey just drop in out of nowhere. Dey probably have some vild story of vhere dey have been and vhere dey are going. All lies. Und den, poof! Dey grab vat dung dey can und are gone! You hat better check your coin purse, young man. Vhere did they say they came from?"

"Morocco. They drove down from Morocco in an old Oldsmobile station wagon. I don't know how they made it. But they did."

"Ya! Just vat I tought."

I looked at him. "So you don't think it would be a good idea if they moved in?"

"I didn't say dat! If dey got de money, den let dem come. Dey won't be here more dan a couple of months, anyway. I can guarantee it. Besides, it vill be gut to have a voman around de house."

Deet was right. It was nice to have a woman around the house. She would set out an occasional flower or two, she tacked up some colorful African *aso oke* fabric like a tapestry and, all of a sudden, our little beach house started to look homey. Barry too turned out to be a nice guy. We would sit out on the beach with our gin and tonics and he would play the guitar.

Barry played well and sang well, so it was easy to like him. He came up with the idea to drive to Ouagadougou in Upper Volta.

"There is going to be a music festival up there in a couple of months and I'm thinking I could be a part of it. It's not just African music, it's all sorts."

I smiled. "Including country and western?"

"Well, I guess we'll see!"

I probably could manage the time off, so I said, "Sounds like fun. Count me in."

CHAPTER 15

NOUGA

About a month after Belinda and Barry moved in, I decided to walk down the beach to the Ambassador Hotel beach bar. The bartender's name was Joe. He was known as "Set 'em Up Joe" and was an affable local man in his early thirties. He seemed to be always smiling and moved fluidly as though dancing to some internal rhythm. He didn't just handle the glasses; he twirled them like a juggler before deftly pouring the liquor and placing the glass in front of you. He asked if I was one of the pilots. I said that I was and asked him how he knew.

"Oh, ya got good heart; ya look like ya know book," he said.

"But really, it's the sunglasses isn't it," I said.

Joe laughed. "Dat's it, old man. Dat's it," he said and danced away. In West Africa it was considered a high compliment to be referred to as "old man" simply because there were relatively few truly old men. Life expectancy among natives was somewhere between forty and forty-five.

"What have you got to eat that's local?" I asked. "Not European, but not bush meat."

"Chop, fufu, and boy yeah, it be too fine," he said.

"Boy yeah? What's boy yeah?"

Joe pointed to a plate nearby. "Boy yeah," he said.

"Oh, boiled eggs! I get it. I'll have some boy yeah. Thanks, and some cane juice." I had given up the struggle of not drinking before 6:00 p.m.

I was halfway through the eggs and my glass of rum when a woman sat down on the stool next to me, blocking my view of the ocean. She looked straight into my eyes.

"You don't recognize me. Do you?" The throaty, deep, sexy voice was familiar. I moved my head slowly indicating no.

"Nouga," she said.

"Major Ahud's wife," I said.

She smiled—she also had perfect teeth.

"And you're here to spy on me?"

"I'm here to have a drink with you."

"How did you know where to find me?" I asked.

"I have friends in all kinds of places."

"Should I be afraid?"

"This is Liberia. Of course you should be afraid," she said.

I signaled for Joe. He danced over and I told him to serve the lady what she wanted. She ordered a gin and tonic, and she was very specific about the gin and the tonic.

"The major sent you to complete the interrogation?"

"He doesn't know I'm here," she said, touching the right corner of her mouth. "I don't interfere in his business, so I don't talk much when he's talking."

"Does he want to know about my new housemates?"

She shrugged. "I suppose he does," she said, "but that's his concern, not mine." She looked directly at me. "Maybe I want to find out about you."

Joe brought the gin and tonic and quickly left to fill other orders. Nouga took the drink gently from the bar and slowly sipped it. A gentle, soft wind was blowing from the ocean. It moved her dark hair across her face. The dim light from overhead created shadows in the hollow of her cheeks and gave depth to her dark eyes.

"The hotel has a small restaurant, but I've heard that it's pretty good," she said.

"Is that an invitation?"

"Yes, it is. Do you think it's too forward of me? Does it frighten you?"

"Not at all," I said. "We are living in changing times, but I am concerned that you are a married woman."

She took another sip of the gin and tonic and looked down into it for a moment. "Ahud and I have an understanding."

"I've heard about these understandings. What's yours?"

"It's simple. I don't especially like circumcised men. They look so . . . so . . . mutilated. It's disgusting. It's hard to find a man who isn't circumcised today."

"And this is okay with the major?"

"He understands," she said with a shrug.

"How do you know that I'm not circumcised?"

She looked at me over the rim of her glass. "I don't, but I'm betting that you're not."

"And if I am?"

"Then we will have a beautiful friendship."

Lack of confidence was not one of Nouga's failings. When one of the major's informants (the major had informants everywhere) told her that I was at the beach bar, she rented a room at the hotel. I suppose it wasn't difficult to predict what I would do or what any single young man faced with the prospect of a beautiful, rather exotic, uninhibited woman would do. Saying no seemed pointless and even illogical.

We had a sumptuous dinner—medium rare lamb chops and green peas with pearl onions and a bottle of Chateau Julian. I asked if she kept kosher.

"Ahud and I are very liberal about such things. We are not orthodox. Sometimes we do, sometimes we don't. We both believe in Israel's right to exist as a Jewish state and we both work to ensure that, but we are not all that religious. It's funny, you know. The first thing people want to know about newcomers to Israel is if are they religious."

Nouga wanted to hear about the flying, and I didn't think I could give away any state secrets by telling her. She was also very interested in the diamond mines, and how the mining, transport, and selling of the diamonds took place. We talked about the role of the Mandingos. I asked her what she thought of the future of Liberia. She said that Liberia was living on borrowed time; that it was essentially a dictatorship even though President Tubman was democratically elected in 1944.

"He's got that useless congress packed with his men and everybody else eating out of his hand," she said, lighting a cigarette. "Tubman is an Augustus Caesar. He came pretty much out of nowhere, like Augustus. He has a genius for government like Augustus, but also like Augustus, his one fatal flaw is his Congo clan, his fellow Americo-Liberians. He has put them everywhere. He wants the dim-wit Tolbert to succeed him, and he's got that wife whose ruthlessness rivals Livia's." She noticed my puzzlement. "Livia was the wife of Augustus and notorious for being ruthless. Tubman," she continued, "probably hasn't got much longer—five, maybe ten years as most. Then all hell is going to break loose."

"What do you mean?" I asked.

"Unlike Augustus, he's got African tribalism to deal with. He's considered the head of his tribe, the Americo-Liberians. They run things here. If you look," she continued, "at a map showing all the Liberian tribes, you can't help but notice there is no Americo-Liberian tribe shown. That's because when the Bible-thumping freed slaves arrived from America in the 1800s, they just took the land they wanted. Nobody here wanted them, and they still don't. And the other tribes, some of them, want to run it their way. They see it as a tribal conflict, not a party conflict. It's almost like a racial thing. The Americo-Liberians consider themselves a little superior to the native peoples, and the native West Africans don't consider Americo-Liberians as truly African. Tubman's kind of politics is not going to solve these problems."

"What about the prosperity here? Do you think these people are likely to cut their own throats—especially the other tribal chiefs?"

"You're right," she said. "As long as he pays them off he can buy peace. He really has captured this Augustan mystique—the people love him, but they hate his tribe.

"The way the other tribes see it, at least most of them, is that the Americo-Liberians are getting it all while they get nothing. The few get much while the many get very little—a dangerous situation." She took a deep drag from her cigarette. "I will say one thing for him though. He hates the communists. You may have noticed that the Russians, the Chinese, even the Cubans are absent from the diplomatic scene here. That's the biggest reason the Americans love him—a strong proponent of capitalism and free market economics."

"I understand that he's not a friend of the Israelis either," I said.

"This is true. We have to be discreet. We have to keep our heads down. But I didn't come here to talk about politics. It's pointless anyway and yes, I am expected to pump you for information."

Nouga had rented a room with an ocean view, not that she gave me much time to enjoy the view.

"I don't want romance," she said. "I want to fuck." She liked clean sex, she said, with no strings and showers before and after. She wanted to shower together, but the shower stall was only large enough for one.

She showered first and was waiting for me in bed.

After breakfast, I walked back along the beach to the house. I didn't feel great about what happened with Nouga, but I had to admit, it was the best sex that I had ever had. She had completely separated any emotion from it. There was to be no affection, no moral responsibility, no obligation, just raw lust and the exploration of ultimate pleasure. There was a kiss and a smile before she left, but no promise of a tomorrow.

I thought about this as I walked along the beach and couldn't help but feel a little abandoned, a little saddened, but strangely, despite my Episcopal upbringing, free from any feeling of guilt.

It was around 11:00 a.m. when I reached the beach house. Deet was sitting in a beach chair swinging a bottle of scotch by his side.

"Vell, my friend. Look at you. It's happened just like I said."

"What's happened?"

"Vell, vhile you were screwing your brains out—Oh yes! Don't vaste your breath trying to deny it." He waved his finger from side to side. "Vhile you were screwing dat Jewish woman—some of the *mannlich* saw you with her at de beach bar—Herr Mike cleaned out de company's account. He even took vhat vas left in de till and has flew de coop." He made a flying motion with his hand.

"Where has he gone?"

"How de fuck should I know? Absconded to America most likely." Deet took another pull on the scotch bottle, which was almost empty.

"Deet, why don't you put that down and come with me."

"Vhere are ve going?"

"To the airport, of course. Let's get the info firsthand." Deet took one more pull from the bottle, clumsily screwed the cap back onto it and, clutching it around the neck, stood up without wobbling. "Dat's a goot idea."

I drove as fast as I could to the operations office at Spriggs-Payne. The door to the office was open. The lounge area was empty. We walked straight to Mike's office. Paterson was sitting at Mike's desk.

"Don't worry," he said. "I can see by de look on your faces. I am not de boss, but this is de only time I get to sit at the boss's desk. He is gone, as you can see. And he has taken everything with him except de pencils."

"Who's running the company?" I asked.

"I am," said a voice behind me. Deet and I turned to see a middle-aged white man looking a bit disheveled and angry, as though he had been roused from a deep sleep. He introduced himself as Mr. de Ruiter.

"You," he said, pointing a finger at Paterson. "Get out!" He made a motion toward the doorway. Paterson slowly stood up, straightened his collar, and left.

"What da fuck do you boys want?" Mr. de Ruiter said, taking the seat Paterson had just vacated.

Deet and I both cringed and gritted our teeth at being called "boys." Was that how he saw us?

"Vhat do you think ve vant?" Deet said.

"I don't know what to tell you," Mr. de Ruiter said. "McCoy cleaned out as much of the liquid assets as he could. He's gone to God knows where. I've been asked to come here and sort this mess out."

There was a long silence except for the rustling of papers.

"Honorable Williams still owns the majority of shares. I see no reason why the company can't continue. The business is here. We haven't lost our major clients. All we've really lost is a few thousand dollars and one asshole. It's just a business like any other business. Will you boys work with me or not?"

"Not if you continue to refer to us as boys," I said.

Mr. de Ruiter looked up at us, his eyes fixed, unblinking and uncomprehending. "Okay, sure," de Ruiter said.

We said that we would stay, but as we were leaving the operations office, Deet expressed his doubts. "Anodder fucking Afrikaner, probably a crook." We walked over to the hangar and spoke to Paterson. He expressed the same doubts but without the profanity. He said that he would stay with the company.

"Okay," I said. "Let's give it a try."

I later learned that Honorable Williams had infused enough cash into the company to meet the payroll and expenses for at least three or four more months.

Deet and I went downtown to Heinz and Maria's for lunch and a beer. It was pretty crowded and I saw a couple of American pilots I knew in the corner of the bar, huddled over the radio. I went over to see what was going on.

"Hey, Bill," I said.

They both turned around to me and said in unison, "Kennedy's been shot! He's dead."

"Holy shit!" I said. "I can't believe it!" I turned to my friend. "Deet, did you hear that? The president of the United States has been assassinated!"

"Ya, ya! I heard, ya. Dat is somezing else! Vhat happens now? A military takeover?"

"God no!" I said. "Vice President Johnson takes over. But this is incredible. I just can't believe it."

I looked around the room, and though there was some general discussion among the Germans about the assassination, no one seemed overly upset by it. At that moment I felt further away from home than ever before.

During that month our business picked up. I had thought that Mike was involved in some shady deals, but de Ruiter went openly into smuggling. I made a lot of trips to the diamond mines. Some of our flights that month were made into Guinea. These were risky ventures. No paperwork was involved, no trail. We would pick up Mandingos from the road along the border. Usually, a Mandingo would come into the office and ask us to pick up his "relative" on the border road. He would indicate where and the time. The road wasn't traveled much, and we could come in full flaps with the engine at idle for silence.

The moment the airplane stopped, the Mandingos would come out of the bush. On my trips, they were always where they said they would be, and they were always on time. Then we would take off without turning around. They had a lot of diamonds on them that they were getting from the mines in Guinea and Sierra Leone.

Usually this kind of pickup went off without a hitch except for one pilot who worked for Stumpy Beizell, another operator at Spriggs-Payne. He landed on a road just over the border in Guinea. He stopped the airplane expecting to see Mandingos, but instead he saw a man dressed in a soldier's uniform come out of the bush. The apparent soldier grabbed the pilot by the neck and pulled him out of the airplane. The pilot took out his gun and fired it in the air in an attempt to startle the man into letting go. It worked, and the pilot, in panic, scampered under the airplane and jumped into the right, front passenger seat. However, the company had removed the controls from the right side of the plane, so the pilot had to lean over to the left seat to operate the controls. He instantly opened the throttle to full power. The man in the soldier uniform ran toward the airplane and jumped in front of the spinning propeller, which immediately decapitated him.

At this point, a woman ran out of the bush screaming. She grabbed the tail of the airplane and hung on, still screaming, until she dropped off as the airplane gained speed. The pilot, severely shaken, flew back managing the flight controls on the left side from the right seat. Blood was still splattered over much of the airplane when he got back. Stumpy, the owner, was upset, of course. It took a whole day to clean the airplane and the prop was a little bent, but he had one of the local auto mechanics hammer it out.

"Actually," Stumpy said, "I think it helped. Before, there was a lot of vibration in it. Now there is only a little."

I later learned that something similar had happed to other air service operators. Their belief was that the Mandingos were being watched; that somebody else wanted a piece of the action, and the soldier's uniform was a disguise.

The Mandingos were not universally loved. Liberians referred to them as the Jews of Africa. They were exclusive, insular, and aloof, and compared to the native population, very rich. It's likely that some of the locals had been watching these pickups, killed or somehow scared off the Mandingos, and waited at the pickup point.

The Mandingos weren't talking. They were always very closed mouthed and conducted themselves as though nothing ever happened.

CHAPTER 16

DEAD MAN WALKING

I was in the hangar looking over some damage done to one of the airplanes when de Ruiter called me into his office.

"There's a village up country that needs a body taken to his home village for burial. I need you to do it."

"Okay, so long as he's in a box."

De Ruiter shrugged. "I wouldn't know."

"How long has the person been dead?" I asked, an important question in tropical Africa.

"I don't know that either. I would imagine not long. But, whatever, you're doing it, right, matey?"

I flew up to a little village due north of Gbarnga. They had a white sheet out indicating all was clear, and I landed without difficulty. A crowd of villagers was waiting for me as I approached. Five of them were dressed up and apparently ready to go to the funeral. It was about a hundred degrees in the shade and this one man was all dressed up in a black suit, tie, and dark glasses. The others sort of carried him into the back of the plane and sat him up straight. Everyone was laughing and shouting, having a great time except the guy in the suit. He would just groan, "Ahhh, ahhh." I figured they had all started drinking for the occasion a little early and this man had gone over his limit of rum. I wanted to get going because it was getting really hot with everyone in the plane.

"Where's the box?" I asked.

"Oh, it at de otha village," one of them said.

"Well then, where's the body?"

"He sittin rah hee."

"Him? In the suit?" I asked. "But he's not dead!"

"Oh, he will be bah de time we get dere!"

And he was.

About a month after this memorable flight, airplane parts started to become scarce. Then the cleanup boys were let go. A few days later, de Ruiter asked us if we could wait two weeks past our normal pay period.

"Das ist it!" Deet exclaimed. "De beginning of de end. I know de signs."

A few days later I was scheduled for a flight up to one of the diamond mines in the north. When I returned, I noticed that none of the airplanes were untied or out on the ramp. The hangar doors were closed. I walked into the operations office and de Ruiter's door was open. I wasn't really surprised to see Honorable Williams there. He was seated at the desk going over a large ledger book. He was dressed in an immaculate white shirt, dark tie, and dark blue suit. He wiped away the streams of perspiration running down his face with a large handkerchief.

"Ah! Ken. I'm glad to see you," he said.

"To what do we owe the honor of your being here, sir?"

He laughed. Honorable Williams was a good-natured man, and a favorite around the airport. We seldom saw him in the operation's office, so I knew this was serious.

"We are shutting down African Air Services. It is unfortunate but it appears that Mr. de Ruiter was as big a thief as his predecessor. The operation is broke, and I have decided to liquidate the company and transfer all equipment and assets to Monrovia Airlines, which, as you may know, is one of my other companies. I'm thinking about using this hangar and office building as a maintenance facility—the Monrovia Airlines office will be strictly operations and this will be maintenance. But don't worry, young man, you will be paid."

Honorable Williams opened another large cloth-bound book. I could see that it was a book of company checks. He scribbled the amount I was owed on one, signed his name, tore it out of the book and handed it to me with a little bit of a flourish.

"Everyone will be paid," he said, "and I want you to know that there is a place for you at Monrovia Airlines, should you want it."

"Thank you, sir. I would like that very much," I said, feeling genuinely grateful.

"Good," he said. "I must tell you, however, that they have a seniority system there. You won't have as much work, at least for a while, as you had here. Is that all right?"

"Sure. Are the others going too?"

"So far, everyone I've talked to has agreed to move over to Monrovia. I'm certainly glad that Paterson did. He's an invaluable asset. I haven't talked to Deet yet, but I hope he will come also. It's not easy to get good men, as you can see." He pointed to the desk. "I have a good manager over at Monrovia—Andre. He's tough but he's fair, and he knows the business. I think you will like him. Why don't you stop by, say Monday about 10:00 a.m. I'll tell him to expect you."

I thanked Honorable Williams. It was a sincere gesture of appreciation. I wasn't ready to leave Liberia. I had the gnawing feeling that I was on the verge of something important. I just didn't know what.

It was Friday so I had a couple of days before meeting Andre. I jumped into Junebug and looked at the check once again. It was a sizable amount, a month's pay. It had to come out of Honorable Williams' personal funds. However, while it was generous, I knew he could make it back in a short period of time. Even the most indifferent operator could make a living with half an effort, and many did.

I drove over to the Airport Bar. It was a concrete block building on the side of the airfield. The dark rectangular openings that served as windows had no glass but were fitted with building contractor's reinforcing steel bars instead. The bars were shaped to resemble palm trees or birds and painted in bright reds, greens, and shades of yellow. Once inside, with the help of overhead paddle fans, it felt open and airy, much like similar public establishments in Key West or Hawaii. Birds flew in and out of the place, easily navigating through the openings. After a beer or two it could be quite pleasant.

The Airport Bar was run by a French woman named Madeleine Roudeau. She was an attractive woman, probably thirty, and had two young children who always seemed to be in evidence. She was divorced from a Dutchman whom no one had seen in years. She had a good bartender, and she kept the place in good condition. It took up most of the main terminal building and wasn't very far from the hangars. The bar sat maybe thirty people. During the day, passengers would fill up the place and wait for the arrival or departure of the DC3 that flew in and out of Spriggs-Payne once a day. There were some native joints along the side of the runway, but most pilots hung out in Madeleine's place after work. After a couple of drinks, we would usually go to a restaurant or bar in town for dinner. Madeleine's also had reasonably good food, and if we happened to be on the airfield around lunch time, Madeleine's was where we ate.

It was early, not yet lunch. I didn't feel like having anything alcoholic, so I ordered a coffee. The coffee was as good as I expected it to be. It was possible, but bad coffee was hard to find in West Africa. Madeleine slipped on to the seat next to me at the bar.

"I heard about African Air Services," she said. Madeleine wore her chestnut brown hair at shoulder length and let the right side fall into what use to be called a peek-a-boo bang.

"Bad news does travel fast," I said.

"Any prospects?" she asked.

"Yeah, I think so. I'm going to see Andre at Monrovia Air on Monday, but it's limited right now—part-time work for a while. Have you heard anything? Anybody hiring?"

"Go over and see Stumpy. He was in here yesterday complaining about his lack of help. He does a lot of work at all of the mines. You will not like him. He's a first-class prick, but it'll be something to tide you over."

I thanked Madeleine for her advice, paid for the coffee, and drove over to Stumpy's hangar.

Harland "Stumpy" Beizell had an artificial leg below the right knee. He had a slight limp that he compensated for by kicking out his right leg, giving the appearance of a sort of half goose-step when he walked. He operated a little air services business consisting of four airplanes, two of which were Lockheed Air 60s that he had convinced investors to buy. They were large tri-cycle gear airplanes and were powered by 340 hp, turbo-charged engines. They had sliding cargo doors that were good for his kind of operation. They were good performers and could haul a lot of goods, making them particularly well suited for the iron mine runs. He also had a couple of Cessna 185s. They looked like they were in pretty good condition.

One of his investors was a Belgian who had lived in the Congo, an older man by our standards. He had plenty of money, and he had put a lot of it into Stumpy's business. Stumpy was American but had been in the country for a while. You could tell from his sagging yellowish eyes, the slow and listless way he moved, and his sallow complexion. Nevertheless, he was still a formidable man with something of the lone wolf about him.

I found Stumpy sitting at his desk in a very dark and grubby little office. The grease on his hands seemed to have spread over every inch of every surface of the room. His head tilted down and was engulfed in a cloud of cigar smoke.

"You Stumpy?" I asked.

"Who wants to know?" he said without looking up.

"I'm Ken. Ken Verrier. Madeleine over at the Airport Bar said you needed a pilot. I was working over at African Air Services, and well, you know what happened there. So I'm looking for some pick up runs. I can start any time." He raised his head to look me straight in the eye. After a long pause, he said, "You haven't been in Africa long, have ya."

"Long enough," I said.

"It's just that you still have a clean, healthy look about you. Anyway, be here a week from Monday—early. I have a run you can take, and we'll see how it goes."

CHAPTER 17

SHEENERY MON

Monday morning came and it was time to meet Andre. I drove over to his hangar, which also housed his office. It was good to see Paterson walking out of the hangar toward me.

"Hey boss!" he said. We shook hands in the Liberian manner.

"How are things going, Paterson?"

"I started work yesterday. It good to have a job, suh. Yes indeed."

"What do you think of Andre?"

He hesitated for a moment. "He is a man of few words, sir, a man of few words. Well, it's good to see you suh. We will be working together again. Dat is good." Paterson extended his hand once again. We shook and I watched as he walked away. A man of few words probably meant the same thing in Liberia as it did in the US—someone who knew where he was going, knew what he wanted, and what to expect.

I walked into the hangar, taking a few moments to notice the aircraft being serviced, then knocked on Andre's office door.

"*Entrez!*" he said in a loud voice without shouting.

He was standing facing a large blackboard—the scheduling board. On it was scribbled all of the pertinent information about the day's flights. I introduced myself.

"Yes, yes, I know who you are. Honorable Williams has informed me. Have you seen our aircraft?"

"Only the ones on the ramp and in the hangar."

"Are you checked out in any of them?"

"Yes."

"Good, that will save us some time. Most of our work is related to the diamond trade but we also have other clients. Occasionally we work with the Peace Corps as well as some private charters—the same work you did at African Air Services. We have also acquired many of their clients. Oh, and by the way, if Honorable Williams or anyone in his family wants to fly somewhere, they fly. Understand?"

I said that I did.

"I don't have anything for a couple of weeks," Andre said. "But what I do need right now is a good mechanic. I'm told that you are qualified in that area too?"

"Yes," I said, "but I thought you had a good mechanic—the boy from the Tourneau Mission, the old Texas Company."

"You're right. Charles. He was good. Apparently too good."

"What happened?"

"He got to be, as I said, really good. They had trained him well up at the mission and he knew what he was doing. He was a real entrepreneur, Charles was. He ended up buying a taxi and hired one employee; and he found a real nice girl he was planning to marry.

"Well, then the military airplanes started falling apart, so what did the military do? They drafted him into their army. He was a Liberian, so they could do it. Then he changed. It was like night and day. They were paying him nothing, maybe twenty, thirty dollars a month. He lost his taxi, his girlfriend left him, and then he went AWOL. Of course they caught him. And then they would chain him up in the hangar at night and make him work on the airplanes during the day. This went on for a while until one night he went berserk. He tried to burn down the hangar and he took a sledge hammer to the airplanes. So, of course, they sent him off to prison. Never saw him again. So, as you can see, I still need a good mechanic."

"I understand," I said, "but I did come here to fly."

"You will fly," he said. "You'll fly so much you'll be begging me to stop. But no one flies if the machines are broken. I have been asking around, but for the moment, I need help."

"I don't have my own tools," I said.

"We have tools." He said. "Come with me. I'll introduce you and show you what we have."

I followed him into the hangar. Andre looked more Vietnamese than French. He was a small man. He walked very fast, and he had coarse black hair that seemed to constantly fall into his face. He introduced me to Koto, his only working mechanic. Koto was from Sierra Leone. He was very thin and looked more like a Somali. Most of his teeth were gone but that did not affect his willingness to smile.

"Koto," Andre said, "this is Boss Ken. He is one of our new pilots and he is also a mechanic from the United States." Koto looked unfazed. "He will be the boss. You do what he says."

Had we been in a maintenance shop in the US, this kind of speech and introduction would have caused instant resentment and led to numerous labor conflicts. Koto, however, smiled his near toothless smile, nodded his head in agreement, and said, "Yes boss, I unnastan. He know sheenery. He know sheenery mo dan me."

Andre rolled the shop's tool chest over to me. One of the qualities of good mechanics is that he handles and cares for his tools like a surgeon handles and cares for his surgical instruments. These tools were a jumble of metal objects covered in dirt and grease.

"I can't use these," I said. "They're a mess. They are all going to have to be cleaned and organized according to function and size. It'll take a day at least, maybe two."

"Then get one of the boys—" Andre said.

"No," I interrupted. "I'd better do that myself."

Andre nodded and started back for his office. I followed.

"Yes?" he said, turning to face me.

"Andre, I don't work just for the privilege of working."

"Since you are a US certified A and P mechanic, I'll pay you fifteen US an hour." Fifteen US dollars an hour was very good money. "Koto gets three fifty. Maybe you can inspire him to get a certification."

I walked back into the hangar, found a large plastic sheet, spread it out on the floor next to the tool chest and dumped the tools out onto it. Koto looked at me, amazed and puzzled. "Wat you do, oh?"

I explained my mission of cleaning and sorting. He shook his head, and walking away, he said, "I got no time fo dah."

I found a bucket of Varsol and spent the day cleaning, sorting and arranging the tools in the proper order. I then cleaned the tool chest inside and out and put clean lining made from tightly woven aircraft floor matting material in the bottom of each drawer.

Toward the end of the workday Andre came out onto the hangar floor. He motioned for me to follow him. He stopped in front of a rather badly battered Cessna 185.

"Charlie Fox has a cracked cylinder. Can you change it tomorrow?" I didn't see any reason why I couldn't. I didn't expect any work from Beizell for another week.

Paterson was outside with one of his boys changing a tire on one of the airplanes. The boy looked up at me and smiled.

"I know you from Mike's operation," I said. "I'm Mista Ken. Do you remember me?"

"Oh, sho do, boss. Sho do. Ma name is Jonathan."

"That's a good name. You know how Paterson got his name?"

"Ya, ah do. Iss da name of some place in Amerika."

"That's right," I said. "Paterson, New Jersey. That's right near New York City."

"Oh, I heard o' New Yor Cetty. So, boss, how bee is New Yor Cetty?"

"Oh," I said, "it's huge! It's big way past Monrovia."

"No!" He laughed. "It can't be big past Monrovia!"

"Oh yeah, it is. They have big skyscrapers."

"Skyscrapers. Wassa skyscraper?"

"Skyscrapers are buildings that go up so high that you can't see the top. They are said to touch the sky."

"Noooo, boss, not possible," he whispered. "No place big past Monrovia."

"Okay, Jonathan, it's big past Robertsport."

Jonathan smiled and exhaled.

Belinda and Barry were both out that evening, so I sat by myself on the porch, gazing out at the ocean. I had a growing apprehension about our planned trip to Ouagadougou for the music festival. Driving to Ouagadougou in that old station wagon? Was I crazy? What if it broke down seven hundred miles short of our destination? We would be out in the middle of nowhere. We would be SOL. No, I would be SOL! Were they even who they said they were?

I had a copy of all the keys, so I went into their room. I found their passports in a dresser drawer along with some newspaper clippings and other papers. Belinda did have a Canadian passport, and Barry had what appeared to be an Australian passport. However, tucked under the newspaper clippings, I found three other passports. Two of them were men, and another belonged to a woman. They were Dutch passports, and one of them had a large, dark brown smear all over a couple of pages. The owners of these documents all appeared to be in their twenties. I hurriedly replaced the passports and left the room, making sure to lock the door on my way out.

I had seen all that I needed to see. I had seen old, dried blood before and didn't need a forensic analysis to tell me what it was. I suspected that the Oldsmobile station wagon had belonged to one of the Dutch passport holders and that they were probably dead. How, or by whom? I did not want to venture a guess. I did know for certain that I didn't want to spend any time alone with Barry and Belinda and especially not out in the bush.

According to their passports, they had been in Morocco, Mali, and Guinea. They had then come in from Sierra Leone (a smugglers' route), which meant that they could have been up to anything.

When they came home that evening, I approached them. I wanted to tell them face-to-face that I wasn't going with them. I wanted to see how they would react. They became very agitated and upset and kept asking me why. I simply told them that something important had come up, and that I couldn't go. I thought things might get violent, so I locked the door to my room and left to go to the Gurley Street Bar. As I had suspected, they were gone when I returned, along with all their belongings.

I thought of going to the Dutch Embassy and reporting it, but that would associate me with them, and once the police got the scent of something, they would destroy things and people for miles around trying to follow their leads—I didn't want to be listed as collateral damage. I decided to push it to the back of my mind—chalk it up to experience and congratulate myself on a lucky escape. I convinced myself, naively perhaps, that if my suspicions were right, justice would eventually catch up with them.

CHAPTER 18

BIG PALAVER

A little bit of maintenance for Andre, some runs for Stumpy, and the prospect of many more flights with Andre brightened my spirits considerably. Andre seemed a solid type, whether he said much or not, and I slowly began to trust him. The beach house was better now too. It was just the three of us—Deet, Tony, and me—with plenty of room and, being pilots, plenty of money.

The isolation that the beach house provided separated me from the mayhem and occasional squalor of downtown Monrovia, which, at the end of the day, was a great relief. Lately, I had been thinking about sketching many of the interesting and beautiful sights in Liberia. I had always, since I was a child, been able to draw. By the time I was in high school I was making regular sketches of everything I saw, which included most of the members of my high school class. My mother was an artist and she had taught me the finer points of sketching and painting. She specialized in acrylics and I learned from her. Acrylics are water soluble and they dry relatively quickly— both good qualities to have in West Africa.

On my way to the beach house one afternoon I, almost on an impulse, stopped at a small retail store in Monrovia that I knew sold art supplies, furniture, model airplanes, and hardware of all kinds, including guns. The place was owned by an elderly Dutch couple, Alida and Geert Koning, who had fled Holland a year before the German invasion. They got on the first ship they could leaving Rotterdam. It was a merchant vessel and after a rough passage, got off the ship in Monrovia and sought immigrant status.

Mr. Koning was a very good business man and always said that if he didn't have it, he could definitely get it from Holland.

Fortunately, he had everything that I needed, and I walked out of his store happily carrying under my arms a large sketch pad with paper, charcoal and a soft lead pencil, an easel, and a set of acrylic paints with brushes. Being able to draw and paint would allow me to bask in the wild beauty of this place without being a part of the phenomenally wealthy or as one of the dirt-poor native Liberians.

The country was growing so rapidly that infrastructure, needed to ensure prosperity, was not or could not be built fast enough. This prosperity, however vast, hardly ever seemed to touch the average, or tribal, Liberian. By the time the massive wealth that was pouring into the country from timber, iron and diamond mines, and rubber plantations got down to street level, it was a drop trickling out of the tap.

This was a wild place. It was like the Wild West in the US, with its gold rush, money, and sense of lawlessness. I could see Monrovia as Dodge City—except for the cars and the loud, incessant sound of radios wherever I went.

I started making regular trips to the iron mines for Stumpy, hauling pumps, huge valves, coils of wire rope, and food supplies. Madeleine was right. He was a real prick. But he paid me for my work, and because I was also a mechanic, I could make sure that the planes could fly. One thing I did like though—I was getting really good at flying. I was getting to know the geography, the weather, and the people, lots of people, seemingly just passing through.

I had gotten to know a ferry pilot, Fred, whose only job was delivering airplanes, and considering the constant need for replacement aircraft, he was always working. He came through town around this time and had his nephew with him—a tall, good-looking young man of about twenty-one, a graduate student at Harvard. We let them stay at the house since we had the spare bedroom. They didn't have a car, so I showed them how the taxi system worked.

Having people stay at your house is always a risk. The last thing you want is to have any sort of run in with the locals. We explained the rules very carefully, particularly about not going to the airfield and messing with any of the women. They are local, tribal, and have families that will cause trouble, or make palaver—big palaver that just won't go away.

"If you want a woman," I said, "go to the bar scene. That's where this kind of business is done and no palaver."

The Beech 18 aircraft that the ferry pilot was transporting had some mechanical problem, so they planned to extend their stay about three days. Sometime late during the second night there was a loud knock on the door. This turned out to be one of the local native policemen, surrounded by a large group of locals from the airfield.

A very tall, wiry man stepped forward and said, "Da college boy, he tay ma girl! He tay ma girl and den he go away. He no got good way. Ma girl no hobojo, oh!"

I turned to the policeman. "What's going on?" I asked, hoping I could glean a little more from him.

"He say college boy play with girl tata, so he wan plenny dolla!"

I got the general gist of the situation and ran down the hallway to the boy's room. He was asleep, so I shook him. I woke up Fred too. I told them what was going on outside and said to both of them, "You get out there! Something has happened here, and it's all your crap."

We went outside and the woman pointed to the nephew. Everyone started yelling again and I took out some money to quiet them down. I paid the woman ten dollars and gave the policeman some dash, and said, "Palaver fini!" He smiled. The others still looked insulted, but they all went away.

It had started to rain by then. Deet had seen the whole thing. He suddenly went into their rooms, gathered up their stuff and threw it out into the road. "Get out now und find your own hotel!" Fred was appalled, and the nephew started to protest vehemently. Deet thought they needed another lesson in the rules of living in Liberia, so he went and got his gun and said to the nephew, "If you don't get de fuck out of de house immediately, I vill shoot you!" The boy knew he meant it and said nothing more.

They left, and I didn't see them again. I asked Deet why he had been so harsh.

"I've seen it before," he said, "und I didn't vant to have to put up vith it—de endless palaver. Vonce it starts, it never seems to end. It vears you down. It vrings you out. Und it can be dangerous."

The next night, Colin, Ozzie, and I decided to go to a movie downtown. I'd heard "Cat Ballou" with Lee Marvin and Jane Fonda was pretty funny, so I suggested it. We all need a little humor now and then. Ozzie parked his car in front of the theater and immediately a teenage boy came up to "guard" our car.

"You hep me small, mista. You hep me small and I guard yo car."

"Yeah, yeah," Ozzie said, "here you go, here's twenty-five cents. You guard my car." Then to us, he said, "Make sure you lock all the doors. I don't want him sleeping inside the car."

It was starting to rain slightly, and as we walked into the theater, the boy climbed up on the hood of the car to keep watch. It was about 10:00 p.m. when we came back out; there was still a light rain. Our boy was sound asleep on the hood, looking very comfortable but hanging on to the windshield wipers so he wouldn't fall off.

"Hey boy!" Colin yelled. "Wake up! Your job is over!" The kid didn't move. Ozzie got in the car and blasted the horn for a good five seconds. The kid still didn't move. Then he told us all to get in the car and started the engine—nothing. I was beginning to feel a bit uneasy. I had gotten to know Ozzie by this time and he seemed capable of anything. Ozzie started creeping down the street with the boy on the hood—still nothing. He sped up to about 30 mph. The boy seemed to have this sleeping death grip on the windshield wipers. He wasn't going to let go.

Ozzie said, "So here's what we're going to do. We're going to go to the airport and see if this guy can fly!"

I was really wishing that I wasn't in the car, but I said nothing. We got to the airfield and we went straight down the runway at probably 40 or 50 mph. At the end of the runway, Ozzie shouted, "Hang on!" and then he stomped on the brakes.

The boy went flying off the hood and disappeared.

Fortunately, he must have made a soft landing because in a few moments after he disappeared from the hood, he popped up into the headlights yelling, "Boss! I'm not asleep, boss! I'm not asleep!"

All I could think was, *Holy shit!*

CHAPTER 19

THE MAJOR

Ozzie drove me back to the beach house. I took a rare shower and dropped into bed. I didn't know anything until I was awakened the next morning by knocking on my door. Deet and Tony were nowhere to be seen so I told whoever it was to wait. I slipped into yesterday's shorts and a slightly stained t-shirt and, after brushing my hair back with my hand, opened the door. It took several seconds for me to recognize Major Ahud. He was dressed in the Israeli manner—casual trousers and a short-sleeved shirt open at the collar. He was clean shaven and his hair was immaculately styled. He was carrying a larger than usual attaché case. I figured that this was it. He had come to teach me a permanent lesson about sleeping with another man's wife.

"Can I come in?" he said.

I opened the door and stood back.

"Look," I said. "If this is about—"

"We can talk about that later. For now, I've come to offer you a deal."

"There's nothing like getting to the point. What kind of deal?"

With that, he opened the attaché case and pulled out a shiny new Uzi submachine gun. I felt a stone-like paralysis sweep through my body. The first controllable thought I had after that was I would not live to see my next birthday. The second one was that it had been a mistake to sleep with his wife.

"Nine millimeter, twenty-five round magazine, blowback operated six hundred rounds per minute, muzzle velocity of four hundred meters per second, two hundred meter effective range, weighs 3.5 kilograms and has a 10.2 inch barrel."

"That's nice," I said, "but . . ."

"Let's go outside. I'll show you how it works. Bring something you don't need or want."

Someone had given me a hardback copy of a Graham Greene novel that I was not able to finish. It seemed appropriate to put it to better use.

I followed the major out to the beach.

"Put it over there," he said, pointing to a small mound of sand. I slowly did as he said. I had the feeling that at any moment he was going to start firing. I forced myself to walk back to where he was standing, holding the Uzi down by his right side. I thought I detected a half smile, as though he might be thinking that this would be a good opportunity to even the score. Every fiber of my being yelled for me to run, but I didn't.

He held the Uzi out so that I could see it. It was a knobby, angular, ugly looking thing that seemed to be more the result of a nightmare than of rational design.

"It was designed by Major Uziel Gal about the same time as the Kalashnikov. Like the Kalashnikov, it was supposed to be durable, capable of rough handling and dirt. To fire it you snap the magazine in place, then make sure the safety lever is pushed to automatic, like this."

He moved the small lever from its position on "S" past the middle click to the "A" position, slid the bolt back to the stop, and then let it go.

"It feeds one in the chamber and is ready to fire. Have you ever fired an automatic weapon before?" the major asked.

I shook my head.

"Well," he continued, "you can pull the stock out or use it as a pistol grip. I think it would be better if you put the stock against your shoulder. Here, let me show you."

He pulled out the metal stock with a snap and I heard it lock into place. Then he held the butt of the stock against his shoulder and fired. Mr. Greene's book disappeared in an eruption of sand and bits of flying paper. The noise deafened me for a moment and caused a ringing in my ears.

"Here, you try it. See how you like it," he said, handing the gun to me.

I put the butt snugly against my shoulder the way I had seen them do it in the movies and touched the trigger. There was a rattle of explosions and the butt hammered rapidly against my shoulder. I didn't hit Mr. Greene's book or what was left of it. I handed the gun back to the major. He very quickly switched the selector lever back to the safe position. Then we walked over to our target.

The book looked like it had been torn apart by a pack of angry dogs.

"This," the major said, holding the gun out to me, "could really ruin someone's day. It's yours. Go on, take it."

The major noticed my hesitation.

"What do you want for it?" I asked.

"Nothing really, but I hear that you're working for Beizell. He is of some interest to us." The major looked directly at me—the look of a predator before it strikes.

"I'm only working for Stumpy, I mean Beizell, part time," I said. "I'm also working for Monrovia Airlines."

"We know that too, but it's Beizell we're interested in."

"What do you want to know about him?"

"We want to know who he talks to, who he meets with, and where he goes. We think he's helping get German war criminals out of Liberia and into Brazil."

"If he is, he isn't doing it for love of the fatherland," I said. "I've learned enough about Beizell to know that he doesn't do anything unless he gets paid."

"If he is getting paid, we would like to know that too, and who is paying him."

"Let me see the gun again," I said.

The major handed it to me.

"Sorry, Major. I won't spy for you, not even on Beizell. But you will know if he's doing something illegal."

"How is that?"

"I'll quit. I don't spy and I don't work for crooks—at least crooks that I know about."

"Suppose I said we could make it worth your while."

"Money?" I asked.

"Possibly."

I slid the firing selector from safety to automatic. "Are we talking about your wife?"

His lips tightened then he smiled. "Nouga is not part of this. We have an understanding. She is free to pursue her interests just as I am mine, but in the end we are partners. We are a team."

"Major, I don't need a weapon like this. I'm not expecting to be attacked by an army. I have no place to keep it. And I'll bet that the moment word's out that I have something like this, it'll be stolen within twenty-four hours."

I knew that the Germans in Liberia tended to support one another, and I had heard that informers were dealt with in traditional ways. However, I suspected that the major had other ways of finding out what he wanted to know.

I pressed the magazine release and removed the half empty clip. Then, after I fired the chambered bullet at the remaining portion of Mr. Green's book, I handed the gun back to him. The major's face looked as hard and as angular as a cut diamond. He wasn't the kind of man who accepted failure gracefully. Though he refrained from threatening me, I had the feeling that he hadn't given up. He took the gun, looked at it, and started to speak, but hesitated. He handed it back to me.

"Take it. No strings attached. Think of it as a gift from Israel to all of those who love freedom. And then too, you may have to fight off an army one day."

He waved his hand in more of a military salute than a friendly African gesture. Then he turned and walked away.

I watched him walk up the beach, toward the house where his car was parked and for just a moment felt a sting of pity for him and for all of those caught up in the cesspool of history—wanting more but unable to free themselves completely.

The major's surprise visit had left me a little shaken, and I didn't know why. I couldn't get over the feeling that maybe he was right. Maybe I did have a moral responsibility, however small, to help punish war criminals. I looked at the Uzi and felt for a moment that I was holding a deadly snake. I looked around to see if anyone was watching but I could see no one. I folded the stock back into the gun and decided to hide it where my free-wheeling friends might not find it.

I put it in my duffle bag along with wads of newspaper to disguise its bulk. Deet and Tony knew that I sometimes kept dirty clothes in the duffle bag, so I knew that no matter how curious they became, they would not look in there.

Unlike most literature, which thrives on conflict, sketching and painting can and often does portray happy, tranquil occasions. Many of the master works of John Constable, Pierre-August Renoir, Mary Cassatt, and Édouarde Manet capture scenes of pure serenity and pleasure, free of conflict.

I took my sketch pad out onto the porch and started sketching the view of the beach with surf. There were several people walking along the beach and I included them. It reminded me of the day we put Arthur's ashes in the Atlantic Ocean just off the beach at Ocracoke Island on the coast of North Carolina.

Every August since I was a child, we rented a cottage there on the beach for a couple of weeks. Arthur liked to swim late in the afternoon when the quality of light turned the surf into a soft, warm, golden color. After swimming he would often sit on the sand, arms folded over his knees, and look out over the ocean until almost dark. It was a day like that, late in the afternoon in August, that we put his cremated remains in the ocean. My mother stood in the water amid the swirl of his ashes. It was her last embrace of him.

There was no religious ceremony. It was strictly a family affair except that Jenny was there. Everyone said something describing how they felt about Arthur except my mother. She could not speak, and did not speak about it for several months after. When she did finally speak, she would not look at me. Summers after that she would often wade barefooted in the surf late in the afternoon. I suppose she was hoping that perhaps an atom or molecule that had been part of Arthur would brush against her feet.

I began to wonder whether something of Arthur might have traveled to this remote beach in Liberia. It was an absurd idea, and I pushed it out of my mind. Instead, I thought of a scene I wanted to paint—an elderly man and woman that I had seen, only for a moment, while I was returning from work, sitting together outside their ramshackle, one-room house. They were smiling broadly, even laughing together, while they held each other's hand. Maybe they were remembering some long ago happy event or the pleasure of having a successful child. Whatever the reason, remembering it was for them deep, pure, undiluted joy.

CHAPTER 20

CRAZY MAN IN THE BIG BELLY

Word got out that Deet, Tony, and I were looking for a good houseboy. Generally, this was done through references, so we were asking friends' houseboys for brothers or friends who wanted to work. One day a local boy showed up at the door with a letter of reference and asked for a job. I did not invite him in but looked at him and said, "What does this letter say? Does it say you are a good worker?"

"Ya, boss! Ah a vey goo worker, oh! But ah na know wad a letta say. Ah na know how ta ree."

"Give me the letter and I'll read it," I said.

The letter read:

This is to introduce Moses Kweat. Do not hire him under any circumstances! He's a shit and he stole from me!

Signed Gunter Schmidt

"You Moses Kweat?"

"Oh, ya suh, boss."

"Well, Moses," I said, "thank you for coming by, but we don't need a houseboy anymore."

Shortly after that, we hired Kumasi, who also served as cook. With his consent, we shortened his name to Ku. He seemed very good, but when he wasn't busy with his household duties, he would sit on a wooden stool in the kitchen and wait for instructions.

A short time after hiring Ku, I went into the kitchen. He was at his waiting station looking at me. I opened the door to our ancient kerosene-fired refrigerator.

"Wha you wan, boss? Ku get it fo you," he said, slipping from the stool and putting himself between me and the contents of the refrigerator.

"Something to eat, Ku."

"No worry, boss." Ku said, "We ha good stew, good meat—no bush meat—and French baguettes, fresh may t'day, from da new market. Vey goo."

"Great, Ku. If you would prepare it, I'll have it out on the porch. That's where I'll be." I retrieved a bottle of beer from the refrigerator, popped it open, and left to find a chair on the porch. Thirty minutes later Ku brought the stew and several slices from the baguette. I had been in Africa long enough to have learned that if something tastes good, don't ask what it is. However, this time I thought I'd try:

"This is great, Ku. A little different, but delicious. What is it?"

Ku grinned. "Oh, boss, don't worry. It white man food. I kno why you askin. It no bugabug. It not time for bugabug."

"Bugabug? What's bugabug?" I asked.

"Bugabug is wha ya call termites."

"Termites? You eat termites?"

"Oh, yeah, boss. Dey good. But dey only come out two time a year."

"How so?"

"Well, you know they live in de big big mounds. Mounds bigga n me. An every now and den, de queen, she decides to move. So dey all move. Swarms and swarms and billions and billions all leave at the same time to find a new home. An das when evybody go get 'em, cook 'em, and eat 'em. Dey real good, boss. Kinda tase lie crunchy chickin."

"Nice to know, Ku, but when bugabug season comes, I'll pass."

Ku came back out to the porch and after clearing away the dishes and handed me a letter that had arrived yesterday. It was from Jenny. We, or I should say Jenny, had managed to keep up a stream of correspondence over the years, and I enjoyed hearing what was happening back home. Lately, it seemed she was asking more and more for me to make some decisions about my (and possibly our) future. I suppose my indecision in that area led to my neglect in keeping up my end of the correspondence.

Honestly, Kenneth, since you haven't written in so long I must assume that you are very sick or dead or, most likely, you have found someone else. That is the probable answer. Your parents don't tell me anything. They say they haven't heard from you either. I want to know how you are and what's going on, so I would like to come to Monrovia. I almost have enough money saved up. As soon as I do, I'll let you know. It'll be great seeing you again.

Love, Jenny

I wrote a quick letter, more like a note, telling her that I was well but extremely busy and that Monrovia was not safe. I gave her a few exaggerated examples and, hoping it would dissuade her, sealed the note in an envelope.

I drove Junebug to the post office and dropped off the letter. I estimated that it would take at least two weeks or more to get there. The last thing I needed now was a visit from Jenny. I simply couldn't deal with what she might expect. I left the US partly to get away from expectations, and I wasn't ready to go back yet.

After mailing the note, I drove over to the Gurley Street Bar. Colin and his merry-makers were there. He waved me over to his table.

"Pull up a chair, ol' boy! Bring this man a cold beer," he yelled to the waiter. Then to me, "Have you heard the latest about good old President Tubman?"

"What's that?" I said.

"He decided that his current residence in Monrovia isn't grand enough. He wants a White House—only twice as big as the one in Washington. I suppose it's a gift from the international companies he has let in here."

"I heard something about it, but not much. Why is he doing it?"

"Hell, all the other despots in Africa are building huge mansions, so why shouldn't he? If you're gonna build the greatest country in Africa, you need the biggest executive mansion, don't you? It just wouldn't do to house the government in wattle huts and have diplomats sit on a dirt floor. He chose a big hill in the city where there were a lot of mud huts and stuff. The construction crews went in with bulldozers one morning and just shoved everybody and their mud huts off the hill. With bulldozers! Hundreds and hundreds of people displaced. And then Tubman built his Executive Mansion. It's being built by LAMCO International, the Swedish-American company. We call it a twenty-dollar saddle on a five-dollar horse.

"And there it is up there, with the big porticos, the long driveway. They are building it really fast. It's almost done already. They flew in everything. I mean everything! If they needed plants from Europe, they flew them in. They even flew in the sod! There were cargo airplanes that did nothing for months but fly in stuff so they could get it all together and assemble this huge building. He wanted it done in time for his twentieth anniversary as president. He is reelected, you know of course, all the time. So they're building this mansion, and I gotta tell you, it is something—floodlights at night and music. It's all concrete—bullet proof and it will probably withstand a direct hit from a Katusha rocket. He had chandeliers flown in from Europe. Can you imagine that? He's spending millions on this place while most of the people here haven't got a pot to piss in." He sighed. "That's just the way it is."

"Well, he knows he's going to get reelected," someone at the table said.

"What's he going to do for security—the army?" I asked.

"The army!" Colin shouted. "That sly old bugger doesn't trust the army, especially after the attempted assignation back in '55. Do you know what the cagey old fucker did?" Colin leaned closer to me. I looked at him expectantly. "He replaced all of their live ammunition with blanks. He now has an army supplied with surplus guns left over from the war, and no real ammo. No coup d'état here!"

"But he does have a secret police," someone else at the table said. "You don't ever see them, you don't know who they are, but they are everywhere. That's his security, mate."

"I've heard that he's putting gun emplacements at strategic locations on the roof. Every approach will be covered," another said.

"Will he load them with real bullets?" I asked, thinking it would be taken humorously. Colin didn't laugh.

"They will be real, all right, and his personal security guard will man the guns."

Everyone at the table nodded and mumbled in agreement.

"Tubman can't live forever. What do you think will happen after he's gone?" I asked.

"Oh, he's already picked a successor. It's the vice president, and when his term runs out there'll be a phony election and some phony opposition, but Tolbert will appear to win. They are all bosom buddies. Truth is, nobody will give a shit as long as the price of rice remains low and a little gelt keeps trickling down from the international sugar daddies."

The waiter came with my beer. I thanked him and asked if he would bring me a bowl of Jollof rice. He smiled and nodded.

"Colin," I said, hoping to change the subject, "what have you been up to lately?"

"I can tell you this, matey. Never carry a crazy man in your aircraft. You know, when you fly down the coast, it is always something different. So I saw the white flag and, yes, I dragged the field to see if they'd cleared the cows off, and to my surprise, they had. So I go in and land. It was a pretty short airstrip.

"The Head Man came out and said that they had this crazy man who, the Head Man said, was a danger to everybody and would I fly him to Monrovia. I had done this sort of thing before, and it is always an unpleasant experience. So, I said that I would do it, but the man would have to be restrained.

"The crazy guy was an average size male in his twenties. He was foaming at the mouth and doing these weird, crazy things, like shaking his head and rolling his eyes. So I told the Head Man, 'You have to tie him up real good!' So they had these big, heavy vines, and they wrapped him up in them. We got him in the back seat, and I'm thinking, I've got my Webley 38. If I have to shoot him, I'll shoot him.

"I was in the 185, and they put him in back and had gotten more vines around him. Then, I took off, and the second I started the takeoff run, he went berserk. His elbow broke the back window and knocked out a chunk of it. So now I had a problem. Was it worth it, I asked myself? Nah, it's not worth it. So I immediately landed.

"They implored me, they begged and pleaded—'I hold your foot' and all that shit. Finally, they came up with some more money. They brought just about every dollar the village had to get him out. So I said I would. 'But,' I said, 'you have to put him in the cargo belly pack, underneath the cabin.' The belly pack has a side door. It opens up where you put the luggage in. It also has a back door to put long things in. The back door is hinged loaded. Have you ever seen one?"

I said that I had.

"Well, you know, it's dark in there. And it's very uncomfortable because there is structural framing. It's made for cargo. They put him on a long pole, and tied him up with so many vines that, I swear to God, the only thing you could see was the very top of his head and the soles of his feet. There was a little piece of his nose sticking out. He's wrapped really secure. Then they pushed him up in the belly pack. I said to the Head Man, 'You could have killed him!' The crazy man looked like he wasn't breathing, and I pointed this out to the Head Man. Then the Head Man says, 'No, no, he no deh, no!' Then he took out a match, and striking it, held it up to the crazy guy's toe. The guy lets out a muffled scream, and the Head Man smiles at me. So they finish shoving him up in there, and I take off again."

"I'm flying along, and every thing's hunky dory. It's about an hour flight. Then, all of a sudden there is this loud *bump, bump, bump* in the belly of the aircraft. Christ! So I did a couple of Dutch rolls thinking it would scare him into submission. But the bumping didn't stop. Finally I did a wing-over, and the *bump, bump, bump* continued. I was getting pretty desperate by now, and worried that something's going to break on the aircraft if the bumping kept up, so I shoved it over then pulled hard on the yoke for a couple of pitch oscillations. Then I heard a noise like *blublublup*. After that, it got very quiet except for the normal aircraft noise. 'Oh shit,' I said to myself. I flew on and got back to Spriggs-Payne as quickly as I could."

"When one of the load boys came up, I asked him to see if there was anything in the belly pack—I didn't have the nerve to look myself. He said, 'No, boss, its empty.'"

Colin's friends guffawed and continued drinking and munching on snack food. "Too bad," one of them said while lighting up a cigarette. "Ya never know what one of them boys will do to an aircraft."

The waiter brought my Jollof rice, but by then I had lost my appetite, so I asked the waiter if he would put it in a container and bring it back. He said that he would, and I paid him and told him to keep the change.

"By God! No wonder everybody loves you Americans. I swear you guys are actually going to buy the world just with tips."

CHAPTER 21

SISTER ANGELINA

I had been in Liberia long enough to feel the novelty wearing off. When I first arrived, there was something new every day. My senses were overwhelmed by new smells and bright colors. I would buy strange fruit and fish from smiling people in colorful clothing. But one day I saw a little baby elephant in a cage; another day I saw monkey hands for sale. Then there was the heat, always the heat. I was beginning to long for just a whiff of cold air from New York State, just for one day. And the palaver. Absolutely nothing got done without palaver—always a small argument over price, over quality, over anything at all. To buy something, first of all, there was always a price for a European and a price for a local, and I accepted that, but there was always discussion, always some sort of palaver. It was beginning to wear me down. I had been stopped by a soldier on the street because my license tag was crooked. "Sorry, mon, here's fifty cents," I'd say. I'd been stopped because my front tire was low. "Sorry, mon, here's twenty-five cents."

None of this seemed to appreciably bother Deet or the others, but I was still not used to it.

And then there was the job. If you had to make a forced landing close to a village with an airfield, maybe you could get out. If you ended up anywhere else, you were probably dead. You have people cheating you all the time. I knew Mike cheated; Mr. de Ruiter cleared out what was left of the company, and I was sure Stumpy was up to no good. Even just going out for a drink could be difficult. When I went to town for a beer, there would usually be some belligerent drunk in the bar.

The worst thing was to get involved with a Big Man at the bar. They drank a lot and loved to gamble. They'd come up to the bar and invite me and whomever I was with to play dice with them. We'd say, "No, no!" And they'd say, "Oh ya mus come, Ya mus come!" and you say, "Ahhh . . . Okay." Then they'd say you cheated. Pretty soon you are going to owe them money.

Everything wears you down one peck at a time. I did not think I could become accustomed to it. There were other people who were. The Lebanese did just fine. The Spanish did just fine. The Germans did okay; they seemed to be able to adapt to it even though they were older than me, all of them.

I was beginning to wonder if I had been in Liberia long enough. These people could be gentle with one another. They could be kind and considerate, yet there was a sharp-edged brutality here that seemed to cut through all aspects of life. And the expats—Colin, Deet, and the others that I had met in Africa—were they the way they were because that's the way they were born or had Africa made them that way? I had to admit, I admired their survival skills, their indifference to danger, their flying experiences, but I did not want to become like them.

I decided to focus on the positive. As far as I could tell, Monrovia Airlines was on the up and up. Andre seemed organized and relatively honest, and he was doing his best to keep the aircraft well maintained. I had a good setup and didn't want to go back to the States yet. I would give it one more go. I had a good feeling about Monrovia Airlines but, if that's all it was, a feeling, and it didn't work out then, like a defeated boxer, I would throw in the towel. I was not going to be swallowed up by Africa

---

I was making regular trips for Monrovia Airlines now. One frequent customer was a Catholic mission on the border of Sierra Leone and Liberia near the town of Hoya Camara. It was known as the Hoya mission. There were five nuns there who ran a small mission school and medical clinic. The youngest nun was Sister Angelina. Every two weeks I would fly her down to

Monrovia. We had an established route that we ran, and she never tired of looking at the world below.

I generally flew Alfa Charlie for these trips. It was slow, dependable, with ample cargo space. It usually gave a smooth ride. Once in town, she would do shopping for the mission as well as post and pick up mail. We would load the airplane up with all kinds of stuff, mostly medical supplies, a few personal items for the nuns, and food—you couldn't get food in the bush.

On one trip Sister Angelina did not meet me at the airplane when it was time to fly back to the mission. I went back to all of the places of business that she always went, but no one had seen her. Then, finally, one of the grocery boys said that he had seen her walking toward the beach several hours ago. I hailed a taxi, since I did not want to waste time walking, and told him to go to the beach. I thought, because of her white habit, Sister Angelina would be easy to spot. She was, and I found her sitting on a palm log that had washed up on the beach. She did not look up at my approach. I squatted next to her. I could see tears on her cheek.

"I've always loved the sea," she said. "I grew up in a little village outside of Stockholm. It was near the sea and I always use to go there when . . . " She did not finish.

"Come on," I said. "We must be getting back."

"Yes," she said. "I'm sorry to have caused you this trouble."

After I had been doing this job for a couple of months, I flew up to the mission, and instead of Sister Angelina, another nun that I had not met before, a much older nun, came out to the airplane. She had one of the mission boys with her who was carrying the mail sack. She motioned for him to put it down. I asked where Sister Angelina was.

"She won't be making the trip," she said, not looking at me, and at the same time directing the boy to put the mail bag in the airplane. I asked if Sister Angelina was sick. She repeated, in a much harsher tone, "She won't be making the trip."

So I flew the older nun—I think her name was Sister Perpetua—to town and brought her back with the mission supplies without exchanging a word between us. I found out later, from one of the mission boys, that Sister Angelina had, in his words, "run off." She had pretended to be sick, and when the other nuns had gone to attend mass, Sister Angelina left with a Lebanese merchant in Monrovia.

Just before getting back into the airplane for the return flight to Spriggs-Payne, I looked around at the pitiful little mission with its mud huts and the flimsy wood-frame structure that served as the clinic and mentally wished her well.

Months later I was in Monrovia having dinner at one of the Lebanese restaurants when an attractive white woman came over to me. She stood in front of me for a few moments then said, "You don't remember me, do you."

I said that I did not.

"I'm Sister Angelina. Or at least, I was."

It still took me several minutes to separate this attractive woman standing before me from the sad, girlish person covered in a religious habit that I had known.

"You're taller than I remember," I said. No longer swathed in her nun's habit, I could see her Scandinavian ancestry from her fine features and her luxuriant blond hair.

"It's the habit. It makes one look smaller," she said, laughing.

"Should I call you Sister Angelina or . . . ?"

"You can call me Greta. That will do," she said.

"What happened, Greta? No one at the mission would tell me. One of the villagers said that you had been eaten by a crocodile."

"Not quite," she said laughing. "I met Amal on one of my earlier trips to town—he's a Lebanese Catholic—and he helped me with my chores. Then it got to be a regular thing. I would go into town and he would be there, at the market, and he would help me. He treated me with every kindness and consideration, which I wasn't getting in the convent where they considered me more of a personal servant. Then something happened within me, almost like a spiritual revelation. I knew with amazing clarity that the religious life was not for me. It wasn't that I lost my faith—I did not. It was just that I knew I had to get out or I would lose it.

"Leaving the convent is not as easy as you would think. I've seen other nuns try to do it. They were all caught and brought back. They were punished and watched. I told Amal what I wanted to do, and what was at stake. He offered to help. He helped me escape. He protected me and offered me a job and a place to live until I could get a grip on things."

"When they realized what had happened, the Church tried to get me kicked out of the country. They pulled every string they could, and President Tubman is a good friend of the Catholic Church. But Amal has powerful friends too, and he called in a few favors. So I got to stay. It cost him a great deal. I owe a lot to him."

She paused with a look of concern. Her right hand began to tremble slightly and she looked nervously around. Maybe she thought that she had told me too much—confession isn't always good for the soul. I told her that I was glad she was all right and that I wished the best for her. She smiled nervously, thanked me, then quickly walked away. I had the feeling that I had been the visible reminder of something she wanted to forget. Like so many of the whites in this country, she was living in the shadows and wanted to stay that way.

I drove back to the beach house very much in need of a shower and change of clothes. I changed into clean khaki shorts and a white short sleeved shirt and, after asking Ku to prepare a large gin and tonic, walked out to the front porch to enjoy a chair and the view of the ocean. Deet was there smoking a cigar. He was unusually quiet—maybe that was part of the reason I felt like telling him about Sister Angelina. He listened, nodding and shaking his head in silent response.

"It ist a shame vat happens here; so many broken dreams, so many failed hopes. I vonder if any of us vill survive Liberia?"

Ku brought my gin and tonic. I wondered if I would ever get used to not using ice. A sense of heaviness had descended over us, and to lighten the mood I told Deet about my attack of diarrhea and landing at the mission and trying to avoid the nuns. This worked and we laughed about it for some time.

"If de dung beetles had gotten to you, vhat vould they have done?" Deet asked, laughing between puffs on his cigar.

"Haven't a clue. I'm told that all they want is your shit. They roll it up in a ball and lay their eggs in it."

"But vith diarrhea there isn't enough *scheisse*, is dere? It's all liquid, isn't it?" he asked.

"But they don't know that, do they. They seem to like it no matter what. Any kind of shit will do. Animal shit, human shit, even if it was tree shit, they roll it all up in a ball and lay their eggs in it. That's what they use it for. The little dung beetles feed off of it, and they become big dung beetles and complete the cycle. It's kind of beautiful when you think about it."

"Sounds like dung beetles are better off than the locals around here. At least for dung beetles, there is plenty of *scheisse* to go around. De dung beetles, dey are in charge. De boys on de street, dey don't get shit—literally."

We were silent for a while as we both stared out at the ocean.

"Oh, by de vay," he said, "your friend Beizell phoned. He has a job for you tomorrow. He says he vants you veels up by zero eight hundred."

I thanked him and finished the gin and tonic. It was getting on toward dinner time. I didn't feel like taxing the already overburdened Ku by having him prepare something from our meager stores of near edibles, so I walked down to the Ambassador's beach bar. Joe was there, smiling as usual, and acknowledging all of the customers by their first names.

"Missa Ken," he said, "still flying high?"

"High enough to hopefully stay out of trouble," I said.

"What can I get fo ya?"

"A large gin and T and one of the Ambassador's famous chicken sandwiches," I said.

Joe did his characteristic juggle with the glasses. When the customers were entertained sufficiently, he finished his juggling act, winked at me, then prepared the drink. Like a magician, he placed it in front of me with the lightest of movements, then called the hotel kitchen from the intercom.

I was enjoying the solitude and the gentle breeze from the ocean when I heard a familiar voice behind me.

"I thought I would find you here."

I turned to see Nouga holding a drink, dressed in a very thin cotton blouse and a loose, airy skirt.

"It's a gin and tonic, I think," she said, holding it up slightly. "I heard the British invented it. They had occupied so many tropical countries, and the best way to treat malaria then was with quinine. So, to make the stuff go down easier somebody got the bright idea of mixing it with a little gin and a slice of lime and look what happened!"

"Your husband came to see me," I said.

"I know. He wants me to get you to spy for him."

"And are you going to get me to spy for him?"

"That, my big brawny one, is entirely your decision," she said.

"Why should I spy for him?"

"Well, for one thing, it would make me happy, and you want me to be happy, don't you?"

"And for another?" I asked

"I want to make you happy, which would make me happy. You see? Everybody will be happy. Isn't that what life's all about?"

"Can I call you Countess?" I asked.

"If you wish, but I'm not a countess. There are no Israeli countesses."

"I know, but you strike me as a countess nevertheless."

She took a sip of her gin and tonic. "I shall take that as a compliment, but there is no need whatsoever for flattery."

"I meant it purely as a compliment. You are one of the most beautiful, most intriguing women that I have ever met. Now, about making me happy, are you sure that your husband is okay with this?"

"As I told you, he is a modern, enlightened man, and he is devoted to his mission."

"Which is?"

"Hunting down Nazis wherever they might be hiding."

"There are a lot of Germans here, as you know, but I don't know that any of them are Nazis. Besides, the war has been over for a long time. They lost. Nazism was defeated, and so was fascism for that matter, except in Spain. Nazism will never raise its head again. Why can't you just forget about it and move on with building a new country?"

"It's a matter of simple justice," she said.

"You mean the old biblical eye for an eye?"

"I mean justice. Crimes were committed and supported by many people, and according to your concept of justice, criminals have to be punished, don't they?"

"But wasn't that done at Nuremberg?" I asked.

"For the leadership and the midlevel bankers and the industrialists, yes, but we didn't get the brutes who carried out the orders—the junior officers, the sergeants, the jail keepers."

"So what do you want to know about Beizell?"

"We strongly believe there is a conduit for escaping Nazis being operated out of Liberia using Varig Airlines. It's a Brazilian airline, and Brazil has made it known, secretly of course, that it welcomes Germans with engineering and technical expertise. Varig makes a scheduled flight from Liberia to Brazil once a week. Ahud wants to know who's getting on those flights and he thinks Beizell is involved."

I turned toward the bar. Nouga came closer to me, pressing her breasts against my arm.

"Think of it as a service to humanity," she said almost in a whisper.

I turned on the bar stool to face her. I touched her hair gently.

"You're a very beautiful woman, Nouga, but I don't want to spy on my boss or anyone else, and I especially don't want to wake up at three o'clock one morning with a Luger in my face and be taken for a ride from which there is no return. I'll tell you, essentially, what I told Ahud: you'll know that something is wrong if I suddenly quit flying for Beizell."

Her face remained expressionless. Then she shrugged slightly. "Ahud will be disappointed, but he's been disappointed before."

"I'm sorry, Nouga," I said.

"Well," she said, "that's Ahud's concern, not mine." She took a long sip of her drink. "I have a room reserved. It's the same one."

CHAPTER 22

THE SANDE

Stumpy Biezell wasn't difficult to work for. He scheduled me for two or three trips a week and the other days I worked for Andre. As an employer, Stumpy treated me well enough, though he wasn't the kind of man you could really get to know. It was strictly business with him. He did have occasional visitors—men in poorly fitting dark suits with hard-set faces and intense eyes that he would hustle into his office. The door was always locked and the shades stayed drawn.

The Israelis obviously had grounds for their suspicions, but no proof. I was tempted. I was very tempted. I hated the thought of ex-Nazi thugs getting away with it. Then again, I didn't really know what they had done, if anything. They could be just scared former German soldiers running headlong from what they believed was the overreaching vengeance of the Israelis. The men Stumpy hustled into his office did not look scared—in fact, they looked quite the opposite. I decided, nevertheless, to take pictures of the next batch of visitors.

I didn't have to wait long. A couple of days later, Stumpy had another late afternoon visit. I waited in Junebug, hoping that there would be enough light when they came out of the operations office. They appeared sooner than I expected, so I quickly got the camera ready and snapped a couple of pictures before they entered their car. I drove over to the Airport Bar immediately and called Nouga from the payphone there. I told her that I wanted to meet her, that it was important. I think she understood. She told me to meet her in our usual room at the Ambassador.

When I got there, Nouga was sitting on the bed, smoking—something she seldom did. I explained what had happened and that I had taken a couple of pictures that she might find interesting. I handed her the camera. I told her that I did not know, nor could I prove, that Stumpy was arranging transportation for his visitors out of Liberia, but that I had to admit that his actions did seem suspicious. She didn't say anything but got up from the bed, put her arms around me, and held me for a long while.

"I know you don't like doing this." she said, "but we thank you, and I thank you from the bottom of my heart."

"I've never liked schoolyard bullies," I said.

A couple of weeks later, Stumpy had a trip scheduled for me. The Firestone Rubber Company owned a very large rubber plantation in the interior, and Stumpy wanted me to fly three of their executives up to the plantation office. They called it Base One.

These men had not stopped traveling since leaving New York two days before. Their suits were wrinkled, and their collars stained with sweat. Nevertheless, they had not loosened their ties. Their faces were office pale and sweat trickled from their foreheads and off their noses. They were clearly uncomfortable flying in a single engine airplane over the African bush.

I found Base One. It had been cut out of the bush like the runways at the iron mines. I landed and cringed, as I always did, when the laterite pinged against the tail and the underside of the wing.

I helped the men with their few bags and started to get back into the airplane for the return trip when one of them—the oldest—came up to me and offered a tip. I thanked him but explained that an air transport is not the same as a ground taxi. He looked puzzled for a moment then turned and walked away.

I had some extra time and the mission where I had taken Sarah was not far off the track. I plotted a quick change of course to it and in less than fifteen minutes I was circling the airstrip. I landed and taxied to the cleared area off the center of the runway. People were running toward the airplane, so I switched the engine off immediately then completed the rest of the shutdown check list and stepped out of the airplane.

"I want to see the Head Man," I shouted above the noise of the crowed.

"Ah take you to eem," a young man said, taking me by the hand. "Come wit me, boss."

"Ya ha good ting for us?" someone from the crowd shouted.

"Not today," I said. "I've come to see the Head Man."

I followed the boy up to the hut where I remembered speaking to the Head Man before. We stopped at the open door. The boy waited. I reached into my pocket and handed him a quarter—my last one. He smiled broadly and ran down the path to the village. The Head Man was standing in the door, his face expressionless.

"Heloo ya," he said, extending his hand. "Goo ta see ya, ma fren." We again shook in the Liberian manner, and he invited me in for the ceremonial coffee.

"We ha new mission man," he said, handing me a steaming, battered cup of coffee. "He young an fulla hope an zeel. He smile much. He also ha young, pretty wife who ee alway looking round scared. Deres a vey young boy who play wit our boys, an a daughta, maybe forteen year, who weep like a lost soul mos de time."

"Does he drink the whiskey?" I asked.

"Na," the Head Man said.

"But he will," I said.

The Head Man laughed. "If he stay long nuff, I tink so," he said.

"I have come to ask about the girl I brought back from Monrovia. Her name is Sarah."

The Head Man's face went blank. His lips tightened a little.

"Is she in the village?" I asked.

The old man shook his head slowly. "Na," he said. "She dead."

"Dead!"

"She wa taken by de Sande."

"The Sande, what is the Sande?" I asked.

"It a secret society o' women. Dey take young girls in de night. Dey take 'em to a secret place where a priestess cuts away some of der private part. The Sande believe dat dis act will make the girls better wives, cause it take away all desire to bed wit oder men. Sarah, she ha ben wit oder men not her husband."

"Did she have a husband?" I asked, hardly able to get the words out.

"Na, she nedder ha no husban."

I had read something of this practice but did not believe that it existed in Africa during the mid-1960s. The Head Man saw that I was now unable to speak, but he knew what I was thinking. He went on.

"Much of de girls die from dis. Dey bleed to death or de corruption enter deir bodies and they waste away in great pain. Sarah, dey told me, died from de bleeding. She ha no ma or pa. Dey ha die o de sickness long ago. So de women o de village took her an bury her. You wan more coffee, Mr. Pilot?"

I shook my head.

"You wan see her grave?" he asked.

"No, no thank you," I said feeling a sudden and painful tightness in my chest. "I must go now."

We stood up and shook hands. At the door the old man said, "Many bad tings happen. De missionaries say dat it de will of God. An we mus pray. But dat not stop de bad things or fix de sickness."

"You're a wise man, sir."

He paused and looked at me as though for the last time. "May good fortune go wit you, Mr. Pilot."

I thanked him and walked back down to where the airplane was parked.

The villagers had dispersed. The only people standing by the airplane were a white man and woman with two children. They were waiting under the wing. As I approached the man extended his hand. I took it.

"I'm the Reverend Joel Burns and this is my wife, Janet; son, Jason; and daughter, Margaret. I understand that you transport passengers?"

I said that I did.

"My daughter, Margaret, is going to live with her aunt and uncle in Lubbock, Texas, until our mission here is completed. Would you take her to Monrovia? She can stay with our mission there until her flight leaves in two days."

"Did you ever know a girl here in the village named Sarah?" I asked. The reverend looked hesitant for a moment. "I've heard of a Sarah in the village, but she died last month. Would that be her?'

"She was killed by a secret society called the Sande. Do you know of them?" I asked.

"I have heard of them," he said. "They practice what is clinically called female genital mutilation or FGM. I thought the practice had died out. We are trying to change that through Christian teachings, but it's very difficult—traditions, no matter how evil, die hard."

"Are you afraid for your daughter? Is that why she's going back?" I asked.

"No, no, Margaret hasn't been happy since the moment we arrived. The change and cultural shock has been too much for her. She misses her friends, her school, all those things she now feels closely linked to. She's too young to understand the importance of our work here. I've tried to explain it to her, but you know how teenagers are."

Margaret was clutching her small cloth bag like someone clinging to a life jacket before jumping into the water. Her mother watched her anxiously.

"I can take her to Spriggs-Payne airfield," I said. "It'll cost fifteen dollars. Can you have someone pick her up at the office of Beizell's Air Service?"

The reverend smiled and nodded. He dug into his pocket and handed me a twenty-dollar bill. "Keep it," he said excitedly. "Keep it. I'll get on the radio now and someone will be there to meet you. Thank you so much, sir. I will pray for you and may God go with you."

The reverend started running up the path to his house, which was little better than a large native hut. His wife and son remained to watch as we taxied to the end of the runway and took off. I climbed straight ahead to about four hundred feet, then did a 180-degree descending turn and made a low pass over the runway. As we passed, Margaret's mother and brother were standing and waving from their midfield position. Margaret ignored them. I did a few shallow Dutch rolls as a parting gesture. Perhaps they thought of it as their daughter waving goodbye.

Margaret, however, was completely uninterested. She sat in the front seat next to me still clutching her bag, her head pushed against the headrest, her eyes closed, her mind counting the minutes until we landed.

Margaret did not open her eyes until we landed a Spriggs-Payne. We taxied to the ramp, and she pushed the door open at the same moment the propeller stopped turning. I watched her run toward Beizell's office. I secured the airplane and followed her. A middle-aged, white man in a gray suit was talking to her.

"Are you the person who is supposed to meet her?" I asked.

"Yes, I'm Reverend Pickle." He extended a hand. I took it and tried to suppress a smile.

"I think I've heard most of the jokes," he said with a laugh.

I turned to Margaret and said, "Do you know this man?"

"Oh yes," she said. "We've been to his house many times."

"Okay," I said. "Have a safe trip home."

I watched as they left the office, the Reverend Pickle with his hand on her shoulder saying, "Don't worry, honey, we'll have you back in Texas before the sun sets over El Paso."

CHAPTER 23

SICK LIKE HELL

I gave Stumpy the paperwork and fifteen dollars, told him I was done for the day, and drove over to the Airport Bar. Madeleine was there and, as always, was very good to look at. I asked for a bourbon and ginger. I had always preferred bourbon and water, but I knew not to drink the water or to come into contact with it in any way. This meant no ice, no fresh vegetables, and make sure they open the beer in front of you. Even then, I would wipe it off with a cloth before I drank it.

"Are you feeling all right, *mon cher*?" Madeleine asked.

"Nothing that a strong drink won't cure."

"Hello mate." I recognized Colin's voice behind me and felt his hand on my shoulder. "Say, mate, you look like something the big cats just dragged in."

"Madeleine, bring Colin whatever he wants."

"Thanks mate, but seriously, you don't look so good. How have you been feeling?"

"To be perfectly honest, like shit."

Colin looked carefully at my eyes and skin. "Let me guess," he said. "Shortness of breath, fatigue—more than usual, I mean—sweating, headache?"

"Yes," I said.

"Have you been taking your quinine meds?"

"Yes. Religiously. My family doctor at home sent me over with Resochin quinine tablets."

Colin sat down next to me. "Sounds to me like you've developed a resistance. You're gonna need a new one."

"Great."

"Welcome to tropical Africa, matey. Whether you like it or not, you've got malaria. You've got all the symptoms. Most people who get it, get it within the first six months of coming here, but you've held out much longer than that. Must be that tough American hide of yours. Funny thing though, some people never get it. And them that do, there ain't no cure, mate. We'll have to get you some new drugs."

"Can you recommend a doctor?" I asked.

"Oh, you don't need one of them quacks. Finish your drink and I'll get you what you need. The dealers around here see it every day. They know what you need."

"You can get drugs without a doctor's prescription?" I asked.

"You don't have to have a doctor around here for anything except signing death certificates, and most people don't even bother with that."

Colin insisted that I ride with him in his car. We stopped in front of a door that looked like the entrance to a fish market—at least it smelled like a fish market. Colin said he would be back in a "jiffy," and I watched as he disappeared through the dark opening. In a few minutes he emerged carrying a small brown paper bag bulging on all sides.

"You owe me twenty quid, mate. The cost of black market drugs is rising."

"Okay," I said. "Just take me to my place. I've got a little cash stashed away."

Colin drove to the beach house. "I'll go in with you and put you to bed. I'll talk to your house boy about what should be done, but I ain't talking to that damn, fucking, Kraut Nazi pilot you live with."

"You don't have to worry about that. He's working and will be drinking tonight at Heinz and Maria's until late."

"Great," he said. "I'll know where to drop the bombs."

I got undressed and crawled into bed. I could hear Colin talking to Ku telling him to boil several more gallons of water and prepare it for filtering. All of the water we used came from our cistern. In order to purify the water, we would boil it for a minimum of five minutes then pour it into a stone tank that had a spigot on the bottom. The stone was some kind of pumice or porous volcanic stone that acted as a very fine filter. It would take a couple of days to seep through the stone, but when it did, all the particles that happened to be in the water were gone. The water was pretty pure. And it tasted good. But this was mainly a European custom and was not done in restaurants or bars. A house boy had to be taught how to do it and, more importantly, convinced that it was necessary.

"Take this money, boy," I heard Colin say, "and get some goddamn fucking mosquito netting and string it up over Mr. Ken's bed or I'll stick this dull knife right up your arse. Do you understand me?"

"Yes boss!" I heard Ku say.

Then I heard Colin leave. A moment later, Ku came into my room, his eyes wide with terror.

"Don't worry, Ku. He isn't going to hurt you, but I think he's right. If you could get some mosquito netting, I would very much appreciate it, and do the water thing. From what I've read, malaria is going to be a rough ride."

"You ha de sickness, boss. My auntie, she know much abou de sickness. She take care o you. I go get her now." Ku started to leave.

"Don't forget the netting," I said as he left. I knew it was like closing the fence gate after the horses had gotten out, but I had no idea what would happen if I was bitten by another anopheles mosquito while I was dealing with this bout of malaria.

Soon after Ku left I started throwing up; every joint in my body was throbbing with pain. I felt cold and started shivering. Then I was sweating as though I had just run a marathon. Sometime later, Ku returned with a large, middle-aged woman that he introduced as Aunty Martha. She took one look at me and told Ku to get as many clean towels as he could find and heat up a pot of water.

"I make you de fever tea right away an you drink it right away," she said.

"Oh, please, no, Aunty Martha. I want real medicine. Not some voodoo concoction!"

"Don' worry, Mr. Ken. Malaria fever tea is good. Is jus local tea leaves wit basil."

"It hep your stomach, boss," Ku assured me.

Aunty Martha did what she could to make me comfortable. She made sure that I took the new Paraquin quinine tablets Colin had bought for me; she made sure there was plenty of filtered, boiled water; she checked the mosquito netting daily; she changed my bed linen regularly and washed it herself. It was five days of agony. Deet and the other pilots would bring Coca-Colas and bottles of ginger ale to keep my strength up. I could barely drink, let alone eat anything solid. When I did, I would inevitably throw it up. On the sixth day the symptoms started to diminish, and I was told by Aunty Martha that I was lucky to have had a mild case of the sickness and that I should take my quinine daily.

On the seventh day I lay in bed, physically exhausted to the point that I could hardly move, but somehow I found the strength to use the chamber pot without help. Later, Aunty Martha came, as she did every day, but this time with a pot of freshly made soup. Whatever it was, it was delicious. I could almost feel my strength returning, but it would be several more days before I could get out of bed with any degree of confidence.

Toward the end of this period, Colin showed up. I was sitting on the porch enjoying a cool ginger ale and listening to the ever-soothing sounds of the surf.

"Hello, mate," he said. "I figured your Kraut friend would be out, so I wanted to see how you were doing, and it looks like you are doing all right. You know, a bad case of malaria can knock people out for months, sometimes forever. About fifteen to twenty percent of the cases are fatal. You are lucky, my man."

"Lucky?" I said. "Lucky is not getting malaria at all."

"Hah! That's near to impossible. Almost everyone here has malaria. It's just a question of degree, especially Europeans. We're sitting ducks. Now, lots of blacks are immune to many of the symptoms."

"Really? Why?"

"The reason, I think, is the sickle cell. It is prevalent in blacks simply because the red blood cells have adapted as a defense against malaria. Instead of being round, they are sickle shaped—they sort of look like a question mark. And the little bastard parasites that cause malaria cannot attach themselves, in that there's no place for them to lodge inside the red blood cell. So sickle cell can be a benefit if they live in Africa, but then, sickle cells don't carry oxygen well either, so the carrier often lacks energy. But sickle cell anemia sure beats malaria."

"I should have paid more attention in biology class," I said.

"Just be glad you didn't get the Asian kind. It goes to your brain. It's called cerebral malaria. Makes you foam at the mouth and your eyes move around like a couple of billiard balls in a hoop and you say funny things."

"Like your crazy man in the cargo pod," I said.

"Aye, I guess you're right." He smiled, thinking about it. "Oh, by the way, in case you're worried, your Kraut friend squared it with Andre. You've still got a job." He hesitated. "Did they tell you about what happened to Varig?"

He must have surmised by my expression that they had not.

"Crashed on approach. Burned. Everybody on board killed except the two pilots. The cockpit section broke off on impact and the pilots scrambled out somehow. How about that for a switch?"

"Any idea what happened?"

"Nothing official, and there probably won't be. The government sent a couple of soldiers to guard the wreckage so that the cops can't steal any valuables lying around, but there will be no investigation. There ain't no FAA here, matey. Tell you what I think." Colin sat in the chair next to me and pulled it closer. "Don't breathe a word of this, but some of us think it was shot down. Some of the people around the airport say they saw something that looked like a rocket going up just as the aircraft was on short final. It could have been a rocket or, more likely, one of those small, shoulder-fired missiles the Israelis have. We think it was the Israelis.

"Anyway, things are happening. Beizell looks like he's getting ready to run. Had a friend of mine who's an official at the port authority tell me that Beizell has made arrangements to ship his car to Florida. He's cashing in his chips, matey."

Stumpy owed me my salary, which he hadn't paid in nearly a month, plus my percentage. It was a substantial sum, and I wasn't going to let him get away with it. I thanked Colin for his help. I went to my room to get my pistol, summoned up strength from somewhere, and drove out to the airfield.

Stumpy was in his office. He looked up when I came through the door.

"You must be feeling better," he said. "I may have a trip for you tomorrow, if you feel like taking it."

"I've heard that you're leaving," I said. He looked at me for a long moment but did not say anything. "I want my money, Stumpy."

"I'm not going anywhere," he said.

"I want my money," I repeated.

He shrugged. "All right, since you insist. You obviously don't trust me. You don't believe me. Come by tomorrow and I'll have your money for you, but as of tomorrow, you don't work here anymore."

"That's fine with me," I said.

I knew that Colin lived on the airfield. I drove over to his place and was lucky to find him at home.

"Colin," I said, "could you let me stay with you tonight?"

"Sure, mate."

"I want to keep an eye on Stumpy. He owes me a lot of money and I think he's going to try to skip."

I didn't know if he would try to leave before paying me, but I wasn't going to risk it. He had an airplane, a Piper Tripacer. It was his personal airplane, and I figured he'd take that airplane along with everything he could stuff into it, fly to Sierra Leone, then get out of the country and the continent.

Colin's porch faced the runway. I waited there for darkness. As twilight approached, a huge number of birds started landing on the runway. I had never noticed this before.

"Colin!" I yelled back into the house. "What are all of these birds doing on the runway?"

"Just wait!" he called back.

After several minutes, I noticed a few cars approaching the runway. They sped up, really fast, then *bump, bump, bump, bump* . . . The cars hit as many birds as they could then came to a screeching stop. The drivers hopped out with big burlap bags and started gathering up the dead and wounded birds. Some of the birds escaped the slaughter, their wings making a huge fan noise as they fluttered away in unison. After the harvest, the cars turned around and drove away. The whole spectacle was over in a few minutes.

"What was that about?" I asked.

"For some bizarre reason, the birds pretty regularly come and stand on the runway in the evenings. The locals eat 'em. I guess clobbering 'em on the runway with a car is the easiest way to catch 'em."

I stayed on the porch and waited until it was completely dark, then I quietly made my way over to Stumpy's airplane. I clamped a set of vice grips on the fuel line to squeeze it shut. I then camped out on Colin's porch, fully expecting to be there all night. About one o'clock in the morning I heard the Tripacer start up, then rev up as though it was being taxied. Then it stopped and I could hear it cranking, *wah wah wah* . . . I grabbed my Llama 9mm pistol and quickly drove over to Stumpy's operation. I could see his airplane on the ramp. He had the cowling up and was looking at the engine with a flashlight, obviously trying to see why it had stopped. I walked quietly up behind him.

"Hi," I said.

He looked up, startled.

"I heard the plane start up."

"Yeah, yeah," he said. "I don't know what the hell is wrong."

I knew that Stumpy was a fairly good mechanic, and I knew he'd figure it out eventually.

"Where are you going?" I asked. "You're not supposed to be flying at this time in the morning. You know you cannot fly till zero eight hundred."

"I'm just running the engine. What are you doing here?" he asked.

"You're getting outta here, aren't you?"

He looked straight at me for a long moment. "Look," he said, "you don't understand. Some people are after me. I've got to go, now."

"Would you mean the Israelis?"

"They're misinformed," he said.

"Because you've been helping your Nazi friends escape?"

"They're not my friends. I was offered a lot of money. It was a chance to climb out of this dump, take my ball of shit, and go back home with something to show for it," he said.

"And where is that—Munich?"

"No!" he said. "I'm an American. Couldn't you tell? I grew up on a farm in Iowa. I know, I have a German name. That's why they approached me. They thought I would somehow be sympathetic. But I told 'em that the German language hasn't been spoken in my family in over a hundred years and that I don't give a damn about their politics or the Israelis or any of that shit. They offered me a lot of money—that's all it was to me—and right now, all I want is to get back to the States."

"You owe me some money."

"Well, I can't pay you," he said.

"Then you're not going to use this airplane," I said. "I know what's wrong with it."

I opened the door of his airplane. I could see that it was full of his stuff. Then he said, "It's in the airplane. Let me look for it and I'll get the money."

"No, no!" I said, "You tell me where it is and I'll get it."

I pulled out my gun, but I did not point it at him. I knew that he too had a gun, but I couldn't see it. It was probably in the airplane.

"I gotta tell you," I said. "I've got a gun."

"You're not going to shoot me," he said.

"You tell me where it is or I'll put some holes in the tires, and put a hole in the fuel tank, and we'll see how far you get."

"It's in the back seat in a metal box. I'll get it for you," he said, making a move for the door of the airplane.

"No!" I shouted. "If I have to use this on you, I will. Please believe me."

I told him to get face down on the ground, and I waited until I could see that he was. I reached into the rear of the Tripacer and very soon felt the metal box. I took it out and told him to get up and count out what he owed me. I kept my flashlight on him until he finished.

"Here," he said, handing me three thousand dollars in tens, twenties and fifties. "That's all I owe you."

"Thanks," I said. "I'll tell you what's wrong with the airplane. There's a vice grip on the flexible fuel line. Release it and you've got your airplane back."

I know he wanted to kill me. I think he would have killed me if he could have, but I backed away from him into the darkness. The engine started and I waited until he took off and watched as his navigation lights moved to the northwest and out of sight. I never saw him again.

I felt the starch go out of my legs and knew that I would probably not be able to drive back to the beach house, so I drove over to Colin's place, settled into the couch on his porch, and fell asleep.

It took another week for me to recover enough to return to work. From then on, I made sure to take my pills daily and to always sleep under netting.

CHAPTER 24

LITTLE BILLY

The wet season had started. Giant, gray storms rolled down to the coast from the hinterland, bringing heavy rains and winds during the afternoon. At night, they would join shoulder to shoulder off the coast and provide some spectacular lightning shows, accompanied by rolls of thunder until morning.

The rain brought increased challenges aside from the normal flying hazards of severe winds, lightning, and turbulence. It generally turned the airstrips up country to muddy red quagmires. Some small airstrips became completely unusable. My workload fell considerably during this time, and when I did fly, the risks were much higher.

The investigation of the Varig Airline accident by the Liberian government did not take long. No public accident report was published. I heard that the Brazilian government was not pleased, but little or nothing came of it. The pilots were sent back to Brazil as soon as they checked out of the hospital. Eventually the guard was removed from the wreckage site and the burned, mangled corpse of the aircraft was left for the locals to plunder. After the accident, Varig stopped all flights into Liberia, leaving the fleeing Germans to find other means of escape. I tried to contact Nouga and was told that she had returned to Israel, but that Major Ahud would call me as soon as possible. He never did.

After that, I was finished with intrigue. I simply wanted to concentrate on work, do my flights, and avoid entanglements. I told Andre that I would take any flight, any time. This was probably a mistake, since there were no legal restrictions in Liberia as to the numbers of hours a commercial pilot could fly at one time. When the weather would occasionally clear, I would fly from dawn to dusk, arriving back at the beach house after dark and leaving before sunrise. When the rains came, I kept to myself and sketched, or painted cloudy, dark seascapes. This went on for several months until the end of the wet season.

Once through the wet season, and Andre felt he had made enough money to call it a profit, he hired Kemo as an office boy. Kemo was a Mandingo. He was short for a Mandingo and a little pudgy, but like all Mandingos, very efficient. He was also very serious and though I tried to make him laugh several times, I never could. Maybe our cultures were just too far apart. Nevertheless, we got on very well together through simple, mutual respect.

I wasn't the only American working and living in Liberia in the 1960s, but unlike the Brits or Germans, we never banded together to form an expatriate group. You could, however, always spot an American on the street or in bars. One of my Brit friends said that it was the way we presented ourselves—the way we stood, the way we walked—something reminiscent of John Wayne. I guess we all felt a bit like cowboys.

Little Billy was especially easy to spot as an American. He was from Oklahoma and over six feet tall. He always wore western boots, usually made from exotic leather such as alligator or ostrich hide, with two-inch heels, tight-fitting western jeans, a western shirt with designs on the pockets, and a large black Stetson hat. He held all of this together with a wide leather belt spotted with silver conchos and a decorated silver belt buckle shaped like a horseshoe.

Andre had hired him at the end of the wet season anticipating an increase in business. It was said, by people who knew as much about him as I did (which was nothing), that he was on the run from the law. After working with him for about a month I could easily believe this, although he never verified it. And I reminded myself that working in Liberia was a bit like being in the French Foreign Legion—no questions about the past.

What Little Billy displayed in sartorial splendor he highlighted in piloting skills. He could handle an airplane as though it were part of his body. It was as though he slipped his arms into the wings and his feet into the tail section and flew. He was also an excellent navigator and did not seem to know what fear was.

I was in the Airport Bar when Kemo found me draining a beer at the long counter. I had gone there seeking relief from the ever-present heat. It was hot—hot as only an afternoon in the West African dry season can be. Overhead, waves of heat radiated down from the metal roof. Even the ubiquitous blow flies could do no more than crawl slowly over the empty beer bottles. From my stool, I could see, by squinting through the security bars at the window, the roof of the airfield control tower shimmering in the sun. I stared across the few hundred feet of baking laterite to our operations office and was obliged to squint. Turning my head inward, I was thankful for the dimly lit air of the bar. I called to Madeleine's new bartender, a boy of thirteen sleeping with his head down on the bar, for another beer. He continued to sleep. Finally, after a number of unsuccessful attempts to rouse him by hurling bottle caps at him, I rose and got the cool bottle of beer from the water tub myself.

Glancing out of the window again, I saw a form slowly emerge from the door of Monrovia Airlines' office and proceed toward the bar. The dark figure moved slowly through the waves of heat. It looked like Kemo, trying his best to hurry without any exertion. With some curiosity, I eased back onto my stool and watched him approach. Only a dire circumstance could have caused Kemo to leave the relative comfort of the office and hike across the airfield to the bar. It was obvious that he was coming to summon me.

Since Kemo was a Mandingo and a non-drinking Muslim, he would never do any business in Madeleine's place. I drank my beer and waited. He finally dragged himself through the wide portal of the bar and approached me. Large beads of sweat rolled off his round face.

"Monsieur Andre say you mus come jus now," Kemo said and waited expectantly.

I knew Andre well enough to know that he would never summon a pilot from the Airport Bar after a slow day unless something of importance had occurred. I drained the bottle.

"Let's go, Kemo, and tell me what the palaver is," I said.

We left the dank heat of the bar and walked, as fast as the heat would permit, across the dusty airfield. The sunlight was so intense that I had to squint even though I was wearing sunglasses. I could barely see Andre in front of the hangar. He was shouting and gesturing to the boys loading an airplane. He was more animated than usual. This was not good.

Kemo, as if reading my thoughts, blurted, "De commissionaire in Guinea got Monsieur Beelly."

This was serious. I could not keep concern out of my voice. "How do you know, Kemo?"

Before he could answer, Andre shouted to us from the hangar, "Come, *vien ici, vite, vite!*"

He paused to shout at the loaders who were pushing one of the company's battered Cessna 180 aircraft backward to the fuel pumps. He then ran over and tugged at my arm,

"Come, *vite!*"

I followed him into the hangar office.

Andre was respected by our Mandingo customers because of his business skill. They called him "the dry man." He got to the point quickly.

"Billy has been caught by a Guinea district commissioner near Kankan."

Little Billy, arrested near Kankan! I tried hard to imagine Billy's Oklahoma accent resonating from the walls of a mud jail in a remote West African village.

Flying the bush in West Africa, we all took our chances. One of the requisites of our job was we had to be willing to try almost anything at least once. We said, usually after too much whiskey at the Airport Bar, that we did it for the adventure, but we all knew, deep down inside, that we did it more for the money. Only a fool would do otherwise.

I had flown a few risky diamond pickups with McCoy, but Andre's focus on the diamond trade was much more intense. Our hangar was, among other things, the western terminus of an enormous gemstone pipeline pouring millions of dollars in diamonds into the Republic. Liberia, being an independent republic for over a hundred years, had been bypassed by the international diamond cartels that set the prices of diamonds in the rest of the world. All prices in the Republic were set, therefore, by the local gem market. Liberia was a diamond smuggler's paradise.

A rough diamond might begin its journey a thousand miles to the east by residing in the bowels of a closely watched native miner who, under the guns of overseers, would swallow the muddy gems and pass them later in the night outside the mining area. From as far away as Chad or Upper Volta, a gem would travel first by overland trails then be sold surreptitiously to the Mandingos. From there, it would move by motorized transport or bush taxi to Bamako or Ouagadougou. It would change hands a few times before beginning the long journey west, possibly in a chartered taxi with a number of Mandingo merchants. They always traveled together for safety. As in the salt and gold caravans of ancient Songhi, it was a dangerous journey. Many Mandingos lost their diamonds and lives at the hands of thieves.

After an exhausting journey of some weeks, the Mandingos and their gems would arrive at the eastern rim of the great rain forest of the Republic that extends, without highways, nearly two hundred miles to the coast. There, as they touched the edge of the thickening savanna, they would let their brothers in the capital know they were ready to be picked up. How they did this without radio, telegraph, or timetables was a complete mystery. What we did know was that when we landed our bush planes on various obscure trails in the surrounding border countries, the Mandingos would materialize from the tall grasses by the road and pile in the airplane with their long robes billowing in the idling prop wash.

The doors would scarcely bang shut before the pilot, pushing in the throttle for maximum power, would roll away, scanning the road ahead for soldiers, cows, or trucks. As the wheels left the ground and the cramped, heavy plane lifted into the air and banked away, heading for the coast, praises to Allah would ring out over the engine roar.

Money is the necessary lubricant of this gem trail. From the president down to the lowliest civil servant, dash was paid in varying amounts. Occasionally, however, something would go wrong. Greed perhaps, or a failure to produce needed cash, or any number of other reasons, had probably trapped Little Billy. To free him would be no mean feat. The alternative, though, was his doing time in a West African prison. And that was fearful to contemplate.

"I want you to go up and talk to the commissioner," Andre said, then waited for my reaction.

I thought about what he had said. It was a euphemism for springing Billy from jail on my own.

"Is that all, Andre? Just talk to him?"

"You're the best I have, Ken. You know it." Then, "The boys have Charlie Fox gassed up and ready." Andre's eyes were now narrow slits.

"Okay, what the hell. Let's do it," I said.

This task was not appealing on any level. Nevertheless, had the circumstances been reversed, I would want to see someone in Charlie Fox, the fastest and most battered Cessna we had, circling overhead at the commissioner's compound.

Andre continued, "Why don't you take Jack with you?"

Jack Dupree, a short, muscular Frenchman who seemed to have no visible means of support, spent much of his time hanging around the Airport Bar or running small errands for Andre. He was a quiet, not very noticeable member of the small fraternity of expatriates that collected around the airfield. His eyes bothered me most of all. They were flat black like non-reflecting painted windows.

I decided that I did not want him to accompany me in the right seat of Charlie Fox. Andre protested but, seeing my adamant refusal, did not press the point. Andre slid back the heavy drawer of the desk. Reaching in, he retrieved a large mass of worn, greasy US bank notes. Counting rapidly, he strapped a rubber band around five thousand dollars.

"Take it, get him back, and don't leave two planes and pilots up there," he said.

I took the thick bundle of dollars, thinking that here was a lot of cash, and hoping that the money was all that *le commissionaire* would want. At least money could always be negotiated, and Andre could supply that.

"Okay, I'm on my way. I'll try to get back by tonight."

I pushed through the office door and almost ran over Dupree who, standing silently in the dim outer office, must have taken in all that had passed between Andre and me.

"Good luck." He smiled, but only his mouth moved. His expressionless eyes remained on me as though they were smearing me with something. For an instant, I felt a wave of menace sweep over me and I hesitated, but the moment passed.

"Thanks," I said, turning to check my water bottle for the trip.

I busied myself with filling my water thermos from the stone filter. Dupree went into Andre's office and softly closed the door. I concentrated on Little Billy's plight. Being detained by an over-zealous officer and his soldiers in our neighboring country was not a unique experience. It was, certainly, an unpleasant experience, but one known to most of us. If one chooses to fly diamond smugglers across international borders without the benefit of paperwork, this was a natural hazard. It was, I thought, typical of our attitude toward such events that I would attempt to rescue Little Billy armed with only a one-liter water thermos and some greasy, ragged money. With no documents, passport, or flowery letters of introduction or guarantees of safe passage, I would try to free my colleague from the grip of a petty tyrant.

I put on my sunglasses, pushed open the door, and stepped into the afternoon glare. The smoke and haze of the waning afternoon obscured the palm trees that fringed the airfield, and the visibility seemed worse than usual. It was bad enough when the gritty, super-heated winds of the Harmattan would blow down from the Sahara, but because the farmers chose to clear their farms in the traditional way, they exacerbated the situation ten-fold. They simply set fire to an edge of the dry forest and let fires alternatively smolder and rage until the first torrents of the wet season stopped the blaze. Wherever the blaze meandered, it would leave behind a blackened strip. That was where they planted the next year's rice crops. Every small farmer did this, and the smoke from the fires combined with the airborne Saharan grit to form an often impenetrable blazing, heated, yellow wall. The dry season seemed to be the worst, but during the wet season, when your body and everything else is molding from six months of rains and dampness, you would gladly forfeit a month's pay for the blessed heat and dust of the dry season.

I walked toward my plane, my boots making small puff balls in the orange dust. I reached the door and swung up onto the worn, grimy seat. It's a bit like mounting a horse; the maneuver can only become graceful with practice. On the ground Charlie Fox squatted on its tail wheel, causing the floor of the airplane to tilt at an uncomfortable angle. This reduced many entering passengers to an awkward crouch and occasionally tripping them into a tangle on the floor.

"Mr. Ken!" It was John Zizzi, one of Paterson's loaders, emerging from the shadow of the hangar. "Plee, can yo tay dis letta fo ma broddah's part?"

He handed me a damp soiled envelope. It was addressed Honorable Joseph Zizzi, Kankan. The envelope bore no stamp or address. It was as if he expected Joseph to step out from the tall grasses along some nameless dirt road in the interior and ask if there was a message from his brother. I had carried other such letters around West Africa and would simply hand them to the nearest local at the destination. Amazingly, they would usually turn up in the hands of the addressee. The locals had no recourse; there was no reliable internal mail service in West Africa.

I put the letter in my hip pocket. John started to give me a verbal message for his brother, but I was rapidly pushing, pulling, and flipping the array of controls listed on the check list—a little like a priest performing a ritual. The starter grinded for a time then, sharply, the engine barked and started, drowning out John's message.

The Russians had built a large and very powerful non-directional radio navigation beacon near my destination at Kankan and the idea of having this kind of assistance was very comforting. I climbed slowly and tuned the radio to the correct frequency but could not hear the identifying code. When I was able to identify the station, I planned to home in on it until I got station passage, then track a bearing from the station until I picked up Kankan visually. I continued to climb, reaching ten thousand feet, nearly two miles above the jungle. Long restricted to ground-hugging in our usual overweight short flights, the idea of flying at high altitude appealed to me and there was nothing or no one to say that I shouldn't do it except the physical limitations of the plane. I urged Charlie Fox higher, to eleven thousand feet.

The plane burst upward, out of the haze, into crisp, clear air. Looking down, the haze now seemed as solid as earth. I was now flying in clear air with unlimited visibility and seemed to be skimming just above the surface of a vast plain of undulating brown hills and valleys, which vanished in ripples toward the horizon. It seemed solid enough to brush my wheels against. Far away toward the horizon where the land and the sky met, a few cumulus clouds could be seen climbing upward like exploding columns of heavy steam. It was as if the entire Sahara Desert had been flung two miles into the air.

Soon, however, the spell was broken. I became aware of the sound of my high frequency radio—a tone similar to the screech of fingernails dragging over a chalk board. The grand spectacle outside my cockpit vanished and the flight was once again the serious business of rescue. The Kankan radio beacon caused the needle on my direction-finder to tremble and swing to the station. From the strength of the signal and flight time that had passed, I knew that the beacon was now very close. Nearly two hours aloft had brought Kankan within a short distance. To descend, I gently rolled the pitch trim wheel a few clicks forward.

Below, the haze had evaporated and the land was changing radically. The jungle had vanished, and here and there, black outcroppings of rock moved past slowly. I passed through seven thousand feet. It was good to look at the earth's floor again through relatively clean air. The needle of my direction finder pointed decisively ahead, signaling that I was very close to the radio station now. I squinted to see the beacon station. There was a small shack, a few fuel tanks scattered in the sands, and a diesel engine. Then a stubby tower beacon repeating *dash-dot* in my headset passed under me.

Billy was being held in a village outside of Kankan. It was about twenty miles northeast of the radio beacon and relatively familiar to me. I started hugging the ground at about one hundred feet. Suddenly, tire ruts swept past my undercarriage and turned away to the east. This track was what I was looking for, and by rolling the control yoke over and pulling back steeply, I followed every turn of the twisting road. A stunted cottonwood tree stood at a bend. I banked again, and the glint of tin roofs flashed in the distance. I reduced the throttle slowly and circled the village. I noticed a jackal below at the edge of the village, sniffing the wind.

The village was fairly typical, although larger than most. There was a circle of round huts clustered near a larger building that I took to be the commissioner's house. A long airstrip, narrow and rutted, pointed directly toward it. A small airplane sat near the end of the airfield; it was Little Billy's Cessna, Foxtrot Papa. I applied full flaps and rolled in a tight circle to a short final approach. I pumped the throttle several times, causing the engine to backfire, hoping to alert Little Billy.

Darkness was now little more than an hour away. If I could free Little Billy from the commissioner's grasp today, a night flight to the coast in poor visibility was possible, but not something I looked forward to. I taxied slowly toward the large house. The villagers had formed a solid wall of humanity at the end of the airfield. They were a solemn, silent lot—very different from the animated crowds that usually welcomed unannounced airplane arrivals.

I cut in by Little Billy's plane, pivoting hard, swinging the tail around and pointing the nose down the dirt runway, then shut the engine down. The silence was strange and unexpected. The villagers slowly, silently surrounded the plane and stared at me, not menacingly but not friendly either. Then the crowd parted and a soldier pushed through and banged the butt of his rifle against the side door. He shouted in French that I must come out. I opened the opposite door, jumped out of the airplane and followed him through the crowd. I approached the commissioner's front door a few feet behind the soldier and entered a long, low, dark building. Along one wall was a rail separating the main room from a knot of spectators. I walked forward alone toward a wide table. Another soldier came up to my side.

"*Attends! Attends!* You way hee. *Le commissionaire viens.* He come soon," he said in a voice that sounded like it started at his feet.

I waited, silent. Feet shuffled in the thin dust on the floor; someone coughed. The roof creaked in the dim light. A soldier came and lit a kerosene lantern on the table. Dusk was making more shadows in the dimly lit building. The lantern revealed a small automatic pistol lying on the table, its barrel pointed directly at me. The silence was becoming uncomfortable, and still no sign of Little Billy. Finally, the commissioner appeared through a curtain behind the table. He was a short, stocky man, somewhere in his thirties with a muddy complexion. He stared at me for a while. I couldn't help staring at his patchy hair, little yellow bloodshot eyes, clammy-looking malarial skin, and the yellow palm oil and bits of rice that soiled the front of his shirt.

"You have been hee before?" he asked. It was an accusation, a way of taking me off my feet.

"Monsieur le Commissionaire, I have never been here before," I said, trying to look firm and unyielding. We stared at each other, a big man's game, but very serious.

He turned his eyes slightly, not meeting mine anymore.

"Your *ami* is under arrest for violating our frontier and for grand crimes against the Peoples Republic of Guinea."

"Perhaps we can settle this palaver," I suggested, knowing that he would understand that this was the preliminary for a money exchange.

"Zat is not possible. He ha violated ze law o ze People's Republic. He mus be made to answer for zis at Kankan."

This was not good. If Little Billy was taken the forty miles to Kankan and imprisoned, it would take the matter out of my hands and Little Billy would surely die. Men didn't survive long in African prisons. I tried to change the subject.

"Where is the pilot?" I asked. If Little Billy was close, perhaps a desperate escape might be the only way. I eyed the pistol on the table and wondered if it was loaded.

"Your *ami* eez safe in our custody," the commissioner said.

He seemed reluctant, uneasy, and I wondered for a moment whether they had already killed him. The commissioner was an enigma. Was he not corrupt? Was he not without a price, or was he a true ideologue intent on serving his country? There was no way I could deal with an honest official. The concern must have showed on my face.

"Unnastan, yo frenn ees in ze compound in ze back o ma house, an you weel hear ze charges agains him."

The commissioner produced a tattered, dog-eared handbook and started to speak. After a minute I realized something was wrong. He was holding the book upside down. He couldn't read, instead reciting the statute from memory.

I resisted the impulse to grab the gun on the table and shoot this little dictator. He droned on. I touched my pocket to check the bribe money, just in case. Instead, I touched a letter I had recently picked up at the post office. It was a rejection letter. The American Express Company had denied me one of their credit cards. *Dear Mr. Vigrier*, it read, grossly misspelling my name, perhaps assuming that I was an itinerant tribesman who would dare presume to ask such a great company for one of their cards. Maybe it would work—a letter from a Big Man is the next best thing. I remembered M. Mammadee Swaree, a rich diamond merchant reputed to have powerful connections in the Peoples Republic of Guinea. The name of M. Swaree emerged everywhere in the diamond business. Perhaps this could be a letter of persuasion from him. The long arm of the powerful could reach out and ensnare this parochial, overinflated tyrant. In Africa, all ran scared, and sometimes terrified, from the Big Men.

"Yo see," the commissioner was saying. "Eet is hopeless. Yo frenn mus go to Kankan on ze nex lorry. I also fine you, yoself, guilty o landing here widdout un clearance an ah fine you one tousand dolla."

"Commissioner," I said, "I have a letter here that I must show you. It is from my good friend Honorable Mammadee Swaree." I unfolded it and held it toward him. The elegant large blue crest seal of American Express was highly visible.

He looked somewhat shocked and bit his lip. "Yo!" he snapped. "Yo mus read it."

"Of course, Monsieur le Commissionaire," I said, clearing my throat. "From the Ambassador Extraordinaire and Plenipotentiary, M. Mammadee Swaree." Then I made up some gibberish about M. Swaree personally guaranteeing me and my companion's safe passage and safety in this Republic. I made it sound as if we were old acquaintances.

"Ah know M Swaree!" the commissioner shouted. "Yo cannot frighten me!"

It was obvious he didn't know him, and was now wary, uncertain of his ground. Instantly, the whole scene changed. The little despot became affable, called for a chair for me.

"*Mon ami.*" He shrugged. "Ah did na know yo were Honorable Swaree's fren. Dese people hee are bush, ah mus deal wit dem harshly sometime, don ya know?" He spoke softly, conspiratorially, as though to a fellow insider. I half expected him to wink.

"Monsieur Commissionaire, may I see my friend now?"

He clapped suddenly and spoke to one soldier in French. Little Billy turned up a few minutes later, slightly disoriented and escorted by a soldier. He was not wearing his Stetson hat, his boots, or his belt. I now wanted to leave in the worst way, certain that Billy would say the wrong thing, or someone would read the letter, which still lay on the commissioner's table, or the ugly little man would have a change of heart. But he sent for beer and custom dictated that we stay and drink. It soon arrived, warm, in tall bottles. We sat quietly, looking at each other in the pale light of the lantern, fanning away swarms of insects, and drinking the commissioner's warm beer.

After a while the commissioner was beginning to feel the effects of the beer, and I was afraid he would turn ugly and not allow us to leave. Every minute's delay put us in greater danger, and I also needed to relieve my bladder.

"Monsieur Commissionaire, we must be on our way, but I must repay you for your hospitality." I laid five hundred dollars on the table. Little Billy started to speak and I stepped hard on his foot. The man stared at the money and scooped it up quickly. I thanked the commissioner for his kindness and consideration, and Little Billy and I strolled casually to the airplanes. It was best not to be seen hurrying.

"Do you know what them bastards did?" Little Billy said. "They took all my stuff, my boots, my Stetson, and my belt, and I want 'em back."

"That's the least of your troubles Billy. We've got to get out of here PDQ or we may not live to see the sunrise. How is your gas? Can you make the coast?"

He looked doubtful. "I don't think so, maybe Wiesua."

Wiesua was the heart of the diamond area, a small town in the center of the rain forest lying a hundred miles toward the coast. It should be lit up from the several generators located in the Mandingo stores.

"We'll figure a course later," I said. "Leave your lights on and I'll follow you."

Outside, dusk had turned to night. A small group of spectators surrounded the planes, still silent but seemingly less hostile. The commissioner followed at a distance with his soldiers, mumbling drunkenly. I swung into the plane quickly, my pulse beginning to race. Nothing was going to stop us now.

"Stop. Stop!" The commissioner and his soldiers ran forward in the dark.

My throat was dry; one hand posed on the starter switch, the other casually pushing in the mixture control. "What is it, Monsieur Com-missionaire?" Little Billy's plane cranked and started. My fingers turned the magneto switch to BOTH. The seat belt dangled out the door.

"Ah mus dash yo." He blurted the words drunkenly. The soldiers handed me a dead chicken and a small hamper of eggs. I thanked him but his response was lost because I hit the starter; the propeller on Charlie Fox rotated several times then caught. With my left hand, I flicked the navigation and landing lights on and pushed the throttle in with my right. The seatbelt flapped wildly against the metal skin of the airplane. I belted myself in, slammed the door closed, and I was away.

I climbed rapidly, turning southeast toward the diamond mines of Wiesua, and found the lights of Foxtrot Papa. Little Billy was good at celestial navigation. He knew all of the major constellations and the orientation of the Milky Way. I stayed with him just aft of his right wing and followed his lights.

After about an hour, a light glow appeared in the blackness ahead. Wiesua! We approached carefully and landed safely. Little Billy later found less than five gallons of fuel remaining in his tanks. That night we slept on old army cots in the room of a small store. We were up fairly early, so I asked the local cook to fry up some of the eggs from the commissioner. He broke the first ones into the pan and immediately pitched them out the door of the hut. The stench of rotten eggs filled the air.

"De yeays are spoil, boss," he said. Monsieur Le Commissionaire, it seems, had the last word.

The cook got some eggs from his own stores and we had those plus a few strips of pork and the local coffee. I gave the cook the chicken from the commissioner, and he took it but eyed it suspiciously. We fueled up from the fifty-gallon barrel of aviation fuel outside of the small shack that served as a flight office. I reached in my pocket to pay the lone attendant, an old man well into his seventies. As I did, I pulled out John Zizzi's letter. I had forgotten to leave it in Kankan. I felt a pang of regret, even though I could not think of any time I could have handed it to anyone. Given the situation, perhaps it was for the best.

We flew home together, this time with Little Billy maintaining a tight echelon right position to Charlie Fox. He was a good pilot, that Little Billy from Oklahoma.

We reached Spriggs-Payne and I contacted Andre over the radio.

"All the sparrows are coming home," I said.

Andre, along with the pilots who happened to be on the airfield, the load boys, the errand boys, and the mechanics were waiting on the ramp. All cheered as we emerged from the airplanes and crowded around us, shaking our hands and asking how Little Billy lost his boots, belt, and hat. I proudly handed Andre the remaining wad of money as well as the American Express rejection letter. One of the load boys loaned Billy his sandals and we all, except Andre and Kemo, piled into cars and drove to the Airport Bar.

Normally, Little Billy didn't drink—I had never seen him drink—but that day at the Airport Bar he downed gin and tonics one after the other and even flirted with Madeleine. He told the story of the Guinea flight several times to any attentive audience until suddenly he seemed to melt in his seat like a piece of warm plastic. Colin offered to take him home and tuck him in, saying that I had done my fair share. I agreed, feeling an overpowering need for sleep myself.

CHAPTER 25

SMALL, SMALL TING

It was late in the afternoon when I awoke. Ku had carefully placed the mosquito netting over the bed.

"No sickness, boss. Ya no wan sickness."

I agreed. I had fallen in bed with my clothes on and, apparently, Ku had removed my shoes.

"I coo big supper for ya, boss. Ya eat notting all day."

"Could you get me a beer, Ku?"

"Yes boss. Mr. Andre call. He ha work for ya tomorra, say ya to be at de airport by eight."

"Did he say what it's about?"

"No boss, only dat ya shou come."

I went through my mail. There was a letter from my dad telling me that everything was all right at home, and that whenever I was ready to return just let him know. There was also a letter from Jenny telling me that she was coming to Monrovia and would be here in two weeks. I was glad Jenny was coming. I didn't think I would be, but I was. For the first time in a long while I was happy. Ku returned with the beer. I told him that we were going to have an important guest from Washington in two weeks' time and that things should be "clean and shipshape."

"Dis person one of yo senators, boss?"

"Hardly, Ku. She's a very close friend."

"Yo fiancée, suh?"

"Not quite, but who knows what the future may bring. It is important that we make a very good impression though. She will have come a very long way."

I arrived at the operations office around seven fifteen in the morning only to discover that the flight had been delayed. The twelve hundred pounds of rice I was to deliver would not arrive for another three hours. That was enough time to treat myself to a decent breakfast at the Airport Bar. Madeleine's chef's du jour was a plate of scrambled eggs, fried pork strips (not quite American bacon but close), and a tomato along with a dish of peeled pineapple and mango, plus a large mug of coffee. I had just taken my first sip of coffee when I felt a powerful hand on my right shoulder. I turned and recognized Honorable Williams standing next to me with a broad, toothy smile that looked like he was going to burst into laughter at any moment.

"Everyone is talking about you, my son! How you faced down the commissioner and rescued Little Billy. How you led him through a stormy night to land at Wiesua just as your plane ran out of gas." I started to object that it wasn't my version of events, but he continued. "Please, my son, join me for breakfast. Here, let us sit at a table like gentlemen."

Madeleine's bartender followed us to the table that Honorable Williams chose near the open doors.

"I will have what this gentleman is having." He smiled. It was meant as an honor. "How I do admire you young men free as birds in the air. So like gods you are, commanding the skies, fearful of nothing. You handle your flying machines as though they are not machines at all. I always wanted to be a pilot, you know. I used to build model airplanes as a boy and fly them from the roof of my father's house, but alas, it was expected that I would go into government as my father and grandfather had done before me. It is the lot of us 'Congo' people to lead this country. It is our burden, so to speak. Without us, the country would descend into civil war, the tribes fighting one other until nothing is left but a waste land." He hesitated for a moment. "You are from Washington, DC, yes?"

I said that I was.

"I spent several years in DC—at the Embassy. I even met President Eisenhower and Mr. Nixon. Before that, I graduated from the University of Maryland and attended law school at Georgetown. When I was at Maryland I use to walk over to College Park Airport when I had some free time and watch airplanes take off and land. There was a small restaurant on the field, or was it at the edge of the field? I don't remember now. I would drink coffee and watch the airplanes. I met some of the pilots and instructors too. They all had names like Buzz or Lucky!" He laughed loudly, holding his hand over his mouth. "God, how I always wanted a name like that, but you have to earn it, I suppose, like Little Billy. Do you have such a name, my friend?"

"Sorry to disappoint you, sir, but I do not."

"Then we will have to give you one." He looked thoughtful for a moment, then his face brightened. "I've got it. We shall call you Spike for the way you handled the commissioner. Is that good? Do you like it?"

He seemed so happy with his decision that I did not have the heart to say anything but yes. Besides, I doubted that it would stick. I had been given nicknames before in school and none of them stuck.

The bartender came with our breakfasts and we ate while Honorable Williams told me about his family. He had two sons, one a student at UCLA and the other training as a pilot at Embry-Riddle in Florida.

"He will, one day, take over ownership of Monrovia Airlines," Honorable Williams said. "And I'm hoping he will start a major inter-African air carrier, but that is in the future and we will see." He hesitated then continued, "You know, I am well acquainted with M. Swaree. I shall inform him of the way you were treated."

"Sir," I said. "I don't think that will be necessary. I'm sure the commissioner was only doing his job as he saw it."

"That may be," Honorable Williams said, "but this is Africa and if you don't remind these petty officials who is really in charge here, things could get out of hand. He'll just get a slap on the wrist, but it'll be a slap that he will remember, and the next time you visit Guinea, the commissioner will consider it an honor."

By the time I returned to the operations office, Paterson had Charlie Fox loaded with two hundred and forty bags of rice in five-pound bags. I took off as soon as I could get strapped in the airplane and headed for the village of Gboyl that supplied the nearby iron mine. I landed at the mine's airstrip around noon. A soldier, a sergeant judging from the faded stripes on the sleeve of his dirty and rumpled uniform, was waiting with two of the village boys. I taxied onto a small ramp at the midsection of the runway. The moment the propeller stopped, the soldier opened my door.

"Do ya ha it all?" he asked.

"Two hundred and forty bags," I said.

"Da good," the sergeant said and called for the two boys to start unloading.

"The usual practice is to pay for the stuff before you start unloading," I said.

"Yo gowana be paid. Come wit me to de jeep."

I climbed out of the plane and followed the soldier to a battered World War II–era jeep, its olive drab paint fading to light green along with the faded white lettering that spelled out U. S. ARMY. The soldier was carrying a US 45 caliber 1911 pistol on his hip. He shouted something to the boys that I did not understand and, although they didn't acknowledge, I knew that they understood.

The sergeant drove the short distance to the village, grinding the gears of the jeep, and not bothering to avoid the holes in the road. We stopped in front of an old army tent that had been patched and stitched in various places.

"Ya stay here," the sergeant said, indicating that I should sit in one of the folding chairs in front of the tent. He went inside, pushing the door flap to one side, and in a few minutes returned with a dirty manila envelope.

"Ah wanna receipt," he said.

I took the cash out of the envelope, counted it, stuffed it in my pockets and wrote, *Paid in full for two hundred and forty bags of rice,* on one side of the envelope, signed and dated it, then handed the envelope to him. He looked puzzled as though he couldn't decide whether to feel insulted, indignant, thankful or just confused.

"Wait!" he said and disappeared back into the tent. In a few minutes he returned. "Go!" he said pointing to the jeep. "Ah tay ya to ya plane."

I was about to hop into the jeep when I heard the sergeant shouting, "Comma hee! Ya! Coma ova hee!"

I looked in the direction that he was shouting. A man had emerged from the bush at the edge of the village. He was carrying a heavy five gallon can on his right shoulder. His short trousers were ragged, and his brown shirt was torn in several places. The man appeared to ignore the soldier. The sergeant drew his sidearm. "If ya no comma hee right now, ah shoot ya dead!"

The man stopped, hesitated for a moment, then turned to face the soldier and walked toward him.

The sergeant holstered his pistol and when the man got to within six feet of him said, "Stop! Put dow dat can."

The man did as he was told.

"Wha ya got in dere?"

"Dis palm oil, boss. Ah go sell it at de mine store"

"Ya go to sell notting less ya pay da tax."

"Ah pay ma tax, boss. Ah pay dem long time hence," the man protested.

"Ya lie," the sergeant said. "If you pay yo tax den show me de receipt."

The man looked frightened and desperate. "Ah got no receipt," he said. "Dey give no receipt wen ya pay de tax."

"Ya lie again. Ya go en get proper receipt or ya pay me de tax an ya get yo palm oil back."

The man protested. He tried to explain to the sergeant that he needed the income from the sale of the oil to buy food and medicine for his family and that there would be no more oil until next season. The sergeant again said that he was lying. The man protested to the point where he was shouting incoherently and crying. The sergeant pulled his sidearm and slid the receiver back and let it go. It snapped back into place at the same time placing a bullet into the chamber. The man understood what this meant and backed away.

"Ya pay yo tax or ya show me da receipt. Now go!"

The man walked hurriedly away, occasionally glancing over his shoulder.

"He canna find a receipt an will na pay de tax. Des bush people," the sergeant said. "Dey are ignorant an will always be so."

I told the sergeant that I would walk back to the airplane. He smiled and, for a moment, looked puzzled. Then he shrugged and disappeared back into his tent, taking the can of palm oil with him. There was something menacing about this place, and I wanted to get back to Charlie Fox and fly away as quickly as I could.

I had no return passengers or cargo, so I decided to fly down to the coast and buy fresh fish for dinner. I landed on the beach with room to spare. I had bought fish from these people before, and they were always very friendly.

"Oh Mista Pilot!" the women called. "Ya wan some fee?"

As always, they were fascinated with the airplane, touching it with their fingertips as though it was a living thing. They wrapped my fish in newspaper and, after a few pleasantries and laughter, I flew back to Spriggs-Payne, turned in my paperwork, and drove back to the beach house.

Once home I handed Ku the fish told him to put them on ice.

"Yes boss," he said, "but is best ah cook dem now." So I said that would be good.

I was enjoying the fish and a beer when Andre called to tell me that he had a job for me tomorrow flying a couple of Mandingos up to the Wiesua diamond mines.

The next morning the Mandingos were punctual and polite as usual. I did a quick preflight inspection of Charlie Fox. I pointed out where we were on the National Geographic map the company provided and where we were going. The Mandingos seemed pleased and nodded their heads in approval. I helped them into the airplane and off we went to the mines.

While the Mandingos were conducting their business, I planned to fly over to a couple of nearby villages to buy some bulk rum. All the villages in this area grew sugar cane and they concocted a potent rum from it, which we, in turn, would sell to the diamond mines for their miners. I was able to purchase six demijohns of rum, which was a good haul. Each demijohn held about ten gallons.

I flew to a mission nearby where we had an agreement to store the rum until we had a buyer at the diamond mines. It was run by a very gentle and quiet elderly missionary who did not drink himself but was pleased to be of help. I would always try and bring him something special as a thank you, something he would not ordinarily have access to, like sweets and good meat. As I started unloading the rum, I handed out little pieces of candy to the kids that were yelling and jumping around me.

Suddenly, I heard a loud American voice shout, "You will not unload that here!"

"Who are you? Where's Brother Stephen?" I asked.

"Brother Stephen has been replaced. The mission leaders didn't feel he was making headway with the native population."

"I am sorry to hear that. He was a very kind, gentle man. This rum is only to be stored here for a week or so. It is not for you or anyone here to drink."

"It is the devil's brew. It is evil and it will not stay here."

This presented me with the immediate problem of what to do with all the rum. The new missionary made it clear that I had no option but to load it back on the plane. I flew back to Baisu, the village where I bought it, and unloaded it there. I could only hope that it would still be there when I came back to get it.

When I arrived back at Wiesua, the Mandingos were still touring the mine and bartering had not yet begun. I had always been a little curious about how this diamond business was conducted, so after landing, I asked the Mandingos if I could accompany them. They nodded in agreement and I followed them, keeping just behind their colorful, long, flowing robes. We stopped at an open structure covered on top by thick layers of palm fawns.

The Mandingoes stood, as majestically as blue herons, waiting for their customers. They began to arrive only minutes after the Mandingos. Each seller, most of them covered in dirt and mud, held a wadded piece of brown paper containing one or several diamonds, all different colors and shapes. The oldest Mandingo, the Head Man whose name was Tajan Gora, withdrew a small scale from a wooden box he carried under his robe.

One after the other, the sellers handed their diamonds to Tajan. He would examine each diamond quickly, then pass it on to the others. They, in turn, examined it and returned it to Tajan, who would then weigh it on his small scale in front of the seller so that he could clearly see what was happening. He would then offer a price based on the diamond's clarity and weight. If the seller agreed, the Mandingos would pay in cash and the bargain was sealed with a Liberian handshake. I watched with fascination while this seemingly orderly process took place.

I never did find out who the "sellers" were. When I asked Tajan, all he did was smile. It was all completed in less than an hour, and we were on our way back to town where the Mandingos would sell their rough diamonds in Monrovia to local Lebanese merchants or to anyone willing to pay the marked-up price. Once back at Spriggs-Payne, I asked Tajan if I could see a diamond. He willingly opened the brown paper wrapping and picked out one of the stones.

"It's a small, small ting, Mr. Pilot, a small, small ting," he said, gazing down at it. After a moment, he placed it back with the rest of the stones. One could see right away they were crystalline, though somewhat dirty and without the glitter of cut diamonds. I asked how much he could get for them, and he said that the stones would fetch thirty dollars per carat from their usual buyers.

"Would you like a small ting, Mr. Pilot?" Tajan asked. "I will give it to you for twenty dollars a carat." I knew that he had not paid more than ten to fifteen dollars a carat. Still, considering the Mandingoes don't give away anything, it was very generous. He held the stones closer to me and I selected a reasonably clean one and put it on his scale.

"Ten carats," he said.

The Mandingos will only deal in cash so I took two hundred dollars out of the cash bag in the airplane and handed it to him. We shook hands and the Mandingos left in a car that had been waiting for them. I went into the operations office with the cash bag and the clipboard with the paperwork on it. I took my last check out of my wallet and wrote it out to Monrovia Airlines for two hundred dollars and put it into the bag. I filled out the paperwork and put it on Andre's desk. He looked up for a moment. Then I told him about buying the diamond.

He shrugged. "As long as your check doesn't bounce," he said to me.

CHAPTER 26

HIM HUMBUG ME

Andre had hired a very large Bassa man, Nathanial, to serve as the company's security system. He was also there for our protection and "debt collection." A number of our customers had the money to fly up to the mines but not enough money to pay for the load. They would tend to let the load sit in the hangar, where we stored it until Andre put enough pressure on them to come and pick it up. If it was there for too long, occasionally the boys would steal some of it. When the customer finally showed up, they would shout, scream, and gesticulate with their fist and accuse Andre of thievery and just about everything else they could think up. That's when Andre would call for Nathanial who, silently and with determined resolve, convinced the customer to be more reasonable and to settle the disagreement by paying his bill. As a gesture of the company's appreciation Andre had a machinist in Monrovia make a very nice aluminum baseball bat for Nathanial. In Nathanial's hands it served as a very effective inducement to ending arguments quickly.

When I told Andre about the new missionary near Wiesua refusing the demijohns on my last trip, he was irate.

"That's it! No fucking missionary is going to get in the way of this operation. You're flying back up there tomorrow morning, you are picking up the rum from Baisu, and you will drop it off at the mission. And you are taking Nathanial with you!"

I was actually hoping we could fly in, off-load, and leave before the missionary could stop us. However, if that didn't happen, I explained to Nathanial what to expect.

"We want this man to understand that we need to do our job. If he says no, then you must convince him, but do not kill him," I emphasized.

We landed and quickly off-loaded the rum and were back in the airplane before the missionary could get there. It was a considerable distance from the mission to the airfield and I thought we could get in and out without interference. However, the missionary's zeal exceeded my expectations. As we got to the end of the runway and turned for takeoff, he was heading straight for us at top speed on his motorbike, leaving a rooster tail of dust and dirt. I shut the engine off and waited for him. The missionary was a big man and obviously angry. He jumped off his bike and was as at my door trying to get it open.

That's when I said to Nathanial, "Nathanial, him humbug me too much!"

Nathanial got out of the airplane from his seat on the passenger side, walked around the tail of the airplane, and came up behind the missionary and hit him over the shoulder with the aluminum bat. It wasn't a love-thy-neighbor tap. I heard the man's shoulder crunch and saw him drop to the ground. The missionary made a struggling attempt to get back on his feet. Nathanial hit him again and again. This time the missionary stayed down.

By now, some villagers who lived around the mission had gathered at the edge of the runway near us. I noticed that they were laughing, jumping, and cheering as Nathanial worked on the missionary. I told Nathanial to get back in the airplane, which he did to the adulation of the crowd. I restarted the engine, did a quick double check and opened the throttle to takeoff power. I thought that the missionary was well clear of the main wheels, which he was, but I had misjudged his position with regard to the tail wheel. I felt the tail of the airplane bounce, *bump, bump,* over the missionary's legs as we started the takeoff run.

He had made the mistake of ignoring the customs and had interfered with a Big Man's charter operation. That was always a sure ticket home. I knew the missionary wouldn't be there on my next trip.

Back at Spriggs-Payne, I told Andre what had happened. He simply nodded and smiled.

I was on my way out when he said, "Got a job for you tomorrow, so don't drink too much and get some sleep—zero eight hundred."

I nodded and waved then drove over to the Airport Bar. The place was crowded, mostly pilots and a few locals. Honorable Williams was there at a table surrounded by laughing pilots. I couldn't hear what he was telling them, but he was very animated and laughing himself. I saw Colin sitting at the bar and came up beside him. He was quietly sipping a beer.

"Hello, mate!" he said. "Would you like to join me for a drink?

I said that I would but there were no more seats and I didn't like drinking standing up. At that he pulled out his revolver, stuck it between the legs of the man sitting next to me and said, "If you don't want your fucking balls blown off, get the fuck out of here." The man, a local, looked momentarily terrified then jumped up and hurriedly left the bar.

"This isn't exactly The Eagle and Child pub in Oxford, old boy," Colin said. "Have a seat." He slowly replaced the revolver in his jacket pocket.

"What do you know of the diamond business?" I asked.

"Only that it's like fucking—almost everybody does it. And if you do it enough you end up dead or dickless. You thinking about doing it?"

"It looks like it might be a lucrative side line," I said.

"Not for me, mate—too many cutthroats. And besides, DeBeers controls the market. The stuff we see around here is penny pound shit. DeBeers is where the real money is and, excuse me for saying so, matey, but you ain't got a snowball's chance in hell of breaking into that racket." He hesitated for a moment. I think he noticed my look of disappointment.

He went on, "But I've got something that'll cheer you up. Have you heard the latest about our illustrious president?"

I said that I had not.

"Well, it seems that President Tubman is scared to death of flying, as you probably know, so he, that is to say the government, bought him a yacht—a hundred-and-twenty-five footer. He had it all refurbished at great expense and he got himself a British captain and a first mate who was, allegedly, a Liberian. They went down the coast once or twice a month carrying the president, so he could go back to his home province. But there started to be a lot of nationalistic pressure from the papers, saying stuff like 'Why don't we have a Liberian captain on the presidential yacht . . .' Well, the government decided that they would. Not long after that, the British captain had enough of the bullshit and just walked off the boat and left the country. So now the president wants to go down to the town of Harper at Cape Palmas—it's his hometown, you know—and his Liberian first mate is now captain. The new captain's only credentials are that he's stood around dressed in an immaculate white uniform on the presidential yacht for a couple of years."

"Now, if you go down the coast, you leave Monrovia, turn left and go about two hundred miles and then you make another left turn and go into the Hoffman River at Harper. It's a tricky entrance. You've got to cross the bar just right. There's a very long line of sand bars on the left with breakers all over them, but once past that there's a big harbor at Harper. And there's a quay where the yacht would tie up. Doable, but not a piece of cake, right? This guy, the new captain, goes all the way down the coast, turns in, gets passed all the breakers, and manages to find the only rock in the harbor. The boat runs hard aground. Bump! The president's on board. The boat lists about ten degrees. So they manage to get the president off and the boat's sitting there. Now it's a joke, sitting up on this rock. Then the paper announced the next day that the captain really wasn't Liberian, he was born in Sierra Leone, so, you see, he wasn't a real Liberian captain after all. He was a foreigner! Brilliant!

"So some fast operator gets involved and brings in this Dutch dive team to try and get it off the rocks. The idea was that they'll blow the rocks up and free the yacht. Well, they only succeeded in blowing up the fucking boat. Then what's left of the boat caught on fire and burned. The Dutch divers realized as soon as it happened what kind of trouble they were in, so they got in their dinghy and headed full speed for the Ivory Coast."

"Did the yacht sink completely?" I asked.

"Unfortunately for Tubman, it did not. It sat there on that rock, a burned-out hulk, as a constant reminder of yet another government failure, and a great source of humor for the locals. So they got a British demolition company to come and finish blowing the thing to pieces. We're pretty good at blowing things up, you know."

"I'll say you are," a voice behind us said. We both turned to see Honorable Williams standing behind us. He placed his hands gently on our shoulders.

"I must tell you that it is a funny story, and I have laughed about it with many of my friends, but if I were you I would be careful how loudly I told it. There are two things the president hates more than anything else, and that is to look weak or foolish. Make no mistake, my friends, I am no great admirer of President Tubman, but he does have ears everywhere."

He must have noticed Colin going a little pale, for he continued, "Oh, I doubt that he would ever harm a European or an American, but you might find yourselves on an airplane headed out of the country with your visas, work permits, and licenses revoked."

"Thank you, sir. I will keep that in mind," Colin said with his relief clearly audible in his voice.

"Not at all, my friends. I want you to stay in Liberia. Your work here is of great benefit to the country." With that he patted us on the shoulders and left the Airport Bar.

"Shew Gawd!" Colin breathed. "But that was a right close one."

"Yeah," I said. "What if it had been Tubman's secretary of state?"

"Or worse yet, one of his whores," Colin added.

I put a couple of dollars on the counter. "It's time I was shoving off," I said. "Got an early flight tomorrow."

"Cheerio, mate," Colin said, draining the last of his beer and still looking a bit shaken. I don't think he would have been nearly as frightened if Honorable Williams had put a gun to his crotch. Colin could deal with that kind of threat. What scared him was what went on behind closed doors in the Big Men's houses.

On the way home I had become enveloped in a sense of dread, and I wanted to shake it off. Had I wandered into some witch doctor's curse? Was there any truth, at all, to bad juju?

When I arrived back at the beach house, Ku was waiting on his stool in the kitchen.

"Ya hav mail, boss," he said, handing me a single letter. "Ya like gumbo fo tonight? I get de recipe straight fom yo stay o Louisiana."

"That would be fine," I said. "Would you fix me a large gin and tonic?"

"Yah, boss, right away."

It was too hot to sit on the porch facing the sun, so I flopped down in the living room community chair, directly under the fan, and opened the letter. It was from Jenny. She was arriving the day after tomorrow at Robertsfield on Pan Am Flight 485.

CHAPTER 27

COFFEE RUN

I was to take a load of mining tools, valves, and spools of wire to an iron mine near the Guinea boarder. I also had a Lebanese merchant with me who wanted to pick up a load of Guinean coffee beans. This coffee was in great demand on the world market, so the Guinean government made it illegal to export without a strict licensing agreement. My pick-up, I assumed, was part of a smuggling operation. As long as the proper dash was paid, the job should go along without a hitch.

The weather was good, and it was an uneventful flight. The loaders were still removing the cargo when I heard the sound of a heavy truck, an old two-and-a-half-ton US Army truck, rumbling out of the bush on a narrow dirt road. The truck pulled up next to the airplane. A white woman with red hair and a beer in her hand was sitting in the front seat between two Lebanese.

The Lebanese men jumped out of the truck, followed by the woman. She was tall; her hair was short and a spray of freckles scattered the bridge of her nose and under her eyes. She was dressed in a man's white shirt and khaki shorts with laced boots. She also had a pistol in a leather holster strapped to her waist. She walked quickly up to the Lebanese merchant, but I could not hear what they were saying.

Then she approached me. "How many bags can you take?" she asked, her green eyes shining with intensity and her eyebrows knitted slightly.

"How heavy are they?"

"Twenty-five pounds each," she said.

"I can take half, maybe more if there is room, and even that is an overload."

She looked disappointed. "Can you make two trips?"

"If the weather cooperates, I can be back in three hours."

"Good." Then, looking over at the Lebanese merchant, she said, "Have your men load thirty bags. He's coming back in three hours for the rest. I'll take the money now."

"No, no, no!" said the Lebanese merchant. "I'll pay you when the job is done."

"All right, all right, suppose you pay me for thirty and the rest when this man," she gestured with her hand toward me, "returns."

The merchant thought for a moment. "Agreed," he said.

When the mining equipment was off-loaded and placed on a mining company truck, the merchant directed the men to start loading the coffee. The woman watched intently, resting one hand on the grip of her pistol and the other on her hip. It didn't take long to load the coffee. I secured the bags with the cargo belts and told the merchant to get in the airplane. He was counting the cash, in US dollars, as he handed it to the woman. After that he climbed into the passenger seat, fastened his seatbelt, and we took off.

"Who is that woman?" I asked the merchant.

"Her name is Sam. She is in the American Peace Corps."

"Peace Corps! I didn't know the Peace Corps was in the coffee smuggling business."

"It is not, but I think that she likes it. She has a gift for it, and I don't know what she does with the money. I do know that she has a lot of contacts in Guinea and she gives the dash to a lot of people. The Guinean government seizes all coffee that they can from the growers and pays them far below the market price. The only way they can survive is to keep some aside to sell to people like her. She pays them the fair market price, and she never seems to have trouble getting the coffee across the border."

Once back at Spriggs-Payne, the coffee was unloaded onto a waiting truck. The merchant gave some instructions to the driver, who then put the truck in gear and drove off with blue-black smoke belching from the exhaust at the rear. When we returned to the mine, the woman and the loaders were sitting on the remaining bags of coffee, patiently waiting. I taxied up next to them and switched the engine off—the propeller, now powerless, ticked over a couple of times then stopped. I popped my door open and the merchant popped his open and we both jumped out of the airplane. I opened the cargo door and the loaders began to load the airplane with the remaining coffee bags. I walked over to where the woman was standing.

"Hi," I said. "I'm Ken." I extended my hand.

She looked at me with complete indifference and, ignoring my hand, said, "How did a nice American kid like you end up here?"

"Not through the Peace Corps," I said.

"Don't get the wrong idea, hot shot. The money this coffee earns goes to the village—most of it to the hospital and the school."

"So what do you do in the village? That is, when you're not smuggling coffee."

She stared at me for a moment, and I thought she might actually take her pistol out and put a bullet through my head. Then a smile flickered across her lips and I had the feeling that she had just, at that moment, decided not to kill me.

"I teach math and science there," she said.

"Oh," I said, genuinely astonished. "Where did you go to school?"

"University of Washington, that's the state of, and how about you?"

"I went to Cornell but dropped out to seek high adventure."

"And are you finding it?"

"Yeah, I think so," I said.

"You planning on going back?"

"Yes, I think so, but I honestly don't know."

The loaders had finished stacking the remaining bags of coffee in the cargo compartment. I went over to the airplane and strapped them down and watched as the woman walked over to the merchant who was paying his loaders. She said something to the loaders that made them laugh. After that she jumped back into the army truck with the two Lebanese men. I walked over to the truck on an impulse. She was now in the driver's seat.

"Do you ever get to Monrovia?" I asked.

"On rare occasions," she said.

"The next time you do, let me know. Maybe we can take in a movie or something." I scribbled my name and phone number on a page in the notebook I kept in my shirt pocket, tore the page out, and handed it to her.

"Maybe I will," she said with a half smile. "The name's Samantha but everybody calls me Sam." Then she waved goodbye, started the truck engine, and disappeared back into the bush.

"What did she say to the loaders?" I asked the merchant on the flight back to Monrovia.

"She told them you have the hands of an old white woman."

CHAPTER 28

JENNY

I drove over to Robertsfield early and was just finishing my drink at the bar when Jenny's plane landed. Two airline employees rolled a boarding stair up to the cabin door and I watched as the passengers started streaming off. Jenny was one of the last. She stood at the top of the boarding stair looking around, her shoulder length blond hair blowing in the hot wind. She was wearing a dress with a full skirt, and as she walked down the steps the wind blew it up above her knees. In the glaring sunlight, her face and exposed arms looked more delicate than I remembered.

The passengers were ushered to the terminal where they would go through Immigration and Customs. Memories of my own chaotic arrival in Robertsfield years ago flooded into my head. Mike McCoy had sent a handler to meet me and get me through this pandemonium. Otherwise, I doubt I would have made it. I began to push my way through the crowd looking for Jenny. As more passengers entered the building, the yelling and shouting rose to a near steady roar. Baggage boys were grabbing passengers' bags, and uniformed Customs officials had started approaching random passengers. Jenny was nowhere to be seen.

Suddenly, the mob separated, and Jenny appeared, calm and smiling as if she were arriving in Washington, DC. She was being escorted by a diminutive, well-dressed black man. The two were chatting as if the crowd was not there.

"Jenny!" I shouted.

She did not look up. Judging from her escort's dark suit and manner, he was a wealthy Americo-Liberian. I watched as the man signaled for porters to come. Two porters, pushing and pulling an empty loading cart, wedged their way through the waiting group of passengers to a pile of baggage. The man, with Jenny next to him, pointed out various bags in the pile and the porters immediately began to carefully place the bags on the cart. The man then pointed in the direction he wanted the porters to go, and he and Jenny followed them as they pushed their way through the tumultuous hordes.

When they were outside the roped area, I waved and shouted again to get her attention. She saw me and waved back with a broad smile on her face. I made my way through the noisy crowd to where they were. The man silently signaled for one of the porters to place Jenny's bag next to her. Jenny held her arms out and embraced me. She felt lean and hard and smaller than I remembered.

"This is Mr. Harriss, Kenneth. Mr. Harriss is an adviser to President Tubman."

"Very pleased to meet you, sir," I said, shaking his hand, "and thank you very much for helping Jenny through Customs and Immigration."

"Please, don't think anything of it. It was truly my pleasure," Honorable Harriss said, not taking his eyes off Jenny. He lifted Jenny's hand to his lips and gently kissed it.

"I do hope you," he hesitated, then added as an afterthought, "and your gentleman friend can attend. Please call my secretary. You have my card."

"Thank you, Mr. Harriss, I will," Jenny said.

I picked up her bag and started walking toward Junebug.

"What was that all about?" I asked.

"Oh nothing," she said casually. "I met Mr. Harriss on the airplane and he invited me . . . us . . . to a reception at the president's mansion this coming Thursday. I think it sounds exciting. Please tell me that you want to go."

"Sure," I said, "I'll go. It may be the most exciting thing around."

"God, I hope not," she said, laughing.

"Jenny," I said, "I can get you a room in a good hotel within walking distance to where I live. I think you would like it better than my place."

"Why, what's wrong with your place?"

"It's got a couple of not very well-behaved guys who come and go all hours of the day and night and who aren't very considerate or respectful of anyone's privacy. And, with a woman there, they may keep everybody awake howling at the moon."

"That explains something," she said.

"Explains what?"

"That I almost didn't recognize you," she said.

"Really?" I asked. "What's different?"

"For one thing, you are all tan, and your hair is so long! Actually, I kind of like it, but you've lost a lot of weight and . . ."

"And what?"

"I don't quite know how to say it . . . but you're kinda grubby looking."

"Grubby looking! I shaved and showered this morning!"

"Yes, but I don't know what it is. You just look different. And look at your clothes—a dirty t-shirt and a pair of torn shorts?"

"Okay," I said, "you got me there. My wardrobe has diminished. But this t-shirt isn't dirty, it's just stained."

Jenny smiled, a little condescendingly. "Is there any possibility at all that you could find a suit?"

"A suit! What on earth for?"

"You know, the reception, the party."

I stopped in front of the Ambassador Hotel and got her bags out of the front of the car. She followed me in. The desk clerk looked up and smiled as though he recognized me. Jenny was given a room on the second floor. It was like most rooms in the hotel: plain, clean, and small with a slight view of the ocean and beach.

"Will you show me where you live?" Jenny asked.

"Sure thing, but let me show you the beach bar first."

She followed me downstairs out the glass doors, across the street and down the short walkway to the bar area.

"Missah Ken!" Joe said with a smile. "An who dis pretty young lady ya ha wit ya?"

"This is Jenny. She's visiting from the States—Washington, DC," I said, anticipating his next question.

"Washington, DC? Oh, I hear about Washington, DC. Oh, so sorry about yo riots. I hear ees very unsafe dere. We are so fortunate not to have gangsters like da in Liberia. Ya will be safe hee. What can I get ya, my dear lady?"

Jenny ordered a vodka and tonic and I ordered a scotch straight up.

"Please, my dear lady, go fine a table an ah wil bring ya yor drinks," Joe said.

We found a table near the end of the concrete deck near the beach. The ocean breeze was pleasant but not sufficient to cool us, and small beads of moisture stood out on Jenny's forehead. She picked up a napkin and gently blotted the moisture from her face.

"You must be exhausted," I said. "Don't you think you should take a nap or something?"

"I'm just a little disoriented. But I'm too excited to sleep. Besides, I want to take advantage of every moment I have here. And perhaps . . . even take the opportunity to convince you to come home."

"I think that might be a conversation for later on."

"You're right," she said, "and right now I want to find out all I can about Liberia."

"Where would you like to start?"

"Is what Joe said true, that they don't have crime here?" Jenny asked, squinting in the fading sunlight.

"Oh, they have crime here. It runs through life here like water."

"How do you mean?"

"Bribery, for example. In the states it's considered a crime. Here it's just a measure of how much you want something. A man can kill his wife, and if he can show he had good reason or pays enough dash, he can get usually away with it."

"Really? I read that Liberia is one of the wealthiest nations in West Africa, has a high GNP, and is politically stable."

"All true," I said. "It's one of the best examples of the trickle-down theory that I know of, and you'll get a chance to see it in action when we go to the party."

Joe brought the drinks and set them on the table in front of us. The light breeze from the ocean moved Jenny's blond hair slightly across her face. She turned to look at the ocean.

"It's beautiful here, isn't it?" she said.

"Yes. It is very beautiful."

"Kenneth, I want to go to the party and I want you to go with me. It'll be a chance to see the people in power close up. It's a rare opportunity, don't you think?"

"I have to admit, it sounds like a cut above the local bar scene or hanging out at the beach, which is all that I can offer."

She smiled and turned to face me, then took a sip from her drink. "This is good," she said.

We talked for a long time about friends and family back home—her parents were doing well. She had spoken to my parents just before leaving. They were concerned since they hadn't heard from me in months.

The president's party was several days away, so before then I wanted to show her the "better side" of Monrovia. We had lunch at Heinz and Maria's bar, where she was a hit with the aging Luftwaffe pilots. Then more lunches at the Gurley Street Bar where the rowdy RAF guys gathered round her. We had dinner at the Ducor Palace Hotel and spent many hours on the beach.

The evening of the president's reception I managed to find a clean, pressed shirt and trousers but had a lot of trouble finding the only necktie I brought with me to Africa. It took several attempts before I remembered how to tie the thing. I buffed the mildew from my dress shoes with an old, worn out sock, then got into Junebug and headed over to the Ambassador to pick up Jenny. She looked radiant in her tropical white dress and white, high-heeled shoes.

The reception was one of several that the president held to celebrate his successful twenty years in office. We stopped at the entrance gate of the presidential residence in Totota. There were two uniformed guards armed with 30 caliber carbines. The guard on my left walked up to my window.

"We're here to attend a social function," I said.

"Hav ya an enveetation?" the guard asked.

"We don't have a formal invitation, but the name should be on your list."

The guard examined the paper attached to the clipboard he held in his left hand. "Wha de name?"

Jenny leaned across me and said, "Miss Jenny Morgan."

"Miss Janni Moogan," the guard repeated as he ran his index finger down the page. "Ah, yas mamah, here t'is, an a guest. Dis mon ya guest?"

"Yes, he is."

"Den you may go in. Pak on de right where ya see de odders," the guard said and pointed in the direction that we were to go. I thanked him and slowly drove through the gate following the driveway to where there were other parked cars. I pulled Junebug into the group of stately Mercedes and BMWs and switched off her loudly banging air-cooled engine.

"It definitely looks like we belong here," I said.

We followed other arriving guests across the parking area and along the newly laid walkways into the residence. Inside, we were directed to a large, central room, which I assumed was the main ballroom. It had been finished in imitation of the French Rococo style, but without the elegance or refinement. Several crystal chandeliers hung from the high, rounded ceiling. Guards dressed in uniforms that looked similar to what might have been worn by Napoleon's generals were stationed at doorways and along the walls. The sound of a string quartet playing chamber music echoed from the marble walls. An elaborate bar with several bartenders was at the far end of the room, and to the side was a lavish display of European and Liberian delicacies. There was an actual roasted boar with an apple in its mouth.

"My dear Miss Morgan," said Honorable Harriss, seemingly appearing out of thin air. He was dressed in a well-fitted tuxedo. "It is a pleasure to see you. I am so happy that you could make it. I've told the president all about you and he would be delighted to meet you." He took her hand and kissed it. "And I see you've brought your young friend?"

Honorable Harriss was, like so many of his fellow Americo-Liberians, well educated and well spoken. He was also very officious and very determined. Being an "advisor" to President Tubman could have meant anything. I knew that President Tubman had many advisors, most of whom had an array of non-specific duties.

He took Jenny gently by the arm. "Come, let me introduce you," he said, leading her away and leaving me standing alone. I started to follow when I felt a familiar hand on my shoulder.

"Mr. Spike! How are you my friend? And what brings you to this grand celebration?"

I turned to see Honorable Williams. He had a drink in his other hand and was showing his usual broad smile. I explained that Jenny was visiting me from Washington. She had met Honorable Harriss during the flight to Monrovia and that he had invited her to this event.

"She couldn't very well come without an escort," I said.

"Of course not, my man. Of course not. Now that you are here, how do you like the president's new residence?"

"Very large," I said

The corners of Honorable William's mouth dropped slightly. "The president wanted it twice as large as the White House. Do you think he succeeded?" Without waiting for me to answer he continued. "I don't think he quite made it, but I'm not really sure. It has what you call the West Wing with many offices for his cabinet and advisors—auxiliary offices, so to speak—in addition to those in the Executive Mansion in Monrovia. I'm told that he has even ordered a copy of President Monroe's portrait—don't know where he plans to hang it.

"I think he had the place designed by one of the top architectural firms in London, working together with German structural engineers. He added a little touch of Hollywood too, don't you think? Fortunately, he used some, but not much, local labor to build it." He went on, "Ahhh yes, the use of local labor however small justified the whole thing. It was in all the papers and on television. He will not let them forget it. And they love him for it."

Honorable Williams smiled a knowing smile and continued, "Just look at this place! What does it say to you? Don't tell me. I know what you're thinking. It says power, authority, great ambition, and most of all, permanence. Our president will be president forever and Liberia will dominate all of Africa. At least," he hesitated, "I think that's the plan."

A server dressed in a white uniform with gold epaulets stopped in front of us bearing a tray full of champagne glasses filled almost to the brim with the golden, bubbling liquid.

"You had better take one," Honorable Williams said. "The president doesn't dispense his liquor easily." I took one of the glasses and thanked the server, who nodded politely.

"I suspect," Honorable Williams added, "that your lady friend will be occupied for some time. Why don't you circulate? There's bound to be one or two others here, besides us, who are interested in the future of air transport in this country."

Honorable Williams patted me on the shoulder and left. I could see that Jenny was being introduced to President Tubman. He had a reputation of being charming with women and I could see that he was pouring it on—all smiles and kisses. He was wearing a tail coat and had a blue satin sash draped over his left shoulder that had various ribbons and medals pinned to it.

He was gesturing with his hand toward a group of people near him. He then led Jenny by the elbow over to them and introduced her. Honorable Williams was making his way toward the same group of people. I finished the glass of champagne—never have liked the stuff—and made my way to the bar. The bartender was someone I recognized: Set 'em Up Joe from the Ambassador's beach bar.

"Hi Joe!" I said, giving him a slight wave. He waved back then came over to where I was standing. "Have you moved up from the Ambassador?"

"Naw, Missa Ken. Dis is a temporary gig fo me and it is no good shit."

"What do you mean?"

"Des rich bastards, dey not pay worth shit."

"That's how they get rich, my friend."

"Ya right bout dat, Missa Ken. Dey get rich off de backs of de little man. Dis ah know, but ah tell you wha, one day dat's gwana change."

"If that happens, Joe, just remember I'm not one of them. I work for them too."

"Ah know, sah. Ah remember ya. Ya tip large."

"That's right Joe, so could you get me one of those rare bourbons?"

"Straight away, Missa Ken, straight away."

I had lost sight of Jenny. For a moment I thought of trying to rescue her, but I knew that the political science major in her was enjoying it. She was probably quizzing President Tubman about the GNP right now. Joe brought the bourbon—he had made it a double. He saluted me with two fingers and a smile, then went to serve other guests.

"And who are you with?" a woman's voice said behind me. I turned to face an attractive woman with dark, straight hair, and blue eyes. "Coca Cola, Firestone, American Iron and Steel?"

"None of them," I said. "I'm a pilot for Monrovia Airlines."

She looked slightly puzzled, as if wondering how I got an invitation.

"One of the president's advisors took a fancy, as my Brit friends say, to my girlfriend and invited her, which had to include me. She's up there now, with him and the president, meeting the Big Men."

"Well, dear boy. I hope you get her back. The president's got a thing for pretty young women."

"Oh, I think she'll do just fine. She likes politics, presidents, and so on. I think she'll see it as a learning experience."

"I expect she will learn a thing or two but, still, you'd better keep an eye on her just the same. Beautiful things have a way of getting lost around here."

A slight sense of foreboding enveloped me. I looked over at Jenny again. She was literally the center of attention—a sea of black suits encircled her. I took a deep breath and turned back toward the woman next to me. She was somewhere in her early forties and about five foot four. I detected a slight Virginia tidewater accent.

"Let me guess, you grew up in the Norfolk area, went to the University of Virginia, and married a diplomat?"

"Close, my lovely boy. I did graduate from UVA but I grew up on a farm near Richmond—well, back in the old days we called it a plantation, but it's not considered polite to call it that now so we just refer to it as the farm. My husband is far from being a diplomat. In fact, I'm not sure he knows what the word means. He's an executive with the Liberian International Ship and Corporate Registry."

"What kind of organization is that?" I asked.

"It's one of those organizations that make it easy for ship owners and corporations to register their businesses in Liberia. That way they can avoid the taxes and fees of their native countries and still do business there. It's like a discount store for the big guys—Liberia gets a lot of revenue and the big boys get to keep the change. Clever, don't you think?"

"Very clever. Makes me wonder why I didn't think of it."

"So what are your plans? I mean, after Liberia? You're too young to settle for this kind of life, and I don't suspect you're running from anything."

"Don't really know. I'm too busy trying not to get killed. But I may return to the States and finish things I started."

"How about your girlfriend, my dear, the one that Tubman is drooling all over. Any serious plans there?"

"Maybe, but it hasn't come up at the moment."

A man in a dark blue suit walked up beside her. He was about fifty, a few inches taller than me and looked at me as though he was stripping the flesh from my bones.

"Who is your young friend?" he asked the woman.

"He's a pilot for Monrovia Airlines."

"A pilot, huh! Does your pilot have a name?"

"I suppose he does. We hadn't got around to that." She looked at me and with a slight smile said, "Dearie, I'm sure you have a name, so would you tell it to little old Jimmy here so that he doesn't start frothing at the mouth."

"Kenneth," I said, extending my hand. He ignored it and glared, first at me, then at the woman.

"Kenneth. Isn't that a nice name, Jim—very American. Oh dearie, you don't have to worry. He's far too young for me and probably far too intelligent for you. Besides, he's got a girlfriend here—see, the pretty one over there, being devoured by the political elite."

The man's jaw clinched like a spring tightening then he slowly backed away. He turned to greet a smiling, good-looking man dressed like the other "presidential advisors." They immediately started talking business between themselves. It was time for me to leave. I excused myself, saying to the woman that it was a pleasure to have met her or words to that affect. As I moved past the two men I overheard the Big Man say to "Jimmy," "Hah! You're right! There is so much money coming in, we just can't steal it fast enough."

I quickly made my way closer to Jenny. She was now chatting animatedly with another group of diplomatic types, all armored in tuxedos and sashes. I elbowed my way to her, making my apologies to the gentlemen in tuxedos.

"I think it's time to go," I said, trying to keep the stress from my voice. She looked at me with some astonishment. "I'm uncomfortable here, Jenny. I feel like I'm in the palace of the czar. Nothing here reflects reality."

Jenny looked irritated. She hesitated for a moment, then made her apologies to the men surrounding her and walked with me out of the president's mansion to Junebug. She flung the door open, making a metallic cracking sound, and flopped into the seat then folded her arms in front of her.

She stared out of the window and was silent during the ride back to the Ambassador. I pulled up in front of the hotel. She glared at me. The dim street lighting outside clearly showed the tension in her face.

"I was having a great time. I was meeting people. I was talking to important people. And you, because of your obvious social inadequacies, forced me to leave. I've missed a great opportunity because of you."

"Jenny, I'm sorry you feel that way. I'm sorry you're angry, but you have no idea what it's like here."

"You didn't give me much of a chance to find out, did you?"

With that she got out of the car and slammed the door so that it rattled like an empty tin can. I watched her as she walked through the open doors of the Ambassador. She didn't look back. I drove away thinking that I would stop by for breakfast and try to iron this difficult wrinkle out.

The beach house was quiet even though it wasn't really that late. Nevertheless, I was thankful since I felt like turning in early and sober. I stripped off my "evening" clothes, checked my bed for bugs and snakes, then crawled in, enjoying the feel of the sheets and pillow. I untied the cord holding the mosquito netting and let it fall. Then, feeling fully protected, I pondered over the events of the evening. I deeply regretted that Jenny was angry and upset, but I still felt that I had acted correctly. I could only hope that eventually she would understand.

The next morning I was awakened by the aroma of fresh brewed coffee and Ku shaking me by the shoulder. "Mornin, boss, something to start de day?" he said, placing the coffee on the night table next to my bed.

I sat up in bed. Several mosquitoes were lodged in the netting. I wondered if they were the malaria-bearing kind. The coffee was life restoring. Then I started remembering the events of the night before. I glanced at my watch on the night table. It was after nine. I hurried out of bed and dressed in my cleanest shirt and trousers. Grabbing the coffee, I rushed out to Junebug, got in, started her up and pointed her toward the Ambassador.

"Sorry suh, Meess Morgan na in her room. She lef bout half hour ago wit two men from de government."

I ran back to the car and drove as fast as it could go to the president's mansion. The guards at the gate stopped me, then ordered me to get out of the car. They had their carbines with fixed bayonets and held them at the ready. I explained that I needed to see Honorable Harriss right away. They wanted to know if I had an appointment.

"Of course I don't have an appointment. This is an emergency!" I shouted. "My lady friend may have been kidnapped."

"Da na fo us! Da be fo de police."

I said that she had been taken by two government men from the hotel this morning and that Honorable Harriss could straighten it out. One of the guards looked thoughtful for a moment then told the other guard to watch me. The guard walked into his guardhouse and used his phone. In a few minutes he returned.

"Ya way hee," he said, motioning to a clear area next to the guard house. "Honorable Harriss, he be down jus now."

I thanked the guard and drove over to the clear area. "Jus now" can mean anything. I expected to sit there for hours. I would wait days if I had to. About two hours passed while I alternately dozed or tapped my fingers on the steering wheel. I noticed a green golf cart with two men in it rambling down the driveway of the mansion. I saw Honorable Harriss get out and talk to the guard who pointed at me. Honorable Harriss walked toward me. I got out of Junebug and offered my hand. He ignored it.

"Two government men showed up at Jenny's hotel and left with her. I think they brought her here," I said.

"Do you have proof of this accusation?" Honorable Harriss asked.

"Where else would they bring her?" I said. "Her father is a big man in Washington and it would not go well with your government if something were to happen to her."

"Who are you to make threats here?" Honorable Harriss's voice had gone up several notes. It was something between fear, anger, and panic. "If she is here," he continued barely able to suppress his rage, "no harm will come to her. I can assure you of that."

"That is well," I said, "for her father has made me her guardian and I am responsible for her while she is here."

This was a necessary exaggeration. I was not her guardian even in the African sense of the term, but as she was here visiting me, I felt I did have a responsibility for her safety in the American sense of the word. I thought it best that Honorable Harriss believed that I had some power to act, if necessary.

"I will be back for her in two hours. If she is not here, I will inform her father who has friends in the American Embassy. I don't have to tell you what that could mean."

He glared at me—it was a staring contest that the Big Men do to underlings until the underlings lower their eyes and back away. I wasn't going to let that happen so we glared at one another for maybe five minutes. Then Honorable Harriss stepped back into his golf cart, his eyes still fixed on me, and motioned for his driver to go. It was the same game I had played with the commissioner in Guinea.

I glanced at my watch. It was hard to read in the shadow of the guard house. I made out 2:00 p.m. The Ambassador's beach bar would be open, so I drove there and parked next to the hotel. It was a good place to while away an hour. I ordered a rum and tonic from Joe, and for a few minutes enjoyed the sound of the surf. It seemed perfect as though nothing could ever destroy the peace and beauty of this place.

I had probably stepped over the line. I may even have gotten Honorable Williams in some trouble. If so, then I probably wouldn't have a job tomorrow, but the only objective that mattered, at the moment, was Jenny's safety. I ordered another rum and tonic. This wasn't necessarily a smart thing to do since Joe tended to fortify them with an extra dollop or two of rum. Joe brought the drink. It was well fortified. I slid a dollar bill over to him. He smiled broadly and held the bill up as though it was a trophy.

My concern for Jenny was more that she might be unknowingly manipulated rather than any fear for her physical safety. I had heard Tubman called a lot of unflattering things but never a rapist. Nevertheless, he was a man with a God complex and he always got what he wanted. I didn't think a minor international incident would be in anybody's self-interest.

I lost myself in the soothing sounds of the waves rolling up onto the beach. I looked at my watch again and was surprised to see that an hour had actually gone by. I thanked Joe and left the bar. I walked through the lobby and out of the front doors just in time to see a government limo drive up and Jenny emerge from the back seat.

"Jenny!" I shouted." Jenny!"

She closed the door of the limo and looked up at me. It was obvious that she was very angry.

"Are you okay, Jenny?"

"I'm fine," she said marching past me, like a storm trooper, toward the hotel.

"I was only worried about you," I shouted after her.

She turned around and faced me like a charging bull. "You ruined a perfectly good opportunity for me. President Tubman is a true gentleman, probably one of the few gentlemen that I've known. They said you made threats. You brought my father into it. How could you have done such a thing?"

"Jenny, they know your father is well connected in Washington. I really think they wanted to get information out of you or use you in some way. But I was also concerned for your safety. This is Liberia. It's run by goons and thugs, and despite how Tubman dresses up, he is no gentleman."

"You're wrong, Kenneth. Just as you've been wrong about a lot of things."

"Tell me this: did they ask you to do anything or say anything to your father or any of his friends?"

"Well, maybe. But it's no big deal."

"What did they ask you do?"

"Well, um, it turns out that Uncle Eddie, Daddy's best friend, is president of a company that Honorable Harriss and President Tubman are anxious to do business with. But I wasn't going to actually do anything or ask any favors."

"So what did they ask you to do?"

"They had a gift for Uncle Eddie, and a letter. That's all. And I was going to take it with me on the plane and give it to him when I got home."

"Do you know what the letter said, or what the gift was?"

"No, but it was small enough to fit in my pocketbook." Her anger subsided as it started to occur to her that I just might have some legitimate concerns. We walked together over to an ornate wrought iron bench that was just outside the front door of the hotel.

"So you think that they were using me as a messenger?"

"I can't be sure," I said, "but that is certainly my guess."

"So it looks like you're not wrong about everything! Just some things."

"What do you mean? Like what?"

"Arthur."

"What about Arthur?"

"I know what you're doing here, Kenneth; why you came here in the first place. You're punishing yourself. You're trying to run away from the guilt you feel about Arthur's death. But there are some things you don't know, too. You know Arthur was in love with me. And yes, he wanted to marry me. We never did have sex, despite what you believe. But what you don't know is that Arthur knew about our feelings, yours and mine, for each other. We had a long talk about it, and I told him I was in love with you. I know it was hard for him, but in the end, he said he understood, and that he was okay with it."

"He knew about us? But there was no *us*. We hadn't dated, or even kissed for that matter."

"I know," she said. "He just knew. And he knew I hadn't been unfaithful and that you had tried to keep your feelings to yourself. He was really quite an exceptional person, when you come to think about it."

"He was, I know. It just makes it all that much worse. Why did he have to die instead of me? I was the one who was drunk. I was the one who called him to come get me."

"The accident wasn't your fault. The man that hit Arthur was drunk. He shouldn't have been driving. You did the right thing."

"I could have stayed," I said. "They asked me several times to stay, but

I wanted to get home. I am so selfish. If I hadn't been so selfish, I wouldn't have insisted Arthur come get me and he would be alive today."

Jenny moved closer to me. "I was with him that night. He wanted to go get you. He wanted to tell you that it was over between us and that you were free to go out with me. He figured you weren't too drunk to talk, but that you were being your usual cautious self and didn't want to risk driving home. Kenneth, when you called, you did not insist; in fact, you talked about staying over, but he insisted on going to get you. It was his idea, Kenneth."

I thought about all she had said. Somehow, I still didn't feel better.

"Well, all this might be true," I said, "but my parents still blame me. I know they don't want to, but it's there. Arthur was their favorite, and I killed him. That's what they think."

"Kenneth, that is just your imagination. They have known everything all along. You just misinterpreted their immense grief and thought they held you responsible. Believe me, you are far from being blamed. You are their cherished only son. If you came home now, you'd be welcomed back as the prodigal son.

"Anyway, it's all in the past now. We can't change one moment of it. We have to move forward with time no matter how much we may dread it. You have to move on, Kenneth." She stood up slowly and started to walk toward the Ambassador, then she turned back to face me.

"I was going to make President Tubman the subject of my master's thesis," she chuckled, "but I don't think that would be a good idea now." She turned around again and headed for the hotel. At the door, she stopped again. "I'm leaving tomorrow," she said, "at the government's request. They're sending a car with an escort. Not exactly how I had hoped to leave."

With that she disappeared through the doors. No kiss goodbye; no wave goodbye; no goodbye.

They would put her on the daily flight out of Robertsfield to Dakar with connections to Europe, then home. I didn't sleep much that night, and the next morning I waited outside the hotel in Junebug at a safe distance until the government car, a black Mercedes, arrived. Two men in dark suits got out of the car and walked into the hotel. In a few minutes they emerged. Jenny was walking beside one of them and the other carried her bags. They waited until she was in the car, then they got in and drove off. I followed them to the airport and remained until I saw Jenny board the DC-4. I realized that this could be the last time I would see her beautiful blond hair flowing in the wind. I continued waiting until I saw the airplane takeoff and turn north.

CHAPTER 29

SAM

I drove over to the flight office.

Andre looked up from his desk. "Ready to work again?" he asked.

"Yes," I said. "I'll take anything you have."

For the next several weeks I flew every job available. One of the good things about flying is that it requires total and absolute concentration. That was what I needed to push Jenny and the events of the past week into the far corners of my consciousness.

I continued at this pace until the wet season arrived and work started to slack off. I had time on my hands. The sun had been swallowed up by milky gray sheets of cloud, and the rain came in curtains of gray liquid. The beach along with everything else was continually wet. I had run out of books, and there are just so many times you can paint a gray-green seascape.

I drove into Monrovia with the intention of rummaging through the local book shop. Most of the books there were used and badly soiled. However, I did find an old but good copy of *The End of Eternity* by Isaac Asimov. I was leaving the book shop when I saw her. She was walking with another woman, and they were both carrying large shopping bags. I ran across the street, dodging several bicycles and a rattling pickup truck.

"Hi Sam!" I said, running up to them. Sam looked at me, clearly not recognizing me. The other woman looked back and forth at both of us.

"Ken," I said ridiculously pointing to myself like a circus clown, "pilot for Monrovia Airlines. We met at Zigida. You wanted me to deliver something."

"Yes, I think I remember you—a sort of mercenary fellow who robs from the poor and gives to the rich."

"You've got me confused with someone else. I'm just a simple college dropout doing a simple job for which I get paid a simple wage."

"Being a mercenary sounds more exciting, Ken. And you remembered my name. That is impressive!"

"I also remember saying that the next time you're in town maybe we could do something—like take in a movie maybe?"

"Would you believe I lost your number?" she said.

"It's plausible, I suppose. It could happen, but no."

She smiled.

"Could I call you then?" I asked.

"The director discourages that kind of thing, and besides, we only have one phone. It's in the office and sometimes it doesn't work."

"Then when will you be in town next?"

"Two weeks from now," she said, glancing at the other woman that I presumed was another Peace Corps volunteer.

"Then let's make plans to meet at the Ambassador's beach bar and from there take in Hollywood's latest creation."

She hesitated for a while then smiled slightly. "Okay, maybe." She reached into her shirt pocket and handed me a typical business card with her name on it, the Peace Corps logo, and a penciled in phone number. "Now we've got to go," she said. "See you later then."

I watched her walk away. Everything around her seemed to focus on her as though she were the center of gravity wherever she happened to be. She was one of those people that everyone recognized as one of the best—her elegance and her beauty were only the outward signs.

I watched her until she was out of sight. It started to rain again. It was pointless trying to run to get out of it. I tucked the book inside my shirt, leisurely walked to where Junebug was parked, and drove back to the beach house with the toy-like windshield wipers beating uselessly against the glass.

I discovered that she was based in the village of Voinjama, near the Guinean boarder, which made sense, given where I first saw her. I checked

Andre's latest flight schedule and found that there was a trip to a village named Malmai, maybe ten miles from the Voinjama. Next day I took two Mandingos up to Malmai, and after saying goodbye, cranked up Charlie Fox to fly over to Voinjama. I found it easily enough but there was no airfield. The dirt road leading into the village looked straight and wide enough, but it would have to be a maximum performance type landing. I decided against it, then circled the village a couple of times and headed back to Monrovia. Back at the operations office I leafed through the paper to check what was playing at the movie theater. The page had been torn out.

I asked Andre, "Is anything playing at the Ravoli?"

He looked up with a slight smile. "One of your American westerns. I think it's *North to Alaska*."

I could use the telephone at home in relative privacy. I dialed the number on Sam's card. An official sounding voice answered, and I asked to speak to Miss Samantha Kay. I was quickly told that she could not come to the phone, but if I would leave my name and number, she would call me back. I told the woman the information, repeating it all very slowly.

I was feeling rather giddy and excited, so I decided to stretch out on the bed. I dropped the mosquito netting, folded my hands behind my head and slowly slipped into a deep sleep. An hour later I was awakened by Ku telling me that I had a phone call from a mysterious woman. I threw the mosquito netting aside, hopped out of bed, and dashed into the hallway where the phone was kept. I took a couple of deep breaths and said hello in my calmest voice.

"Hi," she said in a crisp voice. I paused for a few seconds to make sure I could remain calm.

"Well," she said, "you called me."

"Yes," I said. "Just checking to if you still had plans to come to Monrovia."

"As I said, next week. On Saturday."

"Great. How about that drink and the movie I promised you?"

"I don't know. I've got a lot to do. What's playing?"

"*North to Alaska*," I said.

"Don't like westerns and I especially don't like that phony, draft-dodging, careerist John Wayne."

"Then how about lunch?"

There was a long pause.

"Okay," she finally answered. "I like the little restaurant next to the Chase Bank. They have great fufu and peanut soup, but I may have someone with me. We travel in pairs, you know."

"Great!" I said. "See you at twelve on Saturday outside the Chase Bank then?"

"Okay," she said. "See ya." Then she hung up.

It didn't sound very promising, but at least she agreed to meet me. I went back to bed but was completely unable to sleep. I decided that what I needed was company—loud, boisterous company—the tinkling of ice in glasses and some raucous laughter. For that, I needed the Gurley Street Bar. I rolled out of bed feeling restored and renewed and drove there as quickly as Junebug would take me.

I was pleased to see Colin sitting at the end of the bar. He was throwing back a scotch and not looking very happy. I pulled up a stool next to him.

"Let me get you another one of those," I said.

"Absolutely, mate. That's the most promising vision I've had in the last twenty-four hours."

I signaled for one of the bartenders to come over. I pointed to Colin's empty glass and said, "Two more of those please."

He saluted with two fingers and went to make the drinks.

"Don't ever let that little limp prick Andre talk you into taking a 'special flight.' The little shit, he knows all of our weakness. He knows all he has to do in dangle a wad of cash in my face and I will fuck anybody."

"So who did he get you to fuck?"

"He said it was an easy flight. Christ! I should have run out the door when I heard that. All I had to do was fly these two blokes up to a cut-out airfield near the Sierra Leone border, wait for them to conduct their business, then fly them back. Sounds easy, doesn't it? So I got Charlie Alpha ready in the morning, and these guys didn't get there until after twelve. They showed up in an old truck that looked like it had been used to haul horse dung. They took out a couple of backpacks and two bicycles from the bed of the truck. I just thought they were a couple of eccentrics—you know, we get them here all the time.

"So we get their shit packed in the aircraft somehow and off we go to this toilet at the Sierra Leone border. It was a short runway and I had to hang it on the prop going in. I managed to clear the trees okay and got it stopped before ramming it into the trees on the other end. The two blokes get out without so much as a how do you do, get on their bikes, and head for the border. By this time the locals are swarming all around me trying to sell me shit. I tell them to get away. Naturally, they ignore me so I have to pull my gun. It's funny, isn't it? You can go to the end of the earth and there are always two things people recognize and respect right away: one's a snake, and the other is a gun. So they get the picture after that and back away. I crawl into the back of the plane and close everything up so that the bugs won't get me and try to get some shut eye.

"I fell asleep—more like passed out. When I woke up I was bathed in sweat. The air inside the aircraft smelled like old farts and it was getting dark. I crawled out of the plane. The locals were gone. I did a quick check of the aircraft. Nothing was missing or broken—a fucking miracle. Then I heard this series of muffled explosions from quite a ways off and saw black smoke rising in the distance toward Sierra Leone. I knew from my years in the RAF what had happened. These fucking guys were saboteurs, Israeli saboteurs, who went across the border to blow up something—probably some Lebanese establishment. I started getting the aircraft ready. I wasn't going to wait for those fuckers.

"I was just starting the engine when this taxi pulled up next to the aircraft. Smoke was coming from under the hood and the thing was full of bullet holes. The two guys got out, left the engine running, and jumped into the aircraft shouting, 'Go! Go!' I fast-taxied to the end of the runway. By then it was dark. You know how fast dark comes in the tropics. I couldn't see shit except for the glow of the fire they'd started, and all the time these guys are shouting, 'Go! Go!' So I put in a notch of flaps and pushed the throttle in and held it balls to the wall because there was nothing else that I could do to get more power. I held Charlie Alpha down until I got to best angle of climb speed then pulled it up and hung it on the prop until I figured I was clear of the trees. I must have miscalculated a little because I felt the landing gear hit some top branches and the tail brush against the leaves. We kept flying though. We stayed in the air. All I can say, mate, is thank God for Cessna engineers."

Colin took a long swallow of scotch and continued, "When I got back to Spriggs-Payne there were leaves and sticks embedded in the main landing gear and tail wheel; and there was some leaf stain on the stabilizer as well. I was glad I had forgotten where I had put my gun because I think I would have blown those fuckers heads off I was so pissed."

"What did happen to the two guys?" I asked.

"The instant I shut the engine off they jumped out of the aircraft, ran and jumped into their piece of crap truck and left in a cloud of smoke. When I reported this to Andre, all he wanted to know was how badly the aircraft was damaged and did I want to give back the money that I was going to be paid for the job. I told him to fuck off."

"What did he say to that?"

Colin shook his head slowly and smiled. "Nothing," he said. "The little shit didn't say anything. He just smiled. He knows we're a bunch of whores."

CHAPTER 30

VOINJAMA

As fate would have it, two days before I was to meet Sam I awoke in a cold sweat, followed by all of the symptoms of a malaria attack. Ku came into my room with coffee. He saw my condition and quickly checked the general medicine cabinet.

"Ya nee mo quinine peels Boss. Yo eyes look mos yellow."

I pulled a twenty out of my trouser pocket and wadded it up in his hand.

"Go to the pharmacy," I said, "and get me a bottle of Chloroquine."

He looked at me for a moment, puzzled.

"You can have what's left of the money."

He left hurriedly, jumped on his bicycle, and started for town. The pharmacy wasn't too far away, and I knew it should only take him less than an hour. I went back to bed and pulled the mosquito netting over. I managed to drink half the coffee. It was hot and good and warmed me a little. I then went to the kitchen and retrieved one of the half gallon jugs of filtered water that we kept in the storage locker. I hardly had the strength to carry it. I took it back to my bed and started drinking it through a straw. It tasted flat and a little like chlorine, but I knew that dehydration was a serious result of these attacks and it could make a bad attack worse. I made sure the mosquito net was in place then pulled the bed covers over me and tried not to shake.

I took the Chloroquine as soon as Ku returned. Later that day I started throwing up. If I couldn't keep the medication down I was going to be in truly bad shape. That night, in between moments of near comatose sleep, I sipped water and swallowed the Chloroquine as prescribed. The next morning I was not improved, and I knew that after one of these attacks I would be drained of most of my strength for a while. Ku brought in a cup of coffee and two boiled eggs. I tried the coffee but couldn't finish it. The eggs were impossible. I knew I wasn't going to be able to meet Sam the next day. I asked Ku to call her and tell her what had happened and that I would contact her as soon as possible.

Sometime after this, I don't remember whether it was during the day or night, I slipped into a feverish, coma-like sleep. I was aware that I was standing next to the fireplace in my parents' house. There was a log fire burning, its orange-yellow flames casting flashes of light and shadow into the room. I turned and Arthur was standing at the other end of the room, his face and form dimly lit by the flickering firelight. He walked toward me and stopped at the other side of the fireplace. He was smiling, not menacingly, but the smile of one who understands. I asked him what he was doing there, that I thought he was dead. He laughed and said that he was dead. Then I asked again why he was there. He said that he just wanted me to know that everything was all right, that it wasn't my fault. He was killed by a drunk and that it could have happened to anybody at anytime. He wanted me to know that he was fine and that I shouldn't worry. Then the fire went out. It grew dark and he was gone.

I awoke with a start, covered in sweat. I must have yelled or screamed or something like that because Ku ran into my room shouting, "Boss, boss, you good, you good?"

I told him about the dream. He listened intently then, after a few moments, said, "Your brother he come to ya, he forgive ya, he wan ya to be at peace. Dat's wa it is."

"It was a dream, Ku—a sort of nightmare. That's all it was." I said lying back on my bed. I couldn't stop wondering if Ku had been right.

After several days of sweats, chills, nausea, and aches and pains, the symptoms eased, then passed. I had survived my second round with malaria, and as soon as I had the strength to get out of bed, I called Sam. I was told that she could not come to the phone and for me not to call back. This did not sound good. I shaved, took a much-needed shower, and dressed. Ku was sitting on the steps of the porch smoking a cigarette and looking out at the ocean.

"What did you say to her, Ku? What!" I asked.

He looked up at me blowing a cloud of smoke over his head. "Ah say to her dat ya seek an would na mee wi her, oh," he hesitated, "dee ah not speak de truth, boss?"

"Yes, you spoke the truth, but did you not tell her it was the malaria?"

"Dere no nee, Boss. Every soul here know dat when some soul be seek, ee be de malaria or de dengue fever or a curse. If she been here long, she unnastan."

"Did she say anything to indicate that?"

"Ya, boss. She say to tell ya dat you are de son of bitch an de bastard."

The next day, I drove to the airport early. Andre was in the hangar talking to Paterson. I went up to them, ignored their irritation at my interruption, and told Andre that I had to get to Voinjama and was there a flight scheduled for that part of the country today. Andre said he had not posted the flight schedule on the board yet, but if I would meet him in the flight office in ten minutes, he would let me know. I went to the office and paced around until he arrived.

"What is this about?" he asked, picking up a clipboard and looking at the scheduling paper on it.

"I need to get to Voinjama," I said.

"A woman, huh?" he said, not looking up from the clipboard.

"Is anything going up there today?"

Andre shook his head slowly. "Sorry."

"Have you got something I can rent?"

"Christ, you are desperate. She must be some kind of woman."

"Cut it out, Andre. Have you got something available?"

"You can take Papa Sierra, but you got to pay the full charter price for her—no discount on this one."

"Subtract it from what you already owe me," I said, grabbing keys and clipboard with the log and rushing out to where the airplane was parked.

Papa Sierra was a well-used Piper Tripacer, reasonably fast but noisy. It flew like a box with short, stubby wings and had the glide ratio of a brick. I gave it a quick preflight check—something one should never do quickly. All of the fluids looked good and nothing was loose, hanging, or broken, and no contaminants in the fuel. The airplane was covered inside and out with dust, but that would have to wait. I brushed the dust off the windshield, the seats, and the instrument panel, crawled into the left seat, and started the engine.

When I got to Voinjama, there was a light cloud cover. I stayed just below the overcast, circled the town a couple of times, located the school, and decided to land on a road nearby. I made a low approach over the dirt road. It was not perfectly even, but I could not see any holes or obstructions and it didn't look heavily used. I could not see motor traffic anywhere near it, so I did a descending 180 degree turn into a light wind and dropped it none too gently on the road.

The Papa Sierra rattled and banged but quickly rolled to a stop, leaving a swirling trail of dust behind. I taxied the airplane as close to the edge of the road as I could, then got out and pushed down on the tail of the plane to lift the nose wheel. I then pushed the lowered tail over the edge of the road. This cleared the road for ground vehicles and got me off the hook with the village elders.

I took a couple of deep breaths and walked the quarter mile or so to the school. It was a miserable affair by American or European standards but better than many other local village schools. They were usually one room structures with no desks or electrical lighting or plumbing. The rusting metal roofs often leaked, and the metal sheeting sometimes blew away in strong winds. The school at Voinjama where Sam worked had the advantage of Peace Corps money. Not a lot of money, but enough to furnish the basic necessities for learning.

School secretaries seem to be the same everywhere—officious, busy, and protective. This one was no different. With not even a trace of a smile, she looked up at me as if to say, "Yeesss, what is it!"

"I'm here to see Miss Samantha Kay," I said, feeling a sudden twinge in the pit of my stomach.

After another minute she stopped looking through the papers she had in her hands and looked up at me. "Is this about the attack?" she asked.

"Wha . . . What attack?" I asked.

"Oh! Apparently not. Never mind."

"Seriously!" I said. "I'm a friend. What attack?"

"I am not at liberty to say. I shouldn't have said anything at all. You can ask her yourself."

"Where is she?"

"She is teaching now," she said.

"When will she be free?" I asked.

"In about thirty minutes."

I grabbed the only empty chair in the room and placed it against the tin wall directly opposite Madame Secretary. The heat was oppressive, even though all of the windows were open. My t-shirt soaked up my sweat until it was completely saturated. I focused on a single line of soldier ants carrying little bits of food along the base of the floor and into a small crack in the wall. The minutes passed by very slowly. Finally, I could hear the class emptying out. It was time for their lunch break. The Peace Corps had provided soup, sandwiches, and tea to all of the students. Sam walked up to the secretary's desk

"Anything for me?" she asked.

The secretary motioned toward where I was sitting. Sam turned and a look came over her face that could not be described as friendly.

"What are you doing here? I thought you were sick with beriberi or something like that."

"I need to tell you about malaria."

"I know about malaria," she said. "Come on, let's get lunch."

I went with her to a room that passed for a dining hall. There was a long counter made of plywood where two of the local women were handing out bowls of soup from a communal pot and cups of tea to the students.

"I bring my own lunch. The house woman makes it for a few extra pennies in her pay packet. You're welcome to share it with me if you like." She opened a metal box exposing a sandwich wrapped in wax paper and a ripe banana along with a small bottle of tea.

"Is there somewhere we can have a little privacy?" I asked.

"Sure." She closed the box and led me outside to a large baobab tree with a wooden bench built around it.

"This is as private as it gets," she said. We sat on the bench brushing the flies away from her lunch box. "Want half?" she asked.

"No thanks," I said. "I came down with malaria some time ago. It's the non-cerebral kind. There is little warning of a recurring attack. I take medication to reduce the chances of severe attacks, but so far there is nothing that I know that prevents it. The medication usually eases the symptoms. I wasn't lying when I had Ku call you. Would I have come all the way up here and been willing to subject myself to your wrath if I had been lying?"

"Good point," she said. "Are you okay now?"

"Yeah, fine. The secretary asked me if I was here about the assault. What was that about?"

"I don't think we know one another well enough to talk about stuff like that."

"Sam, I'm here because I want to get to know you better. I want to be your friend. And friends help each other out. And in this case, I just might be able to do that. What happened?

She hesitated for a long moment, then biting her lower lip, she said, "Nothing happened really. We had some construction going on up here a couple of weeks ago, putting up a communications tower. So these workers, even though they were supposed to keep to themselves, would wander around at night. One night, about a week ago, I went into my little house and there was this guy, one of the construction workers. He was one of the blond Arian types with a really nasty look about him. Nobody else was in the house. I told him to get the fuck out, and he gets this expression on his face, and before I knew it he had grabbed me and pushed me up against the wall. You want me to go on?"

"Yes!" I said.

"I screamed, but he covered my mouth and started ripping my shirt off. Thank God Tim showed up just then. And that was it. He left. But the really scary part of the whole thing was, just as he was going through the door, he grabbed my hair, pulled me toward him, and whispered in my ear: 'Don't worry, bitch. I'll find you again. And when I do, I'm going to fuck your brains out!'"

"I can track this guy down. What's the name of the construction company he works for?"

"Doesn't matter," she said. "After this happened he was fired, and no one has seen him since."

The wind had picked up and blew waves of light dust down the road. Sam looked at her half-eaten sandwich as though it were now inedible.

"I'm going to have to talk to that woman about how to make a decent sandwich," she said.

Sam was willing to give me another chance. I flew back to Spriggs-Payne feeling considerable anger towered the construction worker and, at the same time, as lighthearted as a school boy with his first crush. She agreed to meet me in Monrovia the following Saturday. That Friday, I bought two tickets to see *The World of Suzie Wong* just to make sure that I had seats.

The Peace Corps maintained a hostel in Monrovia for Peace Corps workers as a kind of transitioning base for arriving and departing volunteers. Volunteers could also use the hostel when staying over in Monrovia. Controlled access made it reasonably safe.

I met Sam outside the hostel at six and we drove directly to the movie theater. I had paid for balcony seats to avoid a possible rain of beer bottles. I was silently relieved when Sam obviously enjoyed the movie, laughing much of the time. Afterward, I took her to a Lebanese restaurant where we ordered chicken farrouj meshwi and a bottle of Massaya, a rosé from Bekaa

Valley. The waiter brought over a lighted candle and placed it gently in the center of the table. The candlelight softened the bridge of freckles across her nose and gave a look of endless depth to her eyes. She had a way of moving her head when she spoke that made part of her hair fall gently across her face. Then she would almost unconsciously sweep it back with a quick movement of her head.

She told me that she had six more months to go on her commitment and did not think she was going to, even if she could, renew it. As a whole, she liked and admired the Liberian people but felt that she was wasting her time.

"Nothing's going to improve," she said, "until Tubman's government puts some of the billions it's making into the educational system and support for the tribes. We know that isn't going to happen. He and his cronies want to keep them down."

"You've certainly been closer to it than I have," I said, "but I have noticed that the Americo-Liberians have the big cars, the big houses, and the big jobs."

She nodded in agreement. "Tubman and his sycophants had better wake up and smell the shit in their own houses or there is going to be hell to pay."

The owner of the restaurant had apparently overheard our conversation, something I suspect he made a practice of doing for his own survival. He was looking at us intently with an expression of concern and irritation.

"I think we're upsetting the owner," I said.

She glanced over at the owner who continued his intense gaze. "Normally," she said. "I'd tell him to fuck off, but . . ." She hesitated. "These fucking Lebanese, they come here, stick a needle into the bowels of this country, and extract its vital juices. They're a bunch of fucking parasites." She looked at the owner. "Hey!" she shouted toward him. "What's the fucking problem?"

The owner turned, stuffed his dishtowel under the belt of his cloth apron, and walked hurriedly toward the kitchen.

"I think we had better go," I said.

We got up from the table. Sam was still looking in the direction of the kitchen as though she expected to see the owner and a couple of knife-wielding cooks coming for us. I left enough money to cover the bill as well as some dash to appease the waiter, and we made a beeline for the door. Once outside the restaurant, Sam started laughing and running. I looked behind us, checking my six o'clock position as my Luftwaffe colleagues had told me to do. Nobody was following us. We ran until we reached Junebug.

"It's okay," I said, a little out of breath and holding on to the door handle for support.

"Let's go for a drink?" she asked.

"I know just the place," I said.

The Ambassador's beach bar was crowded. A calypso steel band played at one end of the bar. Joe was busy and smiling. I ordered a daiquiri for Sam and bourbon for myself. There was standing room only. I noticed a couple of my air service colleagues at a far table. Deet was with them. He saw us and made his way through the crowd to where we were standing. His eyes and cheeks seemed to sparkle, and his face was red from the sun and heat—Deet could never tan, he simply turned red and remained red. He smiled widely, showing his perfect teeth.

"What's the problem at Heinz and Maria's?" I asked. "The beer gone stale?"

"Nein, too many Israeli spies. Dey're looking under de chairs, de table napkins, even de salt shakers for var criminals. And vho ist dis beautiful *fraulein*?"

I introduced Sam. He took her hand and kissed it, and I thought for a moment that he was either going to click his heels or lick her hand.

"Such beautiful red hair und I adore freckles, just adore dem. You must be of fine Celtic origins. Irish perhaps?"

"On my mother's side," she said, looking at Deet as though he had stepped out of history book and into her presence, which, in a sense, he had.

"Und on your fadder's side?" Deet asked.

"My grandfather was from Sweden."

"Excellent. Gut people, de Swedes. Dhey ver gut to Germany during de var. Adopted many of our aircraft designs and, one must say, some of our ideas, yah. Vell," he said with an air of flippancy, "I must be going." Deet hesitated. "You know you are too gut for him. If he gets too boring, let me know, vill you?"

"Don't count on it, Fritz."

"Dieter, *mein liebling*, Dieter."

"Sure thing, Fritz. I won't forget."

Deet smiled and we watched as he strode back to his table.

"How did he escape the war crimes trials?" she asked.

"I think he might have been innocent, at least of deliberate murder and genocide. He was one of those who truly only followed orders. I think he loves flying airplanes and he had the rare chance of flying the best airplanes of his time."

"I'll bet he hates Jews and deep down he's a Nazi racist."

"Maybe so, but he has to suppress all of that now and move on. I suspect that Deet, despite his swagger, knows what it means to lose."

"Well, it's good of you not to hold it against him."

"I try to make it a practice not to hold anyone's politics or religious or nonreligious beliefs against them. When you get down to it, we all need and want the same things."

"Maybe so, but it seems to me that prejudice and hatred are an indulgence few people can afford."

"It's a bit too lofty for me, Sam. Right now I only want to fly airplanes."

"And that's it? Just fly airplanes?"

"It can be a harmless occupation. It provides a good public service and, when you think about it, in the millions of years of human evolution we, in this fraction of time, have been the only humans to fly. That's something, isn't it?"

"I think that's a great way to look at it, but it seems to me flying is a young person's game, and one's youth is gone before one knows it."

"I have given that some thought too and I agree with you, which is why I plan to do this for maybe a few more years—the money is very, very good—then go home and finish college."

"Sounds like a good plan. What do you plan to study?"

"Aeronautical engineering. I think I might be able to get a job doing that. How about you, when your Peace Corps commitment is finished?"

"Go back to Washington State. Teach, preferably in a private school."

"Why a private school?"

"The kids are motivated. Their parents have put it into their heads what's expected of them, and when kids know what's expected of them, they'll usually perform. That means fewer discipline problems and more assurances of success." She finished her drink and placed the glass on the counter. "Where do you live around here?" She hesitated. "That's not a proposition. I'm simply curious."

"Just down the beach from here. I share a house with a couple of foul-mouthed pilots."

"Did I just meet one of them?"

"Yes," I said.

"Just my luck."

"Ku, our houseboy, does a good job looking after us."

"I'm surprised you haven't taken one of the local girls. Most white men who are here for any length of time seem to do that."

"Too many complications. I have no wish to go through the palaver just to have my house cleaned."

"And your, shall I say, other needs?"

I ignored the question.

"I'm sure someone could explain it." She finished her drink. "Let's take a walk on the beach."

I followed her down toward the beach and out of the light and noise of the beach bar. We walked in silence along the surf line where the breaking waves rush up onto the beach in thin layers of water and rush back again.

"It's a beautiful country, isn't it?" she said.

"Yes, it is."

"I am going to hate to leave it."

"That won't be for some time yet."

"Six months. I told you."

"You could renew your contract or whatever the Peace Corps calls it."

"I'm thinking about it, but I want to live in Monrovia, and there are no openings there."

"Maybe it'll change in six months. That's something I've learned about this place—things can change quickly."

There was a rumble in the air. I looked back to see the night sky lighting up with cloud-to-cloud lightening. A thunderstorm was building and, as usual, it was heading toward the coast.

"I think we had better get back," she said. We started walking back along the beach.

"I want to see you again," I said.

"Can you fly up to Voinjama next weekend?"

"Yes," I said, and I meant it. I would have stolen an airplane, a car, a train. I would have walked through the jungle to see her again.

CHAPTER 31

PINEAPPLE BEACH

We made arrangements to meet almost every weekend after that. I struck a deal with Andre that allowed me to rent Papa Sierra pretty much any time. On those weekends that I flew, I would land on the beach where locals were selling their goods and load the cargo bay up with fish. Sam used some of her "coffee money" to buy everything, and I would usually throw in a few dollars just to help out. After I landed at Voinjama, Sam would distribute the fish to the families at her school. We were always invited to share, and the evening would sometimes take on a festive air. I became known among them as "the blessed one from the sky." When Sam drove the jeep to Monrovia, we would usually meet up with some of her Peace Corps colleagues and eat, drink, and talk way into the night, usually about the current trends in movies, the latest books, and often about the state of affairs in the US.

When we met with my aviation buddies, the conversation tended to go toward affirmations of who was getting laid, how much money one earned in the last month, or the declining state of aircraft maintenance. When she was in Monrovia, we would stay at the Ambassador. One evening, she was standing at the window wrapped only in the top bed sheet, looking out toward the ocean.

"In a couple of months this will all come to an end," she said. "I will go back to Seattle and the cold and the rain. And you, where will you be?"

I had been thinking about it, almost from the beginning. There was only one thing that I was sure of at the time: I was not going to lose her. I knew, without doubt, that with so many miles between us, the curtain would fall.

"I will be with you," I said.

"How do you mean?"

"To put it bluntly, you could move in with me."

She turned around to stare at me. The sheet twisted around her body so that it looked like a royal robe.

"I'll find a place for us. I'll take care of everything."

"I think I rather like the idea of being a kept woman, or," she paused, "are you asking something else?"

"I just want to be with you in any way you want. That's all."

She walked over to me. I was sitting on the edge of the bed. She wrapped her bed sheet around both of us.

"I'll definitely give it some consideration," she said, kissing me.

The wet season, as usual, made flying difficult, but it made driving along the few mud roads of the Liberian interior almost impossible. The only safe way to travel in a ground vehicle during the wet season was to use the mining roads. This usually took one out of the way and added considerably to the travel time but, with planning and perseverance, one could be reasonably sure of making it. When Sam arrived at the Peace Corp hostel, the jeep was covered in mud and there were still some small green branches caught in the hood and fenders of the jeep. She pulled her duffel bag from the back seat.

"Let's get something to eat," she said, tossing the duffle bag into the front luggage compartment and closing the hood with a definite bang.

"Where to?" I asked.

"Any place where they don't serve bush meat."

I drove to Heinz and Maria's and we feasted on sausages, potatoes, and beer.

"I've decided to take you up on your offer. My commitment is done next month. It's the end of term. I've even told the kids. They like me, and they're sorry to see me go, but these kids are used to uncertainty, to disruption, to looking at a very short future. The Corps has starting bringing up the green ones to give them some culture-shock-break-in time before they go solo. I've got to break in my replacement before she goes solo and give her advice, if she'll take it. Then I'm outta there." She hesitated and looked down at her near empty beer glass. "But, you know, I've gotten use to those kids. I found out ways to help them and I don't mean just teaching—I've gotten things for them. Trouble is that no matter what I do for them, it really doesn't make a difference in the long run. Most of them will never get out of the poverty they're in. Most of them will not make it to forty. They'll be exploited by somebody with money and power and robbed by some petty government official or some thuggish tribal leader. What no one in the Peace Corps wants to admit is that no matter what we do for them, most of these kids don't really stand a chance."

"Let's try to think of the one or two kids," I said, "that break out of the mold just because you were there. I think that's pretty hopeful and worth drinking to."

She looked up, her white teeth gleaming through a wide smile. I had made her happy and that had made me happy.

"I'll drink to that," she said, lifting her glass so that some of the beer sloshed out.

A few days before Sam arrived, I had been talking to Madeleine at the airport bar and happened to mention that I was looking for a place to rent.

"I have just the place for you," she said. "It's on the beach near where you live now. It's owned by Mr. Habaka. He owns the Volkswagen dealership plus a few restaurants and a bunch of other businesses. Go by and see him and tell him that Madeleine sent you."

I drove Junebug into the parking lot of Mr. Habaka's dealership and, just as at any car dealership in the US, two men dressed in suits approached me with "let me sell you a car" written on their faces.

"I'm here to see Mr. Habaka about some rental property," I said. Their expressions immediately dropped. One of them pointed to the main office building, a new-looking structure of lightweight metal frames and tinted glass.

"He in de office," one of the salesmen said glumly.

Mr. Habaka was, as I expected, middle aged and balding. He had a heavy black mustache and thick, round shoulders. He was leaning back in his office chair smoking a cigar. I knocked quietly on the doorframe. He looked at me like someone caught by surprise.

"What can I do for you, young man?" he said, putting down his cigar.

"I'm here about your rental house on the beach. I'm a pilot for Monrovia Airlines and Madeleine at the Airport Bar told me that it is available."

"Ahhh, so you're a pilot. I think that is wonderful. I always wanted to be a pilot—such skill, such courage. How wonderful. And how is my friend Andre doing?"

"He's busy. Andre is a good manager and boss."

"Yes, so I have heard. That is good, that is good. And you know Madeleine. How is she?"

"Everyone at the airfield knows Madeleine. She's a very admired woman."

"Yes. Praise God, and she was a beautiful woman in her day." He paused. "She's still a beautiful woman. Truly beautiful women never become anything but beautiful. Don't you think, young man?"

"I haven't thought about it very much, Mr. Habaka."

"Of course you haven't, young man. At your age, why should you?"

"Mr. Habaka, about the rental house?"

"Yes, yes, of course. Why don't we go in your car? You did drive, didn't you? It isn't far. We could walk, but I think I'm beginning to feel a little arthritis creeping into my left hip."

He walked with me to where Junebug was parked. He stopped and uttered an exaggerated gasp.

"Young man," he exclaimed, "you should let me fix you up with a new car. This one looks straight out of a bombing raid."

"It'll get us there, Mr. Habaka."

The house was small but airy. The tiny living room opened up to a porch that looked directly out onto the beach. It was built of concrete blocks and painted white. The small galley kitchen seemed to have the basic necessities and the bedroom was just large enough to fit one double bed and a small chest of drawers. The bathroom had a shower stall that looked more like a three-by-three box stood on end, but the sink and toilet were both clean and new. And it was still within walking distance to the Ambassador's beach bar.

The furniture was midcentury modern, slightly battered and scarred but clean, and functional. I asked him how much. He said $300 a month. I knew better than to agree to the asking price—if you want to be respected in the Middle East you never agree to the asking price. I offered $200. He countered with $250. I hemmed and hawed for a while then accepted his offer. We shook hands, and I drove him back to his dealership.

A week later, Mr. Habaka informed me that the house was ready. I had gotten our usual room at the Ambassador and the next morning, after coffee, Sam and I walked along the beach to the house that we would be sharing. I had already put a deposit down and was told that I could move in any time. It wasn't locked, and I opened the front door to show her the inside. Mr. Habaka had had it cleaned, and there was a smell of fresh paint. I could see that she liked it.

"When can we move in?" she asked.

"Now, if you want. Have you got all of your things?"

"Everything I own is back at the hotel," she said.

"Then let's get it in and put away."

After properly placing Sam's few belongings in the house and in the only closet, we drove to the bunk house. Ku was there as I expected him to be, sitting on a stool in the kitchen.

"I shall be moving out, Ku."

"Eeh-menh! No, boss, No-menh!" he shouted.

"Yes, Ku. I shall be moving. Miss Sam and I are moving in together."

"You can do so hee, boss. Dere be plenty o room hee."

"No Ku, we need more room and we need privacy."

"You have privacy hee, boss. De other boss, dey will not humbug your woman."

"I know that, Ku, but we want to be by ourselves. Like you and your wife."

"Oh boss, ma wife an me, we na ever by ourselves. We ha family always."

"Then what do you do when you make love to your wife?"

"Dey turn way. Sometimes dey leave. Den sometimes dey watch. Dat de way it is hee, boss."

I thought about that for a while and really didn't have anything to say. Then, "Will you come and work for us, Ku? I will pay more."

"No tanks, boss. I ha very much to do an no time fo odder work. But my cousin, Binji, he need work bad—he will work for you, and he can cook too."

"Good!" I said. "Have him come and see me. We are at this address." I scribbled the address on an empty envelope and handed it to him. "It is just down the road. He must know where it is?"

"He do, boss, he do. I tell him today and he come see you jus now."

I really didn't have much in the way of material things. My "cold" weather clothes had long since been ruined by mold and mildew. I had left them out on a table near the road with a sign saying "Free." No one wanted them. I was down to four pairs of footwear—a pair of flip flops, a pair of canvas shoes, and worn out ankle boots that I used when flying, and some badly mildewed dress shoes. I packed my stuff carefully around my Uzi in the duffel bag that I used when I first came to Africa and headed to the new house.

We dumped everything in our small living room and opened the windows to the ocean breeze.

"I think we should name our house," Sam said.

"What a good idea. Anything in mind?" I asked.

"How about Pineapple Beach? Pineapples are all over the place here and they are the traditional symbol for welcome."

"Sounds good to me," I said.

Thus began many months of a kind of indefinable happiness that I had never experienced before. For the first time since coming to Africa, I looked forward to the rain. With the planes grounded, I was able to spend more time with Sam. When I did fly, she would check in with the Peace Corps offices downtown. They were more than happy to have an experienced worker pro bono, and Sam was happy to help.

I knew that she was opposed to marriage, but I wanted to give her something that represented, in a material way, how I felt about her. It had to be something big and with meaning. Fortunately, I had a flight coming up to one of the diamond mines near the Sierra Leone border. My passengers were two Mandingos, one of whom was Tajan, the man from whom I had bought my first diamond. We were almost friends by now. I told him, on the flight up to the mine, that I needed a special diamond . . . rough.

"For a lady?" he asked, smiling.

"Yes," I said, "for a very important lady."

"Don't worry, Mr. Pilot, we will find just de ting."

I landed on the dusty airstrip, taxied to the side of the runway, and shut down the engine.

Tajan and his companion deftly exited the airplane and assured me, again, that they would find something suitable. An hour or so later they returned and Tajan came up to me, opened his hand slowly and with a smile showed me a large rough diamond that I estimated to be at least twenty carats. It was an octahedral stone with a light yellow tint. With proper cleaning and polishing it would make a fine piece. I asked him for the price. Without hesitation he said that the price would be three hundred US—a bargain.

I looked directly into his eyes and said, "Tajan, you are a true gentleman."

He closed his eyes slowly and slightly bowed his head.

I had brought along more cash than I needed and had stowed it in a leather money pouch under my seat. I walked back to the plane, took out the fifteen twenty-dollar bills and paid him. He wrapped the diamond back up in the square cloth and handed it to me. I felt an unexpected sense of pride of ownership. I now possessed something ancient, rare, and beautiful that I could offer Sam.

Once back in Monrovia, I took the stone to my diamond expert, Old Man Louis. Old Man Louis (he was around fifty years old) had operated a jewelry shop since the mid-1940s. He was a Belgian who had fled Europe at the beginning of World War II. He had a thick Flemish accent and looked like he should have been a spy. I asked him to clean and polish it but under no circumstances was he to have it cut. He agreed and said that he could do the job while I waited. It took an hour or longer, but the finished work was excellent. The stone seemed to glow with a deep, pale yellow light yet retained all of its pristine beauty. I bought one of his special diamond gift boxes—finished in red burgundy leather with gold trim—and placed the diamond in the center of its ruffled satin interior. The problem now was how to give it to Sam.

Binji presented himself at the front door, one day, in the pouring rain. "Qua qua, Boss! Qua qua!" he shouted. "Binji heeya! Ee Binji heeya oh! Dews be heavy, so! Dews be heavy!"

I stood there looking at a small skinny boy of no more than fifteen years old. The rain had matted his hair and created ringlets that extended down over his forehead like black dripping icicles. Behind all that he was chattering nonstop in Liberian vernacular, smiling all the while. All I understood was Binji. I stood aside and motioned for him to come inside. Once in, he shook himself off like a dog.

"So you're Binji? Ku's cousin?" I asked.

"Ya boss! Das me, Binji! My man, Ku, he tole me you need a houseboy buku buku. He say yo woman ee too fine! Too fine! An you na wan strangers humbug yo! I cook fo you, I clean fo you, and den I hide. I no humbug you. I fine fine boy. I beg you let me be yo houseboy! I hold your foot!"

"Okay, okay, Binji," I said. "Slow down! You have to talk slowly and with words I can understand. Why don't you dry off and we'll see what you can do. First of all, do you know how to make a gin and tonic?"

Sam drove up as I was enjoying Binji's excellent gin and tonic. She had been in town to buy much needed supplies. I introduced her to Binji and Binji rattled off what he had told me—"I goo boy. I can coo an no humbug yo."

She seemed pleased with Binji. She asked him several questions about his family, about his school. Binji had dropped out of school to work, which was so often the case with the poor in Monrovia. Sam understood this well.

"Well, Binji," she said. "Why don't you start by making us a pot of coffee?"

Binji turned and almost ran into the kitchen. I could hear the sounds of implements slamming around, but I sensed that Binji would figure it out and find everything.

I decided on the direct approach. I would show her the diamond first, then try to explain during the initial shock. I placed the box on the small coffee table in our living room. She put her arms around me and kissed me.

She must have seen the box after she kissed me because she abruptly pushed me away and exclaimed, "What is that? Is that what I think it is? I thought we agreed."

"Why don't you open it before jumping to conclusions?"

She hesitated for a moment, her face completely empty of expression, then slowly picked the box up and turned it in her hand as though she were examining a biological specimen before opening it. She stared at the contents for a long moment, then looked up at me with a puzzled expression.

"It's a rough diamond; it's called an octahedral, pale yellow diamond. It's from a mine in Wiesua. It's for you, if you like it. If you don't, then it'll make a very prestigious miniature paper weight."

With that her mouth opened slightly, and she stared at me wide-eyed.

"It means simply that I'm very happy to have you here. That's all."

"It's beautiful!" she said. "I've never seen anything like it. What on earth should I do with it?"

"Well, it can be mounted as a ring or it can be cut and mounted in earrings. There are a lot of ways to use it. I am glad that you like it."

"Like it? I love it!" she said, clasping the diamond in both hands. "It's the way a diamond should be, just as nature made it. I think I'd like to have it mounted as a ring. You remember friendship rings, don't you?"

"Yes," I said. "I do."

"This will be our friendship ring. Is that okay?"

"I know a good jeweler in town. We'll take it tomorrow and see what he can do for us. As for now, let's celebrate." And, as if on cue, Binji arrived with the coffee.

Old Man Louis looked completely comfortable and unconcerned in his disordered and jumbled surroundings.

"Yes," he said with a wave of his gnarled hand. "I can mount it for you. You want gold, yes?" Sam nodded a yes. "Good, my dear. I will have it for you in two weeks. Don't bother me until then."

"How much, Mr. Louis?" Sam asked.

He held the diamond up to the light from the store front.

"Are you sure you don't want me to cut this for you?"

"Yes, I'm sure," Sam said. "Under no circumstances do I want it cut."

Old Man Louis shrugged. "Whatever you want, my dear. The customer is always right." He looked at the diamond again and said, "I'll mount it for you for fifty US dollars. That's my best price. You won't find anyone what will do it cheaper, I promise you. Wait and I will give you a receipt for it."

The receipt contained a description of the stone, its weight, and a statement that it was owned by the below signature.

"Thank you, Mr. Louis. We'll be by in a couple of weeks to pick it up."

As we were leaving, Sam asked me what would stop him from selling the diamond and telling us it had been stolen.

"We have the receipt, and there is an old law in Liberia that helps protect against such things," I said. She looked at me and I knew what she was thinking.

"It's called 'I'll blow your brains out if you steal from me.' Old Man

Louis has been here since nineteen forty-five and is well aware of this law, and beside that, he's earned a reputation for fair dealing and honesty, and that's what keeps his business going."

CHAPTER 32

TAKE DOWN

The ring was ready when Old Man Louis said it would be, and he had lived up to his reputation for doing good work. We decided to celebrate, so we drove to Heinz and Maria's. It was still early, and the only customers were three men drinking at the bar—they were muscular with broad necks and looked like freelance construction workers.

Sam and I picked an out-of-the-way table and we each ordered a beer from the new, pretty German waitress. The construction workers would leer at her from time to time. One of them, with a mass of unkempt blond hair, maintained a constant smile, or maybe it was more of a smirk, when he looked at her. His left ear lobe was missing and, like a prize fighter, he kept unconsciously flexing his right hand. The other two wore their hair close cropped, which accentuated their angular features.

They kept calling out to the girl, "*O fraulein! Fraulein!*"

The waitress ignored them except to bring them more beer. I noticed the man with the missing ear lobe looking our way several times and I wondered briefly if he recognized us—Monrovia can be a small place.

Sam seemed happy and appeared not to notice the men at the bar. She looked at the ring almost compulsively and touched it with the fore finger of her left hand.

"It's truly beautiful," she said. The waitress brought our beers.

We started chatting about the future and as we did so, entered into our own private cocoon of euphoria. We had a host of options before us, and they were all good. It was one of those moments that would stand still for the rest of my life.

I finished the beer and, as often occurs with carbonated beverages, had to relieve myself. I told Sam that I had to go to the necessary room. She smiled and told me not to be too long. I wasn't long, but when I got back to the table she wasn't there. I looked quickly around. The man with the missing ear lobe was looking in my direction and sniggering. She might have gone to the restroom, so I waited for a few minutes. The man had stopped sniggering and with a look of utter contempt turned back to the bar and ordered another beer.

The minutes passed. She must be in the car, I reasoned, and walked outside toward Junebug. I could see her in the passenger seat. As I got closer, I could see that her head was bowed and that she was trembling. Once at the car I opened the driver side door. She was weeping into her hands. She looked up at me, her eyes swimming in tears.

"That man in there, the big one with the blond hair—he's the one." She broke down into sobs.

"Whuddya mean, he's the one? The one with part of his ear missing? He's the one that attacked you in Voinjama?"

She hesitated then looked away. "Yes, he recognized me. He said that he knew who I was and he was going to find out where I lived then he was going to come and fuck me to death." She started sobbing again.

I felt the skin around my head and face tighten like shrinking fabric. A sense of rage came over me that I had never experienced before. It wasn't simply that he had threatened and frightened Sam into this crumbling emotional state, but he had also entered into our private lives by ruining, forever, an exquisitely happy occasion.

I reached under the driver seat and felt my nine millimeter Llama in its holster, which had been fastened to the underside of the seat. I unsnapped the holster and withdrew the Llama.

"No!" she said. "It's not worth that!"

"This is Liberia and obviously this guy doesn't know the rules. I'll be back soon."

I pushed the gun under the belt behind my back and slowly walked back into Heinz and Maria's. The construction workers were still sitting at the bar. The man with the blond hair and missing ear lobe sipped his beer and did not turn around. I walked quietly but quickly up behind him, took my Llama out and as hard and quickly as I could, hit him in the head with the butt of the gun just above the right ear. He dropped to the floor like a sack of beans. The German waitress turned when she heard the sound, looked horrified, and dropped the plates she was holding. I kicked him in the midsection as hard as I could then turned him over on his back with my foot. The other two jumped off of their seats and faced me. I pointed the Llama at them. They held their hands toward me palms out; nevertheless, they looked like a couple of bulls with their heads down ready to charge.

"Tell your friend when he regains consciousness, if he does, that if he comes near my wife, I'll empty this magazine into him. Do you understand me?"

They didn't move or indicate that they had comprehended what I had said. I shouted at the top of my voice, "*Verstehen sie mich!*"

They both nodded that they did.

"*Sag es!*" I shouted.

"*Ja! Ja! Wir verstehen sie!* Ve vill tell him!"

I backed away slowly then put the Llama back under my belt and walked hurriedly to the car. Once there, I jumped in and drove away, saying to Sam only that I had taken care of it and that she was safe, but she wanted to know what had happened.

"What did you do? What did you do?" Sam shouted.

I told her what had happened.

"Do you think you killed him?"

"I may have. If not, he's going to have one almighty headache if he wakes up."

"We had better get outta here right away. Let's get back to the house, throw some things in a bag, and get to the airport. Cape Town seems far enough away."

CHAPTER 33

CAPE TOWN

Cape Town was as different from Monrovia as it was possible to get. It was a large city in the summer of 1967. It was rich and booming and the political construct of Apartheid was at its height. The blacks, coloreds (these were people of mixed race), and Indians (these included people from India, Pakistan, and Asia) had been forcibly moved from the city center into suburban ghettos. Apartheid went further than that when the government, dominated by the all-white National Party, deprived the black population of their South African citizenship and "resettled" them in what were called self-governing Bantustans. The Apartheid government had the National Party use military and police force to ensure that all government rulings and regulations were carried out.

Sam and I were aware of Apartheid when we arrived in Cape Town, but not fully knowledgeable of the extent of the atrocities associated with it. It was summer in Cape Town, a temperate summer, not the hot, dry season in Liberia, and beautiful, but we were thinking more of escape than anything else. Once there, the idea of escape took on a very real meaning to me, since I truly did not know if I had killed the construction worker. The owners of Heinz and Maria's knew me and would probably keep quiet, but if the construction worker died and the police got involved, they would protect themselves before anyone else. And that included me.

Our hotel was on Lagoon Beach. We had a good view of the ocean, and in the distance we could see Robben Island. Robben Island had been used for about every nefarious purpose human beings could think of. It had been used as a prison since the mid-seventh century. In 1968 it held several political prisoners, Nelson Mandela being one. It had been a leper colony in the more distant past and, at one time, was a whaling station base. All this on a scrap of an island about two miles long and one mile wide. In the distance, Table Mountain seemed to rise from the Atlantic Ocean, looking rather formidable but very majestic, like a piece of flat earth that had suddenly been elevated above the rest of the world.

Since we found ourselves in this beautiful spot, we decided to take advantage of the situation and play tourist. We spent most of our time lounging on the beach, drinking at the bar, and exploring the town. We used taxies rather than renting a car. The drivers knew the town much better than we did, and every night that we went out, they took us to a different club or theater.

After about a week, I pumped up my nerve and called the bunk house and left word for Deet to call me. Several days later, he did. It was early in the morning. He said that he knew that I would be sober and alert. I asked him if he had heard about the incident at Heinz and Maria's.

"Ya," he said. "Everyone knows. You are quite de hero. Bad ass Ken vee vill call you."

"How is the man? Is he dead, badly injured, what?"

"Nein, he got up off de floor, I'm told, shook his head so that de brains rattled around a bit. Den held his head and asked fur a beer. Dere was some blut und maybe some swelling, but dat vas all. Oh, ya! His buddies gave him your message. I tink he listened und understood. I don't tink you vill have to vorry about him again. Oh ya, und anodder bit of news. Jack Dupree, you know, dat mousy frog dat followed Andre around? He vas found dead on the airport road—shot tru de head. Eider he cheated someone, knew too much, or dey jus couldn' stand looking at him anymore."

Then followed the usual question of what we were doing, how was Cape Town, and was "my girlfriend" being good to me.

I slowly put the phone hand piece back on its hook, greatly relieved. I did know that a blow to the head could do a lot of damage, and that complications could show up much later. I would have to keep my fingers crossed, although if the man dropped dead tomorrow I had real doubts that the Monrovian police would care.

I was glad that the man did not die, but I wasn't sorry for the action I took. He had, after all, threatened to rape Sam, and there was no reason to assume he would not have carried out his threat. And it would have been a supreme act of silliness to report the threat to the police.

I pushed the whole matter to a dark, dusty corner of my mind and made it a point of principle to enjoy our visit in Cape Town. It was a matter of great importance, now, that Sam put the incident away too, and I was going to do all that I could to make that happen.

Sam was finishing breakfast in bed when I told her the news. She leaped out of bed and screamed with joy.

"Thank God we don't have to carry that burden around for the rest of our lives," she said, hugging me and kissing me. She stepped back, smiled at me, and said, "You know, Ken, you really are one bad-ass kinda guy!"

With the news that I wasn't a wanted man it seemed safe to return to Monrovia; nevertheless, we were both sorry to leave Cape Town. Despite the rampant social injustices, the blatant economic disparities, and the rigid class structure along racial lines, we did like and enjoy the city and all of the natural beauty around it.

We took a taxi from Robertsfield back to Pineapple Beach. Binji had kept it clean and dusted while we were away. I had paid him for a month, so he essentially had a month's paid vacation, something rare in Liberia. It was late and dark. We groped around for lights, found them, and were delighted to discover that they were working. We were doubly delighted to discover that water was available and, even though we had no hot water, the showers were refreshing. The showers drained what was left of our energy and we fell into bed, barely having strength enough to pull the mosquito netting over us.

CHAPTER 34

DUNG BEETLES

Monrovia Airlines had a couple of British geologists from SLDMC (Sierra Leone Diamond Mining Company) contract with us. They came at the behest of the local government. Their job was to explore all of the creeks up country to find more cashes of diamonds. They would go very deep into the bush with the latest instrumentation and technology. They would very slowly and systematically search for new pipes of diamonds rising up from the earth's core.

Shortly after returning from South Africa, I flew a few of these geologists deep into Nimba country. The village had a hard dirt strip that made it easy for me to land. The Head Man approached and asked if we needed help unloading. I told him that we did and thanked him for the offer. As the boys were unloading the geologist's gear, a young village boy ran up to the plane with a huge smile on his face and his hands spread out like an airplane.

"RRRRRRRRRRRRRRR! RRRRRRRRRRRR!" he shouted.

"That's pretty good," I said. "Are you an airplane?"

"Da ma engine voice!" he said, showing a mouthful of teeth when he smiled.

"Oh, Mista Pilot, Mista Pilot. Can you hep me, oh?"

The boy's mother had finally caught up with him and was, I think, panting and pleading for me do something but I couldn't fully understand her.

"Say that again . . . what do you need?"

"Ya go to Robafee, oh?"

"Robertsfield?" I asked. "No. I'm going to Spriggs-Payne, but its right nearby."

"Okay, da boy, he need to go to his pa in de city," the woman said. "His pa send him to school. Can you do dat, oh! I hold your foot, oh!"

"I can. I certainly can. But it costs money. It costs fifteen dollars."

"Fiteen dolla? Oooo, dat dollar too many. I got fie dolla here. But I can gi yo dash. You wan dash?

"Like what?" I asked.

"Oh, yama, yama! Ting like dry fee, cassava lee, an pawpaw." She uncovered her basket filled with ripe papaya, cassava leaves, and dried fish.

"Okay, Mama. I'll get him there. Tell the boy to get his stuff. And have the Head Man put his pa's name on a piece of paper."

The British geologists were loading up the last backpack, ready to head out. I saw them approach what looked like a dark brown, glistening rivulet crossing the runway. There had been no rain recently, so it was strange to see any kind of water flowing anywhere. One of the geologists had a stick and was walking toward it.

"Hold on there," I said. "I wouldn't do that if I were you."

"Come and look at this," one of them said. "It's not water, it is a zillion ants, all marching in a big fat line. I was just going to see if they would march around my foot if I put it there."

"Then I'm glad I stopped you," I said. "They are driver ants. They are predatory, and they devour any edible organic material in their path. And that would include your foot, mate."

The geologist jumped back in terror and, dropping his stick, ran to where the bags and equipment were being stacked.

The boy loved the flight. He had seen airplanes before but had never flown in one. I realized, as we got closer to Monrovia, that he had never been out of his village. He had never seen a modern building. I radioed ahead to have a taxi waiting for him when we arrived so he could get to his father as soon as possible. The landing was smooth and I taxied up to the hangar where Paterson was waiting. I looked at the boy. His expression of glee had changed to one of terror.

I helped him get out of the cockpit very slowly. He was like a caged wild animal. Paterson said something unintelligible to him and he showed a weak smile. At that moment the taxi pulled up and stopped in front of us. The boy screamed and started running as fast as he could. The taxi, which was a much battered 1955 Ford Fairlane, started following him. The boy let out another scream. I realized that the boy had never seen an automobile before. He must have thought a giant monster was chasing him.

When I told Sam, she confirmed my supposition and said that it was not uncommon for children raised in the bush to have never seen a car but be very familiar with airplanes. She suggested that we go to the beach bar since Colin and Ozzie said earlier that they would be there, and she thought it would be good for us to have a few laughs with them.

"Are you sure?" I asked a little surprised. "I didn't think Ozzie was your favorite kind of guy."

"Friends are few and far between around here sometimes, and some of his stories can be fun."

We walked down the beach to the bar. Colin and Ozzie were there with a couple of other pilots.

"Look who's back! That was some vanishing act you pulled! For a moment there, I though you joined the long list of mysteriously missing persons," Colin said. "Have a seat, mates, and I'll buy you a drink."

"Thanks," I said. "Strangely enough, it's nice to be back."

"I just got back too," Ozzie said. "I've been up country with a team of Yank surveyors."

Sam turned to me and said, "See, I told you he would have a story to tell."

Ozzie grinned and started again. "I swear, these guys must have been financed through bloody USAID. They had loads of food, top-notch camping equipment, some really fine surveying equipment, and they brought along five boys to carry it all. Anyway, we got along just fine, and they asked if I wanted to go along and camp with them in the bush. 'Sure,' I said. I could see that I would eat and sleep better with them than I would at home."

"So what were they surveying?" Sam asked.

"Well, I flew them over to Grand Geheh County southeast of here. They said there were plans to cut a road from Zwedru on down to Fish Town. What they were doing this trip was between Babu and Duabo. The bush is real dense there; I can't see how they're gonna do it. I'm tellin' ya, it was some adventure!"

There was a chorus of "So what happened" from his drinking buddies.

"Okay, so I joined them on Friday and spent Saturday and Sunday with them. We were out in the middle of nowhere. I mean, middle of nooowhere. It was easy going and flat until we got to the edge of a forest when it got really hilly. So we loaded up the boys with all the gear and we start going down this trail. I'm happy as a dung beetle in shit! I feel like a boy scout on holiday.

"So the bearers, they're carrying the loads, and we got to a creek. After crossing it, we were going down another steep trail. It was kind of muddy. And all of a sudden the bearers drop everything and come running back. And we're in the jungle now, mates. I mean, these trees are going up two hundred feet. No place to go off the trail. So they come running by us. What the fuck is that?

"It turned out there was an elephant on the trail with its back to us. Now these are bush elephants. They aren't the huge ones you see in East Africa. But they're still elephants. And it's got its back to us. We could see its tail, and it was making some kind horrible grunting sound. I'm told it's called *musth*. The elephant's in love, you see. It was that time of the year for a male elephant. Their eyes weep, they snort, and they are extremely aggressive. And, you know, of course, they don't want anybody in their territory, and he probably smells a female somewhere or he has a female. Who knows? So, it's obvious we can't go any further."

Ozzie reaches for his beer and takes a long, slow swallow. He knows he has a captive audience. He continues, "This elephant takes up the whole trail. So this Rick guy—I can tell you what, he had cajones. He had a double-barreled shot gun. That was his only armor. I had my pistol. He goes up to it behind the ear, and it's snorting—you know, an elephant is a big animal. And he puts both barrels right on the elephant, you know, behind the ear. *Boom! Boom!* The elephant takes off running down the hill!"

Everyone was silent and focused.

"He didn't shoot the elephant, did he?" I asked.

"Yeah, he shot the elephant. Two shots, right here behind the ear. And the elephant is just stampeding down the trail. It's going downhill. Then Rick says, 'Let's go, let's get it.' And of course, the bearers are nowhere to be seen. I mean, they're half a mile back, watching. So we're chasing this thing, and all of a sudden the trail makes this sharp turn and the elephant isn't there. It's dropped out of sight, off down in the jungle. And we say, 'Shit, what's happening?'

"We start walking back up the trail. And whoa! There it is. The elephant has gone into the bush, doubled back and come up behind us. We're dead ... We are dead meat! And in the panic, in the excitement, Rick didn't reload. All I had was my little 25 automatic—big fucking deal.

"There it was, just standing there. We were all just standing there. And then, just like that, it dropped dead! So it came up behind us and died."

Colin took a gulp from his drink.

"It had come around behind you to settle the score," one of the men said.

"Aye, to settle the score. But I have the tail. The guys took the tusks. And, of course the boys, when they saw that the elephant was dead, they went berserk. They chopped it up with their pangas and saved every edible thing on it. At least they didn't leave it for the monkeys to eat."

Walking home along the beach, Sam was very quiet. Finally, she turned to me and said, "Your Liberia and my Liberia are just worlds apart. The native

Liberians that I have been dealing with out in the bush are basically sweet, kind, and caring people. Their ignorance is not stupidity; it is the lack of access to any kind of modern infrastructure whatsoever. They have little or no electricity, no plumbing, and many times no roads or ready access to clean water. Without the Peace Corps, they would be almost without any education at all. And why don't they have that infrastructure? It's because the Liberians you deal with, the Big Men, the Americo-Liberians keep it all for themselves. My God, the money flowing into this place is staggering. But do any of the kids up in Lofa country see any of it? No. Not one penny!"

"Yes," I said, "but the Ozzies and Colins and Deets, and even me's of this country aren't African. We are just doing a job."

"Do you really think that any of them would be here if there weren't a huge amount of money to be made? Tubman has lured the big international corporations here with assurances of huge profits and tax relief. The only money that trickles down from that wealth is to the company employees and the satellite businesses that grew from them. Very few of them are local people. Oh, I forgot. There is the money that goes to the tribal head men to keep them happy. It's a shitty system. And that's where Ozzie, Colin, and Deet come in. They live in this shit. They all try and hoard their crap so that someday they will be rich enough to leave this shit hole. But they never do. They never will. Why? Because they have come to love living in shit. They are at home here. They are comfortable here. They, the international corporations, the big men are just a bunch of dung beetles getting as much of this shit as they can. You know, Ken, wealth can do some good, but most of the time it causes a lot of pain and torture."

I stopped and looked at her. The moon's reflection on the water lit up her face. She was very serious. "I'm glad you didn't include me in with Ozzie and the rest."

"No," she said, smiling, "you are not the same as they are. I can see that Africa is wearing you down. I don't think we'll be here much longer."

CHAPTER 35

THE GLASS HOUSE

Toward the end of the wet season, Andre started having more contracts than he could fill. I flew every day, transporting Peace Corp volunteers, spare parts for mining equipment and vehicles, bags of rice, boxes of iced fish, Lebanese merchants, Portuguese traders, Mandingos and, on one occasion, a German from Heidelberg who couldn't stop glancing around.

Sam got into the agreeable practice of making coffee in the morning and waking me up with a cup held very near my nose. One morning, however, instead of being awakened by the delightful aroma of freshly brewed coffee, I was startled out of bed by the loud rattle of automatic gunfire. It was coming from inside the house. Trying not to imagine a million things, I leaped out of bed taking the mosquito netting with me and ran toward the sound of the gunfire. I found Sam standing in a pool of water holding the Uzi that had been the gift of Major Ahud. The new toilet looked like a pile of clay and porcelain rubble. Water was spurting from broken pipes, and in the midst of it lay what remained of the body of a rather long snake.

"Coffee is on the stove," she said.

"Never mind the coffee. What the hell happened here?"

"It's a spitting cobra. I've run across them in the bush—very nasty creatures. They spit venom through their fangs at your eyes. They very seldom miss. The stuff is like suddenly having hot sand poured in your eyes, only this stuff can cause permanent blindness. It's also cytotoxic."

"What does that mean?"

"Basically, it won't get through your skin but if you've got an opening in the skin and the venom comes into contact with it, the cells die and liquefy—leaves a really messy wound."

I reached down, next to the remains of the toilet, and turned off the water valve.

"Sorry I had to use the Uzi. With these snakes there is no time to fool around and I couldn't think of anything else. They told us that if we ever encountered one to get at least ten feet away and cover our eyes. Well, that didn't seem too practical since the thing was already in the house. You have to kill these things from a distance. I didn't want to come and get you because by the time I did that and we got to the bathroom, the thing could have gotten anywhere in the house. I am sorry that I destroyed the toilet. I'll pay for it to be replaced."

"Oh, forget about it. I'm glad you killed the vile thing. I don't care about the toilet. I'll call someone and get it fixed."

It was over a week before we could get a replacement and hire a plumber who seemed to know what he was doing. Mr. Habaka was not very pleased either, but he calmed down when I explained that I would fix everything and pay for all damages and that a deadly snake in his house was not his fault.

Binji knew about spitting cobras and at first refused to get near it, but twenty dollars gradually persuaded him.

"Mamba cobra is bad juju, boss, bad juju," Binji said. "Da cobra na sposed ta be here, boss. It sposed ta be in da bush. An de head! Da head, da head still a danger. We got ta burn da head. Ya burn it good."

"We have no way to burn it, Binji. We must bury it. Bury it deep enough so the dogs will not dig it up. Will you do that?"

Binji looked thoughtful for a moment, then nodded. "I do dat, boss. I bury it. But ah gotta talk to juju man fuss. Ya, I talk to juju man."

After that, we formed a habit of checking everything before we used it— the bed, the closet, the kitchen stove, everything. We found a few spiders that looked quite deadly, a nest of cockroaches, traces of rats, and other suspicious sources of plague and disease. Binji didn't like dealing with these things at first. He considered such things in a house to be part of the natural environment. Nevertheless, I offered to pay him a bonus for cleaning them up. Fortunately, in this instance, his love of capital gains outweighed his fear of bad juju.

Later, as we sat on the beach with our gin and tonics in hand, we watched the incessant parade of beach scavengers looking for items to sell. Some little boy would always see us and try to sell us a shell or a dead fish he'd found. I'd always give them a penny or two, so I suppose that's why they kept coming back.

"We always see people walking the beach but never swimming," Sam said. "Have you ever gone into the surf?"

"No. The waves look pretty benign from here, but closer to the surf they are huge. And there is a strong undertow. Every year, one or two bodies wash up on shore. They're usually tourists who didn't believe the locals."

"Good to know. So when are you flying next?"

"Tomorrow I have to run some supplies up the coast to Cape Mount. By the way, would you like to come along with me? There is a village on the coast there where we can rent a dugout canoe. We can get some of the local fishermen to take us out and maybe we can even do some fishing."

"Sure," Sam said. "I'll ask Binji to pack us a lunch."

Our canoe ride was just that, a ride. But it was fun being on the water. We didn't have much luck fishing, but the local fishermen hauled in a net full of wiggling sea worms, which made them happy. These sea worms looked like small red sausages. Once ashore, one of the fishermen started quickly preparing the worms. They were still wiggling when they chopped them up into little o-rings. Then the o-rings kept wiggling. Right away, the fisherman covered them with pili pili hot sauce and began popping them in their mouths.

"You wan one, missa?" the fisherman asked me.

"Not me! Sam, how about you?"

"Sure, I'll try one," she said.

With a show of great bravery, she dropped two into her mouth. I waited.

She was trying to be nonchalant. Then her eyes opened wide followed by her mouth. I thought she was going to scream, but nothing came out but a breathy, "Hey hah!"

"What?" I said.

"Hey Hah! The pili pili is really hah, hah!"

"Yeah, I know it's hot but what do the worms taste like?"

"No taste! Hah, hah. As far as I can tell, no taste at all just hot, hot!"

On the way home, I thought Sam would be interested in the famous, or notorious, Glass House. I altered course to take us near a stretch of isolated beach not far from Robertsport. I landed on the beach, secured the airplane, and led Sam over a couple of dunes to where we could clearly see the house.

It was a small house with a scaled down front porch. The house was made entirely of glass bottles—soft drink bottles, whisky bottles, even perfume bottles—all mortared together as if they were bricks and resembling a three-dimensional impressionist mosaic. The only wood to be seen was at the door and window frames. The roof was made of corrugated metal.

"I'm glad to see it's still here," I said. "I used to fly in here every now and then."

"What is it? Whose is it?"

"It belonged to an ex-Luftwaffe pilot by the name of Diesel. He was here long before I got here. He lived here with his German wife, Alice, and a couple of house boys. He had his own airplane, so he set up his own air transport service, dealing almost exclusively in diamonds. All the air service operations around here deal in diamonds one way or another. Andre does and obviously," I said, looking down at her ring, "I do too. Anyway, Diesel would fly to the Sierra Leone border every morning and pick up the diamond smugglers. Sierra Leone is one of the easiest borders for this kind of thing. It was all set up. There was a customs guy on the Liberian side, and he would collect the big bucks. But it looked legal on paper. So smugglers from Ivory Coast, Guinea, and Mali all came though Sierra Leone. Very close to where

Diesel lived. He had been doing this, very successfully, for quite a long time, until suddenly, one day, he disappeared."

"Did one of the smugglers get him?" she asked.

"Not likely," I said. "The diamond buyers are 99 percent Mandingo. No, the rumor was that he was harboring a bigwig ex-Nazi and the Israelis were on to him."

"What happened to him?"

"Some time after he disappeared, parts of an airplane believed to be his were found washed up on a beach in Sierra Leone but nothing identifiable."

"So it could have been anything," Sam said. "He could have gone down in the ocean or escaped in the bush. Nobody would have ever found him."

"Yes, it could have been anything, but it wouldn't surprise me to learn that Herr Diesel is counting his money in his suite at The Grand Hotel, Punta del Este, right now."

"What about his wife?"

"Alice stayed on. She had a couple of German boyfriends move in with her but never anything permanent. She tried to keep up the diamond business. She didn't have a plane but there was this woman, also German, whom I would fly to and from the glass house from Sierra Leone. We all got to be friends of a sort, and I enjoyed visiting. Then, one day, when I'd flown in the other woman from Sierra Leone, Alice asked me if I would go down the beach to buy some fish from the fishermen coming in. When I came back both women were gone. I never saw either of them again."

"Do you think they left on their own, or did someone kidnap them?"

"Who knows," I said. "I think we've both been in Liberia long enough now to know that that question will never be answered. Rumors, certainly, but no one will ever know for sure."

CHAPTER 36

GUINEA WORM

The wet season was due to start up in another month, and I really didn't know if I could face it once again. It was April, and I wasn't feeling well. I had been dragging for several days and decided to take it easy for a day or so. Binji arrived later than usual. He was excited and nearly out of breath from peddling his bicycle at high speed.

"Boss!" he yelled, "Boss, did ya hee? Did ya hee?"

"Hear what?"

"Merica in revolt! Merica in flames! Merica in bad, bad way!"

"What the hell are you talking about, Binji?"

"De Big Man, boss, King—he been shot dead. Bla people all over Merica in revolt; dey shootin, robbin stores, burnin car—all ting like dat."

Sam walked into the room as Binji was speaking. Her face was distorted. She clasped her hand to her throat—a clear sign of distress.

"Where did you learn this, Binji?"

"It de radio, boss, das wuh make me late."

We didn't own a radio. Radio broadcasts, when the Monrovia radio station was on the air, were usually either exercises in state propaganda or blaring local music. But, I had to admit, I wondered what the Liberian government would make out of this, since President Tubman depended on the US for various forms of aid and, ironic as it sounds, the Americo-Liberians seemed rather proud of their American heritage.

"Should we contact the Embassy, maybe go there?" Sam asked.

"I think the Embassy is probably going to be swamped right now. The hotel has a television in the lobby. That may have something."

Sam and I walked over to the Ambassador as quickly as we could. The lobby was crowded with people all gathered around a black-and-white television mounted on a table. The pictures bore no resemblance to the America I knew—people running wild, smashing in store windows with bricks and chairs, setting cars on fire, and news reporters barely able to conceal their excitement.

"That's it, mates," said someone with a British accent. "America's going down the hole. Serves um right, I'd say."

"They should have learned from us and adopted Apartheid. It works," said another in a South African voice.

"These pictures are coming from Washington," I mentioned to Sam. "I want to try and reach my father."

We left the Ambassador and returned to the beach house. We had a phone there, but I was unable to get through. The Liberian phone company only worked for three to five hours a day and still used the old operator system. Monrovia Airlines had a radio transmitter that could be linked to the international phone system. It was to be used for business only, but maybe I could talk Andre into letting me use it. I drove as fast as I could to the operations office. Andre was there and had heard the news. Yes, I could use the radio.

My father assured me that the rioting was not widespread and that the police were simply letting it run out of steam. "After that," he said, "we can all talk. Nothing to worry about."

I knew that he was lying but, nevertheless, I was somewhat relieved that he was able to talk to me and confident enough to lie. I switched off the radio and thanked Andre. He looked at me and asked if I was feeling all right. I told him that I was fine.

"You look a little pale. Maybe you should see a doctor."

I thanked him for his concern and, without having a good reason or any reason at all, drove over to the Airport Bar. Colin was there nursing a beer. He had heard about the shooting of Martin Luther King.

"Well matey, looks like the US has become just another Latin American style hole that shoots the leaders they don't like. You won't find that in the UK, no sir. We have our problems but nutters with guns ain't one of them."

I didn't feel like discussing it with him, and I certainly did not feel like arguing. I ordered a beer and, for a moment, enjoyed the feel of the cold bottle against my forehead.

"You feeling all right, mate? You don't look so good—not malaria again, ya think?"

"No, it's not malaria, I know malaria, but you're the second person to ask me that today. I feel a little tired, that's all."

I took a long swill of the beer. I noticed Madeleine looking at me.

"I feel fine," I said to her. Almost immediately after I said it I felt myself slipping off the bar stool and on to the floor. I was conscious but did not seem able to move. In an instant Madeleine was around the bar and kneeling next to me. Colin was standing over me, a puzzled look on his face. I could feel Madeleine's hands probing my midsection.

"I've seen this before," she said. She wrote something on one of the bar napkins and handed it to Colin.

"Take him to this doctor now! Do not wait!" she said.

Colin helped me to his car, a red 1953 Morris Minor Saloon. I don't know which was worse, the pain I was beginning to feel in my abdomen or the bouncing, jolting, lurching ride curled up in the Morris. The waiting room was filled with patients all looking wide-eyed at me.

"Umm sorry all," Colin said, "but this in an emergency."

He opened the door to the receptionist office and sat me down on a small wooden chair. He handed Madeleine's note to the receptionist who quickly ran out of the office.

In a few moments she was back with a doctor—a middle-aged man with North African features. He was holding the note in his hand.

"Follow me," he said to Colin.

Colin helped me out of the chair and, with my arm over his shoulders, got me to the doctor's examining room. The doctor told me to undress down to my undershorts and motioned that I should get up onto the examining table. Colin saluted in the British fashion and left the room followed by the receptionist.

"Won't your other patients be upset—putting me ahead of the line, doctor?"

He smiled. "No, they won't be upset with me. They'll think that you are just another white man exercising his privilege."

"We both know that I don't fit into that category. Why did you take me?"

"Madeleine is a very old friend. I owe her from when I first came here. And from the looks of things, she was right to be concerned." The doctor poked and pushed on my abdomen. "You are a pilot for Monrovia Airline?"

I nodded.

"I am Doctor Klatt. I always wanted to be a pilot but I never had the time for it. It must be wonderful."

"It isn't really like that," I said.

"Aaaha!" he said. "Young man, you have a very common malady here in West Africa. You have the hepatitis."

He must have noticed the expression on my face. "If you will put yourself into my care, I will cure you of this disease, but you must do exactly as I tell you."

The doctor injected me with a clear fluid then wrote out a prescription and a long list of stuff that I wasn't to eat or drink. I was to come back in a week.

"I will repeat what I have written here so that it is clear to you. You must come back every week for glucose treatment, no fat of any kind, only lean meat if you can find it, no carbohydrates and absolutely no alcohol. That is very serious—no alcohol, not even a small beer or drop of wine. Is that clear to you?

"Very clear," I said.

Colin was in the waiting room smoking a cigarette and leafing through a magazine. He took me home. I told him that I had hepatitis.

"Oh matey, that's bad. No drinking for the rest of your life! But cheer up, you'll probably be dead soon, so you won't have to suffer long."

Sam took the news as I thought she would: with confidence and optimism. I would not work for the next six weeks. Andre was good about it even though he was losing pilots right and left. Most of his German pilots were leaving to work for a startup aircraft manufacturer in Brazil. He was busy recruiting a recent influx of Spanish pilots who were reported to be very good. For the next few weeks I was too weak to do anything strenuous.

My physical weakness, combined with the frequent rain and high humidity, confined me to what I now realized was a very small house. My visits to Dr. Klatt were something close to agony, but gradually I began to gain strength. The yellow in my eyes started to clear and the thought of anything alcoholic nearly made me throw up. Ironically, Sam got a part-time job as a bartender at the Ambassador's beach bar and became quite proficient at mixology.

I took this opportunity to do some sketching. I made a sketch of Sam that I did not show her. I sketched from memory and from photographs that Sam had taken. I even started painting the "old man with his wife" on a plywood panel.

When I started back to work in June, most of the pilots now working for the air service operators were new. I was considered the old man and with good reason. I had been there a long time by Liberian standards; most of the new pilots were younger than me. There were a couple of American boys from the Midwest, several English lads, a Canadian, and the rest were Spanish. I couldn't speak Spanish but, fortunately, they could speak enough English to operate in the aviation environment. English, for reasons unknown to me, was becoming the language of commercial aviation even in West Africa.

I had just returned from a trip to the iron mines, and we were well into the wet season. I was enjoying a lemonade made by Sam's expert hand when Colin walked out onto our porch.

"What the hell is happening in your country, mate?" I asked him what he meant. Sam heard his comment and stopped what she was doing.

"Some fucker shot Robert Kennedy in the head."

"Is he dead?" I asked

"It's a bullet in the head, mate."

It was difficult, often impossible, to explain to the various people who came up to me in the next few weeks that the United States of America was not descending into chaos, that the military would not take over and there would not be a coup d'état.

Older, expatriate Germans took a particular delight in what they were sure was the collapse of American democracy. I suppose that it was somewhat of a disappointment to them that the US continued with the work of presidential nomination without interruption. I will say, however, that the younger Germans were very concerned and saw the survival of America as the only hope against what they were sure would be an eventual war against the Russians.

The US did not collapse, as I reminded my friends later that summer. However, that August, I did start to have genuine questions about the future of my country while watching the riots in Chicago during the Democratic National Convention. We watched it on the new television set up in the Ambassador's beach bar. Most of the people hanging around the bar were shaking their heads.

"You had better apply for political asylum, my friend, because it doesn't look like you're going to have much of a country to go back to" was the most frequent comment. My parents, who were Democrats, knew what was happening. They knew that there had been a move on the part of the democratic establishment to back LBJ's civil rights act. Therefore, the riots.

Sam, on the other hand, had been in contact with her family in Seattle and, since they were historic supporters of the Republican Party, could have cared less about what the democrats were doing in Chicago and didn't have the slightest fear for the survival of American democracy.

"Ich must say," Deet said to me while downing a hefty glass of scotch, "it does remind me of Germany vin I vas a boy—de Sturmabteilung racing through de streets beating up on Communists and Jews. Ya, just like Germany, no different, my friend. Dis Mayor Daley you've got, he would make a good Nazi!"

America did survive, much to the puzzlement of most of the people I knew in Liberia. Much of my work by the end of August 1968 was training new pilots on the routes, procedures, airfields, and customs of the various groups of people they would have to deal with.

I returned home after a particularly exhausting day. Sam had the night off from the Ambassador's beach bar. I had been experiencing a burning pain in my right leg for some time but passed it off as a strain since I had also been doing a lot of maintenance on the company's airplanes.

I felt a not untypical urge to use the toilet, so I grabbed the closest newspaper I could find and went in to, as is said, sit upon the throne. I was glancing through a report of President Tubman's latest grandstand when I felt a burning, wet sensation in my right knee. I put the paper to one side, and there, wiggling in front of me, was a Guinea worm slowly writhing and twisting his way out of my knee.

Fortunately for me, it was a male Guinea worm—maybe an inch and a half long and about the size of a string of cooked spaghetti. The female is much more formidable at two to three feet long and much fatter. I had overheard some of the pilots talk about this and the best way of removing them. So, I got a match stick from a box of matches on the dresser and, sitting back down on the toilet, began to slowly roll the worm onto the matchstick until I had completely removed it.

I showed it to Sam. She had seen this before in Voinjama where it was fairly common. The Guinea worm, or Dracunculiasis, gets into the body from water contaminated by a very small water flea carrying the Guinea worm larvae. There is no cure or treatment for it except to pull the worms out when they emerge from your body. They can cause arthritis or maybe even death if they die inside you while they are wrapped around your knee or spinal cord.

Sam put her newspaper down and looked at me.

"That's it," she said.

"What do you mean, that's it?" I asked.

She took a deep breath. "Ken, a worm just crawled out of your knee. You've had malaria, hepatitis, and diarrhea. What's next? I know you're not happy with your job anymore. You've been talking more and more about going back to school. This place is wearing you down. It's wearing us down. I'm tired of the heat, the damp, and the constant palaver. Tubman's not going to live forever and when he dies, and who knows when that's going to happen, the shit is going to hit the fan. If these Americo-Liberians would learn from history, they might see that they are not going to have it their own way forever. I want to get out before the deluge."

I had to admit she was right—right about everything. It was time to go home.

I had one more flight. It was to the mission where Sarah had lived. The Head Man was there waiting for me. I told him that I wanted to see Sarah's grave. He nodded and told me to follow him. I walked behind him up the single path to the village cemetery. There were rows of wooden crosses crudely pushed into the loose ground. It had been a few years now and the dirt mound covering her grave was weathered down. I placed a single lily at the base of her cross.

As I was turning to leave, the Head Man put his hand on my shoulder and said, "Ah can see ya a mon of deep sorrow, a mon troubled in his spirit. Ya needn't worry no mo. I know God ha forgive you, ma mon. Ah know it. Ya can go in peace now."

I thanked the Head Man and flew back to Spriggs-Payne. I taxied Charlie Fox to the ramp at Monrovia Airlines and let the engine idle for a few minutes, listening to the propeller slowly beat the air. I pulled the mixture control and as I turned the ignition switch to off, realized that I had survived seven years in West Africa flying the bush. I would never again be as good at something as I had been at this. The burdens of the heart had been lifted and now it was truly time to go home.

THE END

MERICO ENGLISH DICTIONARY
(LIBERIAN ENGLISH)

All too: Both

Be so: Let it be as it is

Big Man: Rich politician or businessman; usually an Americo-Liberian.

Big past . . . : Expression to explain quantities or size.

Boc boc: May I come in?

Boy: most natives, not connected with power

Boy Yaah: Hard boiled eggs, usually sold by street vendors

Breeze: Wind

Bugabug: Termites

Buku: Plenty, much

Bush: Forested land

Bush meat: Meat from wild game in the bush

Cane juice: Local rum, very strong

Cartoon: Cardboard box

Cassava: Local potato-like root pounded into fufu

Caynoo: Canoe or dugout

Chop: local food

Chunk: Throw or hit

Cotta cotta: Miscellaneous stuff

Dash: Small bribe, usually to a minor government official

Dews be heavy so: Rain

Fee: Fish

Fineo, or fini one time: Event is over

Fixa hee: Repair something

Good heart: Nice person (he got good heart)
Gowana hee: Go on ahead
Grona: Urchin, delinquent

Haloo ya: Standard greeting
He know book: Smart, literate person (he can read)
He know sheenery: Description of a mechanic or a pilot
He like palaver too much: Description of an argumentative person
Hee: Ahead (gowana hee) or Hill (Bomi Hee)
Help me small: I want a discount on business, or a small bribe.
How you keeping, ya: Standard greeting
Humbug: Bother, annoy

I beg you, ya: asking or imploring
I hold your foot: Strongest expression of imploring or begging for
something.
I say, my fren: Start of a conversation or argument
I swear, whaaat?: Surprise expression

Juju: voodoo magic
Jus now: Soon

Machine that beating: Any engine or motor
Machine voice: Engine exhaust
Mamba: Species of snake, but can be used for any snake
My Saturday: dash, bribe, tip, extortion

No be fine self: Something bad
No got goo way: Bad person

Old man: Person of skill or substance of any age; mark of respect
On the side: Let me out of the Taxi or bus (with hand banging on vehicle)

Qua, qua: A visitor's knock on the hut when no door is present

Rogue: Thief
Runny Stomach: Diarrhea

Small boy: Street person
Small small ting: Raw diamond
Spoil da ting: Destroy or ruin something

Tapadoo Stew: Rat stew
TIA: This is Africa
Too fine: Good, very good
Toos: Tools

Waterside: Waterfront
Wawa: European expression when confronted by African issues (West Africa Wins Again)

Whee: Cart (with wheels)

Yama Yama: Miscellaneous stuff or junk. Sometimes as yama yama business
Yana boy: Street peddler
You best me: You are right and I am wrong

Zootin: All dressed up; showing off

ABOUT THE AUTHOR

A retired Aviation Safety Inspector for the FAA, Daniel V. Meier, Jr. has always had a passion for writing. During his college years, he studied American Literature at The University of Maryland Graduate School and in 1980 was published by Leisure Books under the pen name of Vince Daniels. He also worked briefly for the Washington Business Journal as a journalist and has been a contributing writer/editor for several aviation magazines.

Dan and his wife live in Owings, Maryland, about twenty miles south of Annapolis and when he's not writing, they spend their summers sailing on the Chesapeake Bay.